T0349387

Rejoice with me; I have found my lost sheep.

—Luke 15:6 (NIV)

MYSTERIES OF COBBLE HILL FARM

Digging Up Secrets
Hide and Seek
Into Thin Air
Three Dog Knight
Show Stopper
A Little Bird Told Me
The Christmas Camel Caper
On the Right Track
Wolves in Sheep's Clothing
Snake in the Grass
A Will and a Way
Caught in a Trap
Of Bats and Belfries
Stray from the Fold

MYSTERIES OF COBBLE HILL FARM

Stray from the Fold

CYNTHIA RUCHTI

Mysteries of Cobble Hill Farm is a trademark of Guideposts.

Published by Guideposts
100 Reserve Road, Suite E200, Danbury, CT 06810
Guideposts.org

Cover and interior design by Müllerhaus
Cover illustration by Bob Kayganich at Illustration Online LLC.
Typeset by Aptara, Inc.

ISBN 978-1-961442-49-8 (hardcover)
ISBN 978-1-961442-50-4 (softcover)
ISBN 978-1-961442-51-1 (epub)

Printed and bound in the United States of America

MYSTERIES OF COBBLE HILL FARM

Stray from the Fold

GLOSSARY OF UK TERMS

beck • stream or brook or creek

bloke • man

brolly • umbrella

car park • parking lot

codswallop • nonsense

dustbin • garbage can

fairy cake • cupcake

fortnight • two weeks

innit • "isn't it"

mug off • deceive or take advantage of

skiving off • skipping school, work, or other responsibilities

telly • television

torch • flashlight

wellies • Wellington rubber boots

CHAPTER ONE

Pastor Fitzwilliam "Will" Knight reached into a turquoise-striped box and gently lifted out the most beautiful cupcake Dr. Harriet Bailey had ever seen. His hazel eyes watched her carefully for her reaction to the small cake in a turquoise baking paper, lavishly decorated with pale yellow frosting.

"This is what you're suggesting for the wedding cake?" She made sure her amusement didn't come across as shock. "It's a bit small, isn't it? How will it feed all our guests?"

"We'd have a much larger version, of course." He held his hand over the cupcake to give her a visual. "Or a tower of these fairy cakes, perhaps?" Fairy cake was the common term for cupcake in England.

"Where did you get this? I haven't seen anything like it in White Church Bay." She scooted aside papers to create a larger free spot on the clinic's reception desk, far from where a cat crate or birdcage might ever sit.

Will's face registered his delight. "The Happy Cup Tearoom and Bakery is capable of making anything we choose," he reminded her. "They can also make the cake and frosting whatever colors we want. What do you think?"

Harriet rotated the small, scalloped plate in her hands as a kennel club judge might examine the best of show. "It's flawless. Elegant, but not over the top."

"That's why I like it. We're not over-the-top people."

"How can you say that when I'm wearing my best shoes?" Harriet tapped the toes of her wellies against the floor, offering proof with her footwear. She would have left them on the mat at the door as usual, but the week had been so dry that she wasn't worried about whether she'd track anything in.

"Forgive me. I meant no offense. Does the cake meet with your approval for our wedding?" Will asked.

"The cake is really lovely, Will," Harriet assured him. "And I like the idea of individual cupcakes for our guests, with perhaps a larger one for the bride and groom. I'd like to follow the tradition of saving some to share on our first anniversary."

"Excellent idea, Harriet. That's step one—the design."

She chuckled. "I didn't realize there were steps. What's step two?"

"Taste." He retrieved a turquoise fork from the box, cut off a bite of cake, and offered it to her. "Earl Grey sponge with seedless blackberry jam and lemon frosting."

She closed her eyes, savoring the flavors. The cake itself tasted beautifully of the hearty, slightly citrusy tea, which emphasized the tart lemon in the frosting. The tangy blackberry added another note without overriding any of it. "Oh, Will, it's incredible!"

"I think so too."

"Have I interrupted an important wedding conversation? Should I come back later?" Polly Thatcher—now Polly Worthington—leaned against the doorframe, grinning.

"Not at all. In fact, it's just the kind of thing we need the matron of honor's input on," Harriet replied.

"Is this fairy cake for love or for the wedding?" Polly asked as she approached.

"Both," Will and Harriet answered in unison then smiled at each other.

If Harriet had known such happiness was possible...what would she have done? Moved to England sooner to take over her grandfather's veterinary practice, perhaps learning from him directly before his passing? Would she have stopped resisting her heart's tug toward Will months earlier and hushed the inner insecurity that warned her to keep her distance? Yes and yes. But she supposed everything had happened in God's perfect timing.

Swooning over lemon frosting would have to bow to the need of the moment. "Do you have time to place our order with the Happy Cup, Will?"

"I do." He winked. "Good practice, that. 'I do.'"

She shook her head, grinning. "Thank you. At last count, we have one hundred and fifty RSVPs."

"What do you think, then? Order enough to serve two hundred? I don't mind a year's worth of leftovers in the freezer. I've been assured the cake will keep, as long as we store it properly."

"Sounds perfect. Thank you for taking care of that."

"You don't need to thank me. This is my wedding too, and there's a lot to be done. It shouldn't all fall to you."

A car pulled into the parking lot. Harriet peeked around Will to see if her suspicion was correct. "If you two will excuse me," she said, "I believe my first patient has shown up a little early. A much-loved cat named Millie has a suspicious growth on her abdomen. We noticed it on her last visit, but her owner, Estelle Payne, called yesterday to tell me she thinks it's grown bigger just over the last few days. I told her I'd see them first thing this morning before our scheduled appointments start to arrive for the day."

"Should I prepare the surgery?" Polly shed her light jacket and geared up for the workday as she spoke.

Harriet thought for a moment. "Let's get through the exam first. I should know fairly quickly whether we'll need to operate."

Will scooped up the bakery box and headed for the exit. "I'll leave you to the fun. And don't worry about the cake, Harriet. I won't eat any more until we can share it."

"Thanks. Love you," Harriet called after him.

"Love you too," he said as the door swung shut.

Polly grinned at Harriet. "Is it my imagination, or did Will finally figure out how to be romantic?"

Harriet toed out of her wellies and slid into her work shoes. "I think he always knew the specific kind of romance that speaks to me. I am so blessed."

"We both are." Polly sighed. "Eloping was the right choice for Van and me, but cake like that might have changed my mind."

"You've been a newlywed for less than a month. It's not too late for cake," Harriet replied on her way to finish her prep.

With the cat's exam completed, Harriet braced herself for the discussion with Millie's owner.

"We won't have the results back from the regional lab for a week or more, but it looks suspiciously like a mast cell tumor, Estelle. But you know cats. They love to surprise us. And Millie just might."

"I'd rather she surprise me with a bulb from my garden, like she did yesterday. Not something serious."

"Before we let our concern get out of hand, let's wait on the results of the biopsy. Until then, the painkiller I've prescribed for Millie should ease her discomfort. And she may become even more fond of lap time than she was before. Polly will give you instructions for caring for the biopsy site."

"Thank you, Dr. Bailey. I appreciate your kindness. I've a wee gift for you." She extended a package wrapped in what Harriet recognized as a recent issue of the *Whitby Gazette*.

"Thank you, Estelle," Harriet said as she opened the package. "I'm touched by your generosity. A pair of mittens! How very thoughtful."

"Mittens? In the middle of summer?"

Seated at her desk in her office, Harriet ran her hands over the cream-colored, deeply textured surface of the mittens. "Sheep wool. The real thing. They're so beautiful. Besides, it's not like mittens expire. These will be wonderful this winter."

"Well, you know knitters," Polly said. "They can't really help themselves. What's the saying? 'I could stop any time. I just choose not to'?"

"That's another topic entirely, but yes, I can see the tendency in knitters too."

"Mittens in July is something I never would have thought of."

"Technically, July doesn't start until tomorrow. They're beautifully made," Harriet went on. "With damp weather always around the bend here, I may be able to use them sooner than I expect."

"One never knows," Polly said, affecting an attitude of someone three times her age. "Ah, there's the phone. I'll get it." She headed for the reception desk as Harriet's aunt, Genevieve Garrett, entered.

"Hello, Aunt Jinny. How are you?" Harriet was delighted to see her. Any room felt brighter with her presence.

"Busy, much like you are, I imagine. The summer crowds are prone to need a vet as well as a physician's comments on whether their mysterious rash is poison ivy. More are traveling with pets and service animals than ever before, aren't they?"

"They certainly seem to be. What can I do for you?"

Aunt Jinny tapped a file folder in her hand. "I have your lab results from your NHS annual physical."

Was it her imagination, or had Aunt Jinny's eyebrows lifted higher than normal, toward her strawberry-blond hairline? As a healthcare provider, even if Harriet's patients were of the mammal, aviary, and reptilian nature, she was required to remain current with her license and her personal health checks. "And?"

"All good."

Harriet wasn't holding her breath. "Good" was the expected response.

"Except for one small detail."

That was unexpected. "Which detail?"

"Your blood pressure, my dear," Aunt Jinny said. "It's a Bailey trait. Generations of us have struggled with it."

Harriet snorted. "I'm too young for blood pressure issues. I'm not even in my midthirties. What young people do you know who have blood pressure problems?"

"Ones who carry undue stress or are related to this family."

A sudden chorus of bird calls, barks, and meows rose from the reception room. *Right on cue.* Stress? Couldn't be.

"All right. What do you suggest—cut down on salt except for the chips at Cliffside Chippy? Drink more water?" She hefted her ever-present water jug to emphasize that she was already on the case. "If you've seen me wrestle a lamb through a birth canal, you know I don't need to add more aerobic exercise."

Aunt Jinny crossed her arms over her lab coat. "Knitting, actually." She eyed the mittens on Harriet's desk. "Have you started already?"

Harriet grabbed the mittens and stuffed them in her roomy lab coat pocket. "No. These are a gift from a grateful animal owner. Really, Aunt Jinny? Knitting? With this crazy on-call schedule and a wedding to plan? I hardly have time to commit to a new hobby."

"That's all the more reason for you to do it. I'm prescribing regular doses of time to sit and knit. I'd give you the option to read instead, but, knowing you, you'd read veterinary journals and turn your downtime into more work. So knitting it is. It has similar effects on the mind and body as meditation, but I know you'd never be able to sit quietly without doing something with your hands."

Harriet sighed. For the life of her, she couldn't think of a reasonable argument against it. She'd tried knitting the previous December and maintained a passing interest in it, but she hadn't had time to dedicate to it. She still didn't.

"Food for thought," Aunt Jinny said as she turned to leave. Then she raised her index finger as if adding an important point. "*Low-salt* food for thought."

Harriet would have tossed a comeback her way if Polly hadn't filled the door, her eyes wider than normal. "Doc Bailey, you're needed in the car park. Stat."

Harriet took the side door to avoid the pets and owners who waited for their nonemergency appointments. She quickly walked around the corner of the building and saw a dour sixtysomething man standing beside a pickup truck, one strap of his overalls undone and hanging over his barrel chest. She strode up to him and extended her hand. "Good morning, Alfred," she said. "What brings you here?"

Alfred Ramshaw lowered the tailgate of his pickup to reveal a goat sprawled in the bed. "I need you to tell me what caused this, and if you tell me it was Arlene Pendergrasp, you'll not find me arguing."

"Oh dear. Is he gone?" Arlene's last name was Pendergraf, not Pendergrasp, but this hardly seemed the time to point that out.

The goat raised his head and twitched one foot as if to convince Harriet he was still kicking, literally and figuratively.

"Tell me what happened to him," the man growled. "I've never seen an animal so sick."

Harriet pulled disposable gloves from her pocket and climbed into the truck bed.

"Wish I'd had a pair of gloves. You think he's contagious to people? Or contaminated? What if it's nuclear fallout from some unfriendly country's testing?"

Harriet swallowed her laughter. He was being serious. "I'm fairly confident it isn't radiation sickness." She did her best to examine the limp goat, searching for a wound or other evidence. Harriet palpated his abdomen. Most animals would flinch at the very least or try to wiggle free from her grasp. Nothing. He smelled oddly foul, more so than an average goat. "He might have been struck by lightning, I suppose."

"Ain't seen lightning in more than a fortnight. Can't be that, Doc." Alfred shook his head, as if that should have gone without saying.

"I need to make a more thorough examination and run tests."

"I'd think less of you if you didn't," he said, his voice less gruff than it had been. He obviously cared about his animals.

"What made you mention Arlene Pendergraf?"

"If anyone were up to no good in Yorkshire, it would be her." The gruffness was back in full force. "I think she's up to something."

"Why is that?" Harriet felt along the goat's spine for misalignment, but it seemed fine. Her relief was something she didn't dare express to the worried farmer.

"I got another goat who's unwell. Not this bad, but she's breathing like she grew up in a coal mine. I can't afford to lose her, or this one. And I've been seeing more than one crazy squirrel near the trees by my stone fence, the one that separates my land from Pretendergraf's. Maybe she infected the squirrels with something, and they're spreading the plague. If what ails this goat is spreading to my herd—" He turned his face away.

Harriet laid a hand on his shoulder. "I understand, Alfred. If it helps, I think he's stable for right now. I need to get him into the kennels until I see to the scheduled patients waiting for me inside and can devote my full attention to him."

"I can haul him there." Before Harriet could reply, Alfred lifted the goat. He grunted and struggled but managed to carry his goat all the way to the kennels in back.

Harriet bid him goodbye with a promise to let him know what she discovered with a full examination. The fact that he had more than one ailing animal with different symptoms—to say nothing of "crazy" squirrels—told Harriet that this was no ordinary ailment. Diagnosing and mystery-solving were often separated by a fine line. It seemed she'd just been invited to do both.

As his truck rolled out of the parking lot, she turned her attention to the sounds of a dog disagreement in the clinic behind her.

Harriet stuck her hands in her pockets as she made her way back toward the door. In the left pocket, her fingers touched the beautiful mittens from Estelle. "Knitting. Sure, Aunt Jinny. That's the answer to all my problems."

CHAPTER TWO

H arriet headed back to the vet clinic and waved at Aunt Jinny, who was returning to her dower cottage directly across the way. Flower beds framed the building in summer beauty. Aunt Jinny both lived and worked in the cottage, which also housed her doctor's office. Harriet had always loved the idea of a homey medical facility.

How had her aunt managed to maintain both a full patient load and a full personal life without short-changing either? When did she find time for the kind of rest she recommended to Harriet?

Harriet's new short-term intern, Lyle Brody, joined her in the parking lot. "Would you like me to make sure the goat in the kennel has water? I assume you don't want him eating until after the exam."

"Yes, please, Brody. That's thoughtful of you." What a blessing he'd been. June was a rough month for him to start, but with the small vet clinic in Saltburn-by-the-Sea closing after their vet's sudden retirement to Jersey, Harriet was more than happy to inherit another set of hands and eyes, even temporarily.

"I assume water is enough for now, but not an excess of it," he went on. "We don't want to dilute any samples we need." Brody, who preferred to be called by his last name, was highly skilled for someone so young in his career. Extra time for orienting him to the practice and protocols had put additional strain on the month when

Harriet was also squeezing wedding preparations into her schedule. But it had already been worth it for his assistance. Only a few days on the job and he was already becoming essential.

"Very good. Thank you."

He hurried away. The gentleness with which he handled animals spoke well of his future in veterinary medicine. Brody was a godsend in so many ways. It was true that training him and answering his steady stream of questions added to her responsibilities, but his exuberance for the work to which she'd devoted her life more than made up for that.

She stood a moment longer in the parking lot, surveying the property her grandfather had inherited from his father and tended with the same care, the buildings he'd used for his family and his art and to care for animals and their owners.

A soft summer breeze lifted the hair around her face. The roses had outdone themselves, scenting the air with their delicate perfume. Gardens at every turn burst with glorious abundance. She caught a whiff of salt in the air from the nearby North Sea. Would she ever tire of the peace that singular aroma brought her?

Perhaps she didn't need a so-called restful hobby as much as she needed more of this—more moments standing still in the middle of her heritage, the land of her ancestors, the beauty of a Yorkshire summer, with the promise of a wedding right around the corner.

A flutter of happiness grew in her heart. The flutter was familiar and welcome, a sweet reminder of the joy that had come unexpectedly with her move to White Church Bay. Marriage had been the last thing on her mind when she'd taken up where Grandad had left off at the Cobble Hill Veterinary Clinic. If anything, she'd found the word *marriage* distasteful back then, so soon after Dustin Stewart had broken their engagement. But that was a distant memory now.

There was so much to settle before the wedding. She had the music, her gown, the reception, her parents' visit, meeting Will's father, and a million other details to worry about, despite all that had already been decided.

But first, she needed to address the patients in her waiting room Mondays were always her busiest day.

She started toward the front entrance, intent on apologizing to the animals—and their people—who were waiting.

But before she reached it, a squat bulldog trailed by a smiling Effie Lynn exploded through the door.

"I'm so sorry, Effie. I'll see you as soon as I can. Delays are inevitable in this business, I guess."

"Not to worry yourself, Doc," Effie said as she hurried to keep up with her dog's waddling gait. "The Duke of Earl is quite happy to trot around outside for a little while, as you can see. We're early for our appointment anyway."

To Harriet's surprise, the reception roomful of animals and humans followed Effie and the Duke out.

"Mind if we wait out here, Doc?" one called. "It's such a gorgeous day."

"I don't mind at all," Harriet replied, trying to hide her confusion.

Brody was ahead of the game, hauling folding chairs to the grassy area near the entrance.

Polly was last out the door. She came to join Harriet. "You're probably wondering what we're all doing out here."

"I figured you'd tell me when you got a chance," Harriet said, a hint of amusement creeping into her tone.

"I'm calling it creative problem-solving," Polly said, her eyes twinkling. "People were starting to get antsy, and their animals were picking up on it. The dogs were getting a bit nippy with one another, so I suggested we all come outside for some fresh air and more space before anything got too heated in there. Although I'm not sure how I'll keep an eye on things out here and in there at the same time."

"Find yourself a shady spot under that tree and don't give it another thought." Harriet patted her friend's shoulder. "I'll take care of it, and I'll call you if I need you."

"Your handyman volunteered to help, since he was here for that loose cabinet door anyway," Brody said, handing Harriet a clipboard and pen. "He's around back getting some chairs off the patio."

"What? That's nice of him. He doesn't have to do that."

"He said he owed you more than that for being so gentle with Zelda." He set up another chair. "Why would he bring his wife to you instead of your aunt? No offense."

Harriet laughed. "None taken, Brody. Mike's not married. Zelda is one of his two pet swans. It was touch and go for a while, but Zelda was able to rejoin her mate after a very tricky spinal surgery. We took a video of the procedure, if you'd like to study it sometime."

Brody's eyes lit up. "Really? I'd like that. Thank you."

Harriet perused the collection settled around the makeshift triage, each of them squinting in the sun. Several owners had let their dogs into the fenced-in yard to run off excess energy, and all were keeping a close eye on their pets. With that settled, it was time for Harriet to get back to work.

Since everyone was enjoying the outdoors so much, she might as well get started. She squatted to eye level with a guinea pig who sat on its owner's lap. "Lovely to see you this morning, Godfrey."

To her surprise, the guinea pig snarled.

Harriet held steady but knew better than to draw closer. "Foul mood?" She couldn't remember hearing a guinea pig snarl before.

"It's the distemper, innit?" Wendy Minnert said, wrapping a well-worn bath towel tighter around the animal. "My husband says Godfrey caught it from me."

"Distemper?" The contagious virus was quite serious, causing issues with nearly all parts of its victims' bodies. But it tended to affect wild animals, and Harriet couldn't imagine how a domesticated guinea pig might have caught it.

"I had my grandson look it up." Wendy sighed. "Foxes, wolves, mink, ferrets, skunks, raccoons, and dogs can get it, but my grandson didn't find a single word about guinea pigs." She stroked her pet with a gentle fingertip. "Oh, Godfrey, love. I'm sorry if I gave you something so horrible."

Harriet ventured a little closer to the animal. Godfrey chattered his teeth, indicating that he still wasn't happy, but it was a downshift from his earlier growl. She gently began to examine him, making soothing sounds to help him relax. "I believe your husband was pulling your leg, Wendy."

"He wasn't! He's quite concerned that it'll spread to our other pets."

Harriet smiled and sat back on her heels. "Well, the good news is that you have nothing to worry about. It's Godfrey's front paw that's the problem. Not distemper. See how red the pad of that paw is? Should be soft pink. And it's polydactyl too. What do you know?"

Brody, leaning over Harriet's shoulder, said, "Never seen that before on a guinea pig."

"We had a polydactyl cat several months ago," Harriet said. "Soon after I arrived. She was quite special."

"Oh dear," Wendy said. "Godfrey, my darling, is this the end for you?"

"Polydactyl simply means he has an extra toe on this paw," Harriet said. "It's not dangerous at all. Would you mind lifting up his chin so he doesn't bite me?" Harriet withdrew her ever-present forceps from her pocket. "Hold still, Godfrey. There we are. What a brave boy you are. That wasn't so bad, was it?" Harriet held aloft a small piece of broken pottery for the animal's owner to examine. "This was the problem all along."

Wendy's face blanched. "This is my fault after all. I thought I'd swept it all up. I must have missed a piece."

"Dropped a plate?" Harriet kept her attention on the paw, watching for bleeding or evidence of infection. Perhaps she would prescribe a round of antibiotics to be safe.

She looked up in time to see a flush creep into Wendy's cheeks. "Threw it, actually. My husband said the lamb chops I fixed him would make great tiles for our slate roof should it ever get to leaking. Normally, I'm not so short-tempered, but if he has a problem with my cooking, he can make his own dinner."

Harriet buried her face in her elbow, pretending to sneeze so she didn't laugh. "Will you look at that? The pad is already starting to improve. Less red than it was even a minute ago. I'll have Polly provide an antibiotic ointment as a precautionary measure, but otherwise you two are good to go."

"And then we'll need to schedule surgery for that extra toe?" Wendy asked anxiously.

Harriet walked a narrow balance beam of meeting patient needs and caring for their owners. "It won't hurt him at all to leave it as is. I try not to do unnecessary surgeries. There's no reason to risk infection or other complications if we don't have to. You simply have a special little guy. Let's not do more than we need to."

"He's special, that's for sure." The woman pressed her lips together. Her chin quivered before she stroked a quiet Godfrey and said, "Thank you."

Harriet's own words sank in. *Let's not do more than we need to.* Her work ethic was strong, but was Aunt Jinny right? Did she sometimes allow too little time for recreation? Did that, and the stress of the wedding, make her harder to get along with and less patient?

Will seemed not to notice his beloved's imperfections, unlike Wendy's husband. Harriet pressed a hand to her chest, grateful for Will's gentle nature and generous outlook.

She didn't deserve a man like the Reverend Fitzwilliam Knight. She'd never imagined herself as a pastor's wife. She'd seen herself in the States, married to a veterinary colleague, tending to small animals in a large town. Never in a million years could she have foreseen herself in White Church Bay, a village clinging to the cliffs of the North Sea, dealing with a wide range of dilemmas that kept her head spinning and her imagination piqued.

To say nothing of preparing to marry a minister. Honestly. She never once asked for such a thing before she met Will. She could pull a pottery shard from a small animal's paw and coax triplets from a ewe. She could mend an eagle's broken wing and treat a dog's allergies.

But could she tend as well to the spiritual needs of the congregation Will served? Could she tend to the needs of his congregation as well as she could tend to her patients with a scalpel and stethoscope? Could she look to the needs of her husband's heart so he could serve well?

Harriet made her way around the group of those requiring her attention. Before long, it was clear who required more in-depth care and who merely needed a few words of advice.

As natural as the task seemed, as easily as counsel flowed from her mouth and her training, as smoothly as her hands worked, no souls were at stake in her role—unlike in Will's occupation and passion.

Although, from the faces of grateful pet owners, they might disagree.

She had no time for thoughts like that. No time to talk to God about it either. Her skills were needed by a feverish feline. She would figure it out later. If she could.

CHAPTER THREE

By the next morning, Alfred Ramshaw's goat was still a little out of sorts but much improved—almost like a human might be the day after eating something they were allergic to.

Harriet searched online for the kinds of things to which a goat might develop a sudden allergy. None of her findings offered a clear answer, which was more than a little strange. Poison didn't seem likely, despite Alfred's insistence. But she also couldn't discount it either. Even if it was a case of poisoning, in a farm setting, accidental poisoning was far more likely than intentional.

And there was the matter of the female goat who was not well. Harriet made a note to call Alfred to see how she was faring.

As if reading her mind, Polly poked her head in. "Alfred Ramshaw is on the phone. I'd put him off, but he's beside himself over his goats."

"I actually wanted to talk to him anyway. Thanks, Polly." Harriet picked up the receiver on her desk. "Hello, Alfred. I was just getting ready to call you. How are things this morning?"

"Almost *lost* a goat last night. That's three sickly ones."

"I'm so sorry."

"She gave birth then keeled over. She's starting to come around, but that was too close. And it wasn't like normal labor troubles."

"How's the baby?"

"Babies," he corrected. "She had two kids. And if it's a disease or some such, I'm not eager to have them drinking her milk."

"Do you need me to come help get the twins settled on bottle feeding?"

He huffed. "I know how to get them to nurse on another mum. I wasn't born yesterday."

Harriet dismissed his tone. "What is it you need me to do, Alfred?"

"What can you do?" he snapped. "Write it down. It's evidence for when I sue Arlene Prendergrass for poisoning my animals."

She couldn't get into a debate about his assumptions, as there was no actual evidence of anything. "Perhaps your goat lost too much blood during birth. We can try a transfusion to help her feel better. I'd need to see her to make sure that's what it is before we do anything drastic though. I don't know Arlene Pendergraf well, but she doesn't seem the type of person to poison anyone's goats."

"I'm almost sure of it. She'll do anything to make my life miserable."

Harriet rubbed her forehead. What was she dealing with here? "Let me check my schedule. Since you have the twins to care for, don't worry about bringing the mama goat in. I should be able to come out to your farm in a few hours and take a look at her."

"Might be too late by that point."

"I thought you said she was coming around," Harriet said, puzzled. "Is she on her feet?"

"Barely. Breaks my heart to see her like that. The poison's invisible, I tell you. Did my buck...?"

Harriet was grateful for better news to share. "He's doing much better, but I've found nothing definitive. I'd like to keep him another day or two and run some allergy testing on him."

"Guess that will have to do. Allergies? This plague isn't allergy-related. I can tell you that much."

"I'm sorry, but I couldn't find anything suspicious when I examined him."

"Don't you find *that* suspicious? That you couldn't find a reason? What kind of vet can't figure out why an animal is doing poorly?"

Not an unfamiliar question. Harriet had often asked it of herself.

She loved a good mystery—following clues, turning over evidence, listening and drawing out health information—and this wasn't an easy one. There was always more pressure to solve a mystery when it was related to an animal's health.

A third goat had been affected. By the same malady? It seemed unlikely. The symptoms of the goats she knew about didn't seem related, although they shared some common ground—literally, since they all lived on the same farm. But Alfred was clearly distressed. And that was enough for Harriet to press forward. His poison assumption seemed far-fetched at best. Arlene Pendergraf was a kind, soft-spoken woman around Alfred's age. To Harriet, she seemed the least likely suspect in all of White Church Bay.

"I'm not giving up yet, Alfred. I have blood test results to view later today, in fact, and there are more tests I'd like to perform. Perhaps while I'm at your farm, I can take a look around. Maybe I can gain some insights from the terrain or—"

"Nothing wrong with my terrain. It was fine for my father, my grandfather, and my great-grandfather before that. They raised Aberdeen Angus, but my pop had to sell them off along with nearly half his acreage to pay some debts, and that left me with more tangles than pasture."

"Perfect for goats."

"So you do know a thing or two." Before she could think of an appropriate response, he continued. "Let me tell you how important this is. I landed a sweet deal with a fellow who supplies some fancy restaurants between here and London—places that know the superior value of high-quality goat cheese."

"I'm a big fan of goat cheese myself."

He grunted. "I almost lost my best milker today. And she can't even feed her own kids until we figure it out. If this keeps spreading, or if the milk I send to the cheese maker ends up contaminated, it might well spell the end of my farm."

"I'll let you talk to my receptionist, Polly. She knows my schedule."

There was a long pause. Finally, he said, "Doc, if she gets worse before you get here, it's on your head."

"We'll get to the bottom of this," Harriet said. "I'll do everything I can."

"I just hope everything you can do is enough."

Me too, Alfred. Me too.

Her first of what Harriet felt might be many visits to Alfred's property was brief, to say the least. She'd prioritized seeing his "best milker" immediately, since he'd informed her she couldn't stay long.

She examined the nanny, who was rapidly recovering rather than worsening, just as the others had. Whatever had hit them was short-lived. Serious enough to render them out of commission for a little while but not serious enough to leave permanent damage, it appeared.

Harriet conducted a brief assessment of Alfred's operation and noted only one thing that seemed odd. What was Betsy Templeton doing on the property, and with a metal detector? Harriet recognized her because Betsy owned a foul-tempered chicken who occasionally required medical attention, but Harriet had no idea what else Betsy did with her time.

"My cousin," Alfred explained. "She's a little annoying, but harmless. She's convinced that there's some kind of buried treasure on our land. Our great-grandfather claimed he found some gold pieces back in the nineteen twenties. Every now and then she gets it in her head to go looking for more. That can last for weeks. Then she'll set aside her interminable search for a while before she picks it up again."

"Has she uncovered anything?" Harriet asked.

"Oh, sure," Alfred said. "She's found herself a hatpin from the 1800s and a few coins from the sixteenth century. She's determined. I'll give her that."

Harriet watched the woman stoop, waving the metal detector slowly over a patch of dark green grass. Apparently, nothing registered. She stood and stretched her back.

Alfred checked his watch. "Have to go now. Betsy has a bloke coming to her place to fix her fireplace, or so she hopes. I need to get her to her house before he arrives. Don't know why her son or daughter-in-law can't come get her."

"Can I take her for you?"

"It's the opposite direction of the clinic. I don't mind so much. Did you get what you came for, Doc?"

"For now. I still need to go much more in depth with water supplies, tools, equipment, goat hiding places, their habits, and other such things. But I guess that'll need to be another day."

"Guess so."

What a conundrum of a man. One minute, his goats were the most important thing in the world to him. The next, he needed her to leave before she learned anything so he could drive his cousin home, even when Harriet offered an alternative.

With blood samples she feared would offer her no insights, she climbed into her Land Rover and returned to the clinic.

Within twenty minutes, she was back to her normal routine.

"Your dearly beloved is here." Brody's choice of words was almost as startling as Polly's latest stripe of hair dye, a vivid green.

Harriet took the chart Brody offered her and gestured for him to set the crate in his other hand on the exam table. She recognized the crate style from the local animal shelter. The volunteer must have remained in the reception area.

"Would you mind telling Will it'll be a few minutes before I can talk to him?" Harriet asked, eyeing the small, shivering dog through the crate door.

"Already told him," Brody said. "I hope that wasn't overstepping. Pastor Will insisted that he's in no hurry. And he and I both know your dedication to your clients." He nodded at the crate.

"Thank you, Brody." She was dedicated to her animals, but that didn't mean she was less dedicated to the man she would soon marry. It was all about the priority of the moment.

After they married, would she have the freedom to make those choices the way she did now?

No, wait. That wasn't fair to Will. She fought to erase all evidence the doubt had even crossed her mind. *Stress.* Aunt Jinny could always be counted on to gently put her finger directly on the sore spot.

For now, it was Harriet's responsibility to remove the raggedy animal from its protective case and find out what ailed it. Will knew that her absence at the moment didn't indicate a lack of interest or respect. She gloved up as she scanned the preliminary information on the chart.

It was a good reminder for both of them. His occupation was as priority-driven as hers. What a circus they'd create, juggling human and animal needs.

Within minutes, Harriet knew that the pup inside the crate, who'd been found on the side of the road, was malnourished and dehydrated at the very least. Dehydration could skew lab work, so she started an IV of fluids, nutrients, and minerals and postponed further investigation until the dog was stable.

With the puppy in Brody's more-than-capable hands, she removed her gloves, washed her hands and freshened up, and sought out Will in the waiting room.

"He just left," Polly said between coos to Jocelyn Field's baby and clucks at the colorful parrot sitting on her arm. "He left you a message." She drew a folded paper from her pocket. "I didn't peek. Promise."

Harriet accepted the note, a little disappointed to have missed him.

Polly leaned toward the new mom and whispered, "This love-bird is engaged."

"Ah, yes. Sweet times." Jocelyn beamed and cuddled her baby.

The young parrot snagged Polly's woven bracelet with its beak.

"I didn't mean you, Rufus." Polly deftly dislodged the parrot and returned him to Jocelyn's older son, who sat beside his mom.

Harriet noted Rufus's protruding upper beak. The curve may have grown too long for the bird to pick up and crack open his food, although he obviously had no trouble grabbing things like bracelets. It might be time for a beak trimming.

She ran her palm over the note Will had left for her. Funny how someone's penmanship could make her happy. She opened it on her way to her office.

> *Harriet,*
>
> *I've been called away unexpectedly by a parishioner. Please forgive me for not waiting. Conflicting priorities and all that. I hope you understand.*
>
> *Yours,*
> *Will*

She understood all too well. It was the same difficulty she'd been batting around herself all morning.

She texted her love and support to her "dearly beloved" before returning to her busy practice.

Replacing fluids had made a huge difference. The abandoned pup wasn't cured, but already his eyes had more life in them. She launched into next steps. Clean the dog so they could examine him more closely for any injuries. Check bones, teeth, and gums, palpate the abdomen, see if they could get the pup to stand and eat a little...

As she worked, she could hear Aunt Jinny's voice in her head. *The same is true for humans too, Harriet. Stay hydrated. Choose a drink of water over medicine for a headache.*

Harriet hadn't had two feet on English soil before Aunt Jinny was quoting her favorite advice. "Aunt Jinny!" Harriet had quipped, gesturing to the bottle in her aunt's hand. "Water over tea? What will the neighbors say?"

Aunt Jinny hadn't lost a beat. She hefted a thermos Harriet hadn't even noticed. "Not in place of tea, my dear. Alongside."

And thus had resumed Harriet's relationship with her father's sister, one that had been long-distance for too many years. They shared a love of medicine, an appreciation for Grandad's landscapes and animal paintings, a fascination with the incredible setting of Cobble Hill Farm, its breathtaking views of the North Sea, the ever-changing yet ever-beautiful gardens, and White Church Bay's warm and friendly people.

Harriet would always miss her mother and father, being an ocean away. But Aunt Jinny's presence in her life was a gift she would never take for granted.

Which reminded her that it was time to rehydrate. Tea or water? She decided to follow Aunt Jinny's example.

As she put on the kettle and drank deeply from her water jug, she reflected that maybe hydration was Alfred's livestock problem. Could they be strangely and suddenly dehydrated for some reason? Electrolyte imbalances could cause a wide variety of ailments. But in three separate animals? As if they'd consorted together to revolt against their owner? And that theory wouldn't account for the differing symptoms.

Dehydration sounded like a theory Alfred Ramshaw would come up with himself when he was stumped by the facts of the matter. Harriet wasn't stumped yet. Was she?

CHAPTER FOUR

Thursday evening, Harriet took a deep breath of briny sea air. Alfred's nanny goat was on her feet and cleared for motherhood. Harriet was operating on a temporary assumption that the animals' illnesses were unrelated. After two more long days of wedding planning and caring for patients, she soaked in the welcome July warmth, drinking in the kind of contentment that came with a moment of relaxation after extraordinary productivity.

The scene was enhanced by a light breeze off the sea and a rolling green landscape of hill and dale, draped like a thick wrap over pastures, farmlands, and distant moors, which would soon be awash in pink and purple heather blossoms. It was the perfect backdrop for Will and Harriet's walk after an impromptu picnic supper of leftovers from their combined kitchens.

"This is my favorite time of day," Will murmured. His hand tightened around hers as they walked the path along the cliff side of the Bailey property in quiet companionship.

"Your mother would be proud," Harriet said as they walked.

He glanced at her, startled. "I'm glad you think so, but what brought that up?"

"She was a Jane Austen fan, wasn't she?"

"An avid one."

Harriet lifted their locked hands. "She would have approved of such a gentlemanly and tender expression of your love."

Will grinned. "Mum did appreciate sincere and heartfelt romance. I wish you could have met her. You would have found her 'most agreeable,' as Jane would have said. She would have cherished you—the woman who finally captured her son's heart."

Suddenly, Harriet had the idea to work a Jane Austen nod into the wedding as a tribute to Will's mother. Polly might have an idea for her. Or Aunt Jinny.

Wasn't there a distinct, iconic handkerchief or ribbon or something in one of the classic Jane Austen books? Or she could find a book itself. A first edition, or an edition with a painted edge. Where would she even begin to look? And just when would she find the time to hunt down a treasure like that?

Will leaned forward to catch her gaze. "Have you drifted off into thoughts of celebrations around the bend or far across the Atlantic and all you left behind?"

"No. I'm simply savoring the moment." She took a deep breath and caught a hint of jasmine. It had all but engulfed one of the tree stumps at the far end of the property. A neighbor had dubbed it "invasive," but Harriet thought its scent was invasive in the best way possible.

"Will, do you think it's too late in the day to take the path through the woods?"

He checked his watch. "We should have time for a detour and still make the threshold of your home before dark."

"I would like our walk to last longer."

"Soon it will last a lifetime."

As they emerged from the canopy of old-growth trees, they were met by the sound of tires squealing out of the Cobble Hill Farm parking lot. Aunt Jinny, fists on her hips, stood between them and the departing vehicle.

Harriet's mind spun. What was going on? She looked toward the art gallery. An interrupted robbery attempt? No. She could see Ida Winslow and a gallery volunteer in the doorway, nonplussed but obviously as startled by the unexpected noise as Harriet herself had been. Harriet waved to them as if she and Will had it all under control. Ida and the other woman retreated into the gallery building.

As Harriet and Will quickened their pace and approached Aunt Jinny, Will called out, "Trouble?"

Aunt Jinny pointed to the gravel in front of her. "You could say that."

At her feet lay a chipmunk that had seen better days. Its tiny chest rose and fell slightly, but that was the only sign it was alive.

"Did Alfred Ramshaw drop this off?" Harriet asked her.

"No, it was a couple of teen lads. Why would it be Alfred?" her aunt asked.

"He's had some trouble lately with his goats randomly taking ill. And he said there were squirrels on his property acting strangely. He's convinced it's sabotage from his neighbor, Arlene Pendergraf."

Aunt Jinny's eyebrows rose an inch. "Well, this wasn't my friend Arlene or the grouchy Alfred. As I said, it was a couple of teens."

Harriet frowned at the poor creature, its dull eyes matching the listless way it sprawled on the stones. It looked disturbingly like it suffered from a miniature version of the ailments she'd witnessed in Alfred's goats. "I'm going to have to apply more time and effort to figuring out what's going on at Alfred's place."

"You don't seriously think Arlene is involved, do you?" Will rubbed his forehead. "She's the sweetest woman in Yorkshire."

Both Aunt Jinny and Harriet tilted their heads in his direction.

"Present company excluded," he added.

"I only know her from church," Harriet said. "She's invited me for tea, but I've always had a conflict of one kind or another."

Aunt Jinny tilted her head Harriet's direction now. "I've told you so many times that one never turns down an invitation to tea. Old Doc Bailey's granddaughter refusing tea? We mustn't let the *Whitby Gazette* get wind of this." She affected a look of mock horror followed by a knowing grin.

Harriet drew disposable gloves from her jeans pocket. She was thinking that if the chipmunk was suffering what had ailed Alfred's goats, it would likely get better on its own, as the goats had. But she couldn't be sure of that until she examined it. It might require her intervention after all.

"Of course you keep a pair of gloves handy at all times," Will said, smiling fondly.

Harriet bent to retrieve the limp creature. "And how far are you from the nearest Bible at the moment, Will? A vital tool of *your* trade?"

He patted his breast pocket where she knew he carried a small New Testament. "Fair enough."

"If you two don't mind," Aunt Jinny said, "I'm heading inside to my snug sofa, my fresh cuppa, and my book."

"Isn't that a little warm and cozy for a midsummer evening?" Harriet teased.

"My fan offers any coolness I crave. It's all about balance, my dear, as I believe I've been telling you." Her aunt waved as she started back toward her cottage.

"Enjoy your evening, Aunt Jinny," Harriet called after her. She cradled the chipmunk in her gloved hands and turned to Will. "Reverend, would you be willing to lend me your services?"

He tapped his breast pocket again. "Always at the ready. Perhaps I can read him something from Luke 12. Not even a sparrow escapes God's notice." His eyes twinkled with amusement.

Lord, help me to never tire of his sense of humor, or he of mine. "I'm sure he'll appreciate that. Let's get him stable, okay? Would you disarm the lock on the clinic entrance and switch on the lights? Let's take care of this little guy."

Harriet worked quickly and brought the chipmunk back to its usual wild energy. Then she and Will shooed it out the door and watched it scamper off into the night, its tail straight up in the air like a live exclamation point.

Will took her hand. "I appreciate that you care for the smallest animal as if it was the most important," he said.

"They're here in God's world," she replied. "Of course they're important."

He kissed her temple.

"What was that for?"

"For reminding me every day that proposing to you was one of the best decisions I've ever made."

After they said good night and he headed home, she listened to the music of insects and frogs, evening birds, and the not-so-distant waves as she got ready for bed. She was troubled about the rash of unexplained illnesses. Had the chipmunk come from Alfred's property, even though he wasn't the one who had brought it to her? Nothing would have surprised her at this point.

Harriet sighed. She needed to relinquish her concerns to the God who, as Will had reminded her, tracked every sparrow. He would lead her to what she must do.

Her heart fluttered in her chest. In less than a month, she and Will would share her home at Cobble Hill Farm. She'd been apprehensive about it when she first brought it up, but Will had immediately asserted that they should live in her ancestral home, much to her relief. Soon, he would be listening to the same night song through the bedroom's open windows as they fell asleep side by side. He'd see the same angle of the sun pour across the kitchen tiles in the mornings like spilled honey, hear the same pattern as rain fell and trickled into the downspouts.

Her phone pinged. If she didn't check it before she went to bed, she'd wonder who was trying to reach her. What if it was an emergency?

But it was her mother with another question about wedding details. Mom had found her mother-of-the-bride dress after an excruciating search. She hoped Harriet would approve and that the color wouldn't clash with the flowers or the matron of honor's dress. Did Harriet want her to send a fabric swatch to make sure it would work?

Harriet smiled. It was only about six o'clock in Connecticut, which was five hours behind Yorkshire. If it had been urgent, her mom would have called, but she knew Harriet would be going to bed right about now. She had texted so she didn't forget to ask the question but that also meant she didn't need an immediate answer.

Harriet's mom had always been incredibly considerate, but she was also unflappable. She probably wouldn't even flinch if Harriet told her she was going to wear a wedding gown with an untraditional feature. Like pockets for a tissue, a mint, a nervous bride's hands, or perhaps a spare pair of vet gloves. Harriet chuckled, imagining Mom's response. "Whatever makes you happy, dearest. Make sure they're deep." She could picture her mother's response to that—or to a scene like the one Harriet had experienced earlier that evening.

Skid marks in the Cobble Hill Farm parking lot when teens dropped off a sick chipmunk. That really couldn't be connected to the goat illnesses at Alfred's, could it? Had she missed clues of other animal grievances that were part of a plot concocted by a couple of summer-bored teens? But if they were involved in something, why would they risk discovery by dropping off an ill wild animal? On the other hand, if they weren't involved, why would they hurry away?

She'd have Van Worthington, the local detective constable, take a look at the skid marks in the morning if he was free, although it was hardly worth engaging the law. Harriet jotted a list of reminders on a notepad she kept on the nightstand. *Call Van. Order more disposable gloves. Ask around about teens who might be causing trouble.*

She'd called Estelle earlier that afternoon with the results of Millie's biopsy. The woman had shed tears of relief when Harriet told her it was a fatty, noncancerous tumor and perfectly harmless.

Harriet's eyes had barely closed for two minutes when she sat up again, switched on the lamp, and added to the list. *Set up appointment for wedding gown fitting and order shoes.*

Elegance and minimalism—the wedding's themes—were apparently contradictory terms in the bridal industry, but she would figure something out.

Did wellies come in bridal white?

She chuckled. If anything indicated that she was in dire need of rest, that thought was it.

CHAPTER FIVE

Harriet conquered some of her middle-of-the-night list before the clinic opened Friday morning and began another list, which included checking in with the lab in Whitby about the samples she'd sent from Alfred's goats.

Drawn by the perpetually unfinished behind-the-scenes tasks at the clinic, she almost dove in. But instead she decided to follow Aunt Jinny's suggestion to pay attention to her workload and recreational imbalance. She asked Polly to hang the Closed sign on the door and move any non-urgent appointments to the afternoon. She'd stay a little later if needed today.

The church knitting group was on hiatus for the summer. Harriet was tempted to use that as an excuse to appease Aunt Jinny. But on her way to Galloway's General Store the day before, she'd noticed a whiteboard easel sign in the window of the local yarn shop, Purls of Faith. KNIT THE SUMMER AWAY IN OUR AIR-CONDITIONED CRAFT ROOM. BEGINNERS WELCOME.

Harriet had noted that Friday mornings featured "casual, open knitting with friends," and she thought she might at least try it. When the lab reported no results yet, she made her way to the yarn shop.

Soon she wrestled with herself in the back room of Purls of Faith, staring at fingers that would not cooperate. At least the atmosphere was relaxing, with several women in various plush chairs, the murmur of conversation punctuated by the click of knitting needles. The craft itself—not so much yet. She made a mental note to tell Aunt Jinny so as she stabbed the point of her right needle into the stitch on her left.

"You're holding the wool too tightly, pet." Arlene Pendergraf, one of several self-appointed knitting instructors, tugged on the strand of wool pinched in Harriet's clenched fingers. Her presence had been a pleasant surprise for Harriet. She figured Aunt Jinny couldn't fault her for intending to relax and accidentally stumbling into productivity. "Loosen the tension. This craft is supposed to be relaxing. You'll be much happier with the finished product if you let the wool slide naturally through your digits as you knit."

Betsy Templeton straightened her rounded shoulders as best she could. "It's not nice to call her an ijit. She's just inexperienced." Her voice was gravely and rough.

"Digits," Arlene said patiently. "Not idiot, Betsy. Turn up your hearing aids, please."

"Not wearing them today. Quieter that way."

Another woman chirped, "Gracious! What are you doing in a room full of talkers without your hearing aids, Betsy?" Harriet figured that since she hadn't met her, the woman must not own animals or attend White Church.

Betsy grumbled something unintelligible as she continued to knit.

"Is this better, Mrs. Pendergraf?" Harriet held her knitting so Arlene could see it.

"I'm not married, so it's just Miss Pendergraf. But you can call me Arlene." She perused Harriet's efforts. "That's much better. You're a natural, Dr. Bailey."

"Please, call me Harriet. Thank you for walking me through this. You and the others make it look easy, but so far it feels like it's eluding me. I'm afraid I'm not very skilled with handicrafts."

Alfred, you must be wrong about her. The side benefit of getting to know Arlene better might make Aunt Jinny's knitting prescription more productive than Harriet had first assumed. And from what she was hearing, she couldn't imagine Arlene risking any animal's health.

"Nonsense, my dear. Remember your suture thread."

"What?" Harriet glanced at her work. The black Shetland wool clinging to her needles looked less like a caterpillar than a few moments earlier, but she couldn't see what it had to do with suture thread.

Arlene smiled at her. "I assume you've developed a feel for the kind of thread you use to sew a wound closed on your various patients. Cats, dogs—"

"Goats," Betsy added, glancing up from her project. The expression on her face gave away nothing, but her eye twitched. Alfred said she was often on his land. Likely few others were. She didn't look like a saboteur, but she certainly had access. "At least someone can sew around here, Joyce. Especially important sewing."

"Mother Templeton, that's hardly fair," the young woman protested. She must be Betsy's daughter-in-law, the one Alfred had mentioned. If Betsy often spoke to her in such a way, Harriet could understand why Joyce might not want to be around her to help her run errands and such.

"I suppose a goat, yes." Arlene squirmed.

She squirmed? And Betsy twitched? Harriet ticked off her mental checklist. Could be sciatica. Arthritis. Or guilt. The last option made no sense though.

"Sewing up wounds. You have a feel for it, don't you, Dr. Bailey? Harriet, I mean?" Arlene picked up her own project again.

"Yes, I see your point." Harriet could envision the incisions she'd closed as a first-year veterinary resident. "Tight is right" was not the clinic's motto. Too tight, and the scar would pucker. The edges wouldn't heal naturally, quickly, and smoothly. She had indeed developed a sense of how much tension produced the best results for the animal's recovery and minimal scarring.

She consciously relaxed her grip and imagined herself bent over an operating table rather than the ball of wool in her lap.

As the women chattered around her, Harriet fell into a more comfortable rhythm and focused on deeper breathing with longer exhales. She thought less about how to make the stitches and more about how they felt to create, trying to lock it into her hands' muscle memory. She kept her ears alert for anything that might reveal more related to Betsy's random outburst about goat surgery. As far as Harriet knew, Betsy didn't own any goats herself, just one cranky chicken. Perhaps goats had been on Betsy's mind because of her interactions with Alfred.

"How's the temperature of your feud with our dear Alfred, Arlene?" Betsy asked, as if her question was a natural accompaniment to the discussion about the advantages of homespun versus four-ply and circular needles versus straight.

Her daughter-in-law set aside her knitting project and left the circle with a huff. She made her way to the tea and treats on a table near the window.

"I do not have a feud with your cousin, Betsy," Arlene said, her sweet face darkening. Judging by her tone and expression, Harriet suspected this was not the first time she'd had this conversation with Betsy. "It cannot be a feud if it's completely one-sided I can't fathom why he would ever imagine I'd wish him harm in any way."

"Oh, you have plenty of reason, which is why…" Betsy started then stopped herself. "I apologize, Dr. Bailey. With you soon to be the reverend's wife, I shouldn't gossip around you."

From near the tea table, an indistinguishable mumble drifted toward them.

"Why should that make a difference, Betsy?" Arlene stilled her needles.

"Why shouldn't it?" Betsy demanded.

"We should treat Harriet—and all people—with respect no matter what their station, profession, or marital status. Wouldn't you agree?" Arlene must have measured every word to make sure it landed softly, rather than as a reprimand.

This was the woman Alfred suspected of foul play?

Betsy's cheeks pinked. "I was simply pointing out that among us is one who will soon be married to a clergyman."

"So gossip is acceptable in front of the average person, but not in front of members of the cloth and those they choose to wed?"

"Arlene. Mrs. Templeton." Harriet smiled at them both. "I will be exactly the same person a month from now as I am today."

Her comment started a fit of laughter around the small circle of knitters.

Arlene silenced the cackles with a wave of her knitting needles. "I believe what Harriet means is, that at her core, who she is will remain the same, even though every other aspect of her life will undergo adjustments and changes. Am I right?"

"Yes, of course," Harriet replied.

Arlene raised her chin and closed her eyes for a moment. "None of us need watch our words more carefully around Harriet than around the Good Lord Himself. Wouldn't you agree, Betsy?"

Aunt Jinny, are you sure knitting is the best prescription for my prewedding anxiety?

Harriet glanced at her watch. She'd have to leave soon—and she'd dropped several stitches when she'd turned her wrist.

A text from Polly quickened her steps from Purls of Faith back to the clinic. She was urgently needed at a local farm. Walking had seemed like such a good idea until now. Initially, her stroll into town had been part of her relaxation. She should have known it would leave her at a disadvantage in an emergency.

She stopped several times to catch her breath while the influx of summer tourists to White Church Bay passed by her on the narrow walkway. They all seemed to delight in the steep decline toward the bay. They would change their tune with the climb back to the upper area designated for their parked vehicles.

Her calf muscles ached—less so than when she'd made the climb a year ago, she noticed—but the unfolding view was worth it as she neared home and the clinic. How many steps down and up? And from the beach to the Upper Bay plateau? She'd promised herself she would count one day, but the view always stole her good intentions.

The English roses flourished. She could smell them while still a dozen yards from Cobble Hill Farm. How many roses had her grandparents planted with their own hands? And how long ago? Grandma Helen had been gone years before Grandad passed to glory, gone before Harriet was born. She'd heard they made quite a team until cancer took her from him.

Townspeople reported that, for a while, Grandad had stopped painting. But one day, his inspiration suddenly rekindled with even more light and depth, as if relinquishing his beloved wife to the care of a loving Father made room for an infusion of creativity after a season of darkness.

Harriet lengthened her stride as she fully crested the hill, double-checking the text message for the address of the farmer in distress. When she finally reached the clinic's parking lot, she climbed into the Land Rover—which she'd affectionately nicknamed "the Beast"—tossed her knitting bag on the passenger seat, and took off for the moors.

When she arrived at the address, she was surprised to see Alfred Ramshaw standing at the end of the drive, signaling her to turn in as if landing an airplane. The SOLD sign beside him looked as if the paint hadn't yet dried. What was he doing here? The farmer who'd called in the emergency was named Jeb Hawks, according to Polly's message.

She rolled down the driver's side window. "Alfred? Am I at the wrong address?" *Again?* After more than a year here, one would think she could easily navigate the charming lanes and lack of signage.

"No. This is it. Jeb is waiting for you."

"Is he a friend of yours?"

He coughed in a way that almost sounded amused. "I'm just here for the show. Make your way around back and see what that lad's got going. Or not."

She wound through a maze of small outbuildings, each one more dilapidated than the last.

The little bungalow where Jeb must live leaned decidedly to the left. The closest outbuilding—a machine shed?—leaned at about the same angle, but in the opposite direction, forming a welcome of sorts to the rear of the property. She drove between the leaning buildings and at last reached a fenced-in section, the newest thing she'd seen so far.

Harriet parked, pulled on her wellies, and grabbed her medical bag.

Alfred had trotted along behind her. "That's him. Over there," he said, pointing. He leaned over, hands on knees, and drew deep drafts of air. If Harriet had realized he'd be coming too, she would have offered him a ride.

Harriet shielded her eyes from the sun and watched as a young man approached the fence with an alpaca trailing on a lead behind him. "He's an alpaca farmer?"

Alfred snorted. "Just wait. It gets better."

Before she could ask what he meant, Jeb approached with the alpaca. "You must be Dr. Bailey," he said.

The alpaca didn't have the courtesy to acknowledge Harriet's presence. It seemed to have other things on its mind. She couldn't put her finger on what was wrong with it, but the animal's spark was definitely off.

"I am What's going on here?"

"I think I may have harmed my one and only. This beautiful creature." He gestured mournfully to the alpaca. "Or, she was beautiful, until I became responsible for her."

"Responsible," Alfred mimicked.

"Alfred, please," Harriet said, stepping closer to Jeb. "She's still alive, standing, walking. Although she does look"—she searched for a word but returned to the fitting one—"forlorn."

"Didn't I suggest depression when you told me about her at Chippy's? Didn't I?" Alfred asked Jeb. He turned to Harriet. "The boy described her symptoms to me, and I said to him, 'You think you got problems, son? I almost lost my best doe. And something's acting like nerve gas on a couple of my other animals.'"

Poor Alfred. More of his animals had been affected? This had to stop. Unfortunately, Harriet didn't have any answers for him. Yet.

"Your problem, Jeb?" Alfred said. "That's fixable." He folded his arms over his overalled chest. "Tell him, Doc. Tell him what his animal needs."

"Give me a chance to examine her, Alfred. Jeb, may I?"

"Yes, please. Alfred here said you were the vet to call."

Harriet was surprised by that but tried to hide it. Since she hadn't been able to fix what was wrong with Alfred's animals yet, she wouldn't have thought he'd be willing to recommend her to anyone. "Let me take a look."

She opened the gate and let herself into the corral. She approached slowly so as not to startle the animal, but it seemed beyond startling. The fawn-colored alpaca was female and appeared to be about a year old. She was a suri alpaca, the rarer of the two alpaca breeds. Huacaya alpacas were more common, featuring the crimped fiber associated with their teddy-bear-like appearance. Suri, on the other hand, were known for silky fiber that grew in long lengths down their bodies. This animal's wool was beautiful but struck Harriet as rather dull, and her eyes weren't as bright as Harriet would like.

"What's her name?" Harriet asked as she worked.

"Lovie," Jeb answered.

"Have you kept her away from your other alpacas? To lessen the possible spread of disease, if that's what this is?"

Movement caught her attention. Alfred had slapped his hand over his mouth.

"She's my one and only, like I said." Jeb seemed oblivious to Alfred's behavior.

Harriet wasn't about to draw attention to the older man, though she believed she knew what the problem was now. "Jeb, how long have you had one alpaca?"

"Just a few weeks. Oh, I intend to get more. I can't grow my herd with just the one. Even I know that."

Harriet hung her stethoscope around her neck. She didn't want to insult the young man's intelligence, but she needed to figure out exactly how much he knew so that she knew how much she'd have to teach him. "Jeb, may I ask how you got into alpaca farming?"

"I lost my job in Whitby. A friend of mine sold me this farm and Lovie dirt cheap because he moved to a beach house in central Texas."

Harriet closed her eyes. "Are you familiar with what central Texas is like, Jeb?"

Jeb ducked his head. "Come to think of it, Texas is pretty big, isn't it? Not like here, where there's always water within spitting distance. So if he's in the middle of Texas, he couldn't have a beach house, could he?"

"How long had you known this friend?"

"I'd just met him, actually."

Alfred drew closer. "In a pub, no less."

Jeb stroked the unruly fluff on top of Lovie's drooping head. "And she's a rare breed, I hear."

"Well, that part is true. Did this friend give you any advice about raising alpacas?"

"I figured I could look it up on the internet."

Alfred snorted.

Harriet suddenly didn't feel bad about not offering him a ride from the front of the farm. She faced the crestfallen Jeb again. "Do you know how I know that you will be a great farmer one day?"

"How?"

"You care about your animal."

"He just can't care *for* her." Alfred smirked. Then he backed away from Harriet's glare, his hands raised.

"Don't listen to him, Jeb. Caring about animals will take you a long way," Harriet assured him. "But we need to close the gap between what you know and what you need to know."

"I've got a lot to learn, Doc. I know that. But one step at a time, right?"

"Well, in this case I'd start with two."

"What do you mean?"

"Jeb, alpacas are extremely sociable animals."

"Yeah. She's real friendly. Well, she was."

"They're sociable with other alpacas in particular. They don't do well alone. I don't see any signs of disease or injury. Just her broken heart. She needs other alpacas the same way you and I require food and water."

Jeb's eyes rounded. "I think my friend mugged me off. I had no idea about a lot of things, I guess."

Harriet had heard the phrase "mugged me off" before, and she remembered that it meant someone had been tricked or deceived.

Alfred shook his head, but the quirk in his eyebrows showed an unusual softness. "You've been well and truly taken in, my boy."

"Alfred, I don't know what I would have done if you hadn't helped me down at Cliffside Chippy. Thanks for suggesting I call Dr. Bailey. And Doc?"

"Yes?"

"Please tell me there's some hope for Lovie. Can she recover from this?"

"From friendlessness? From being unloved? We all can." She heard a sniffle behind her but refused to see if Alfred was genuinely emotionally moved or mocking her. "We need to act quickly. In fact, I would suggest that you consider letting a local alpaca farmer keep Lovie for a while so that Lovie can hang out with her herd. She could foster her until you can afford to purchase another couple of animals."

Hope lit in Jeb's eyes. "It sounds like you have someone in mind."

"Yes, I do. My neighbor, Doreen Danby. She's been raising alpacas for years and has a wonderful herd. Lovie will be safe and happy with her until you can bring her home again, and I'm sure Doreen will let you visit her as much as you want."

"Doreen makes a top-notch apricot scone too," Alfred added

"And as far as purchasing new animals, it won't be the bargain price you paid for Lovie, but it'll be worth it."

"To say nothing of this magnificent farm," Alfred said, sarcasm dripping from his tone like the leaky eaves on the ramshackle house. Then his voice and expression became earnest. "But I can help you with that. I like spiffing up an old piece of history, and I'm always looking for projects in which to invest my considerable means."

Alfred Ramshaw? Considerable means? Generous? Caring about someone else, much less the young man he'd spent the last few minutes mocking?

A day full of surprises, that was for sure. And it wasn't even noon.

CHAPTER SIX

It wasn't yet dawn, but Conrad Stokes needed to have all in order by first light if he had any hope of conquering the yawning mouth of the North Sea without being noticed. That inviting sky called to him.

What he would give to have met Wilbur and Orville Wright before they'd returned from Europe to the United States the year before. But he'd studied their work, noted their successes, analyzed their failures, and had to respect their fortitude even if he didn't agree with many of their theories about flight.

The cliffs near White Church Bay were formidable, but exactly the elevation he needed to catch the updrafts required for his spider-like flying machine to take flight. Too many others devoted their time to flight research near Dover and

Sheppey to the south. They had the advantage of a shorter distance between them and France. He had the advantage of fewer prying eyes.

Conrad wasn't interested in duplicating someone else's accomplishments. His pulse raced with the thrill of what hadn't yet been done.

What he shared with Orville and Wilbur was the disdain and ridicule of those in their homeland they most wanted support from. They had their younger sister Katharine on their side, and all of Europe now touted their celebrity. It remained to be seen if America would finally embrace them for their ingenuity and how far they'd come.

Conrad had none but Elizabeth on his side. And even she had voiced her eagerness for him to hurry and realize his dreams so they could finally wed. If her parents knew those dreams were his life's work and not just a curious and dangerous hobby, they would never have given their consent for him to court their only daughter.

And he would need to keep them in the dark on that subject until it was his name splashed across the headlines, his accomplishments extolled by the press, his inventions sought after. He longed for the day when his endeavors could provide an income for a young couple rather than drain the lifeblood out of a single man striving to balance a machinery apprenticeship and a driving passion for flight.

As he ran through his preflight checklist, he reminded himself that he wasn't without support other than Elizabeth's. His friends—dreamers, as he was—were essential to every test flight. He could only pray they would maintain the silence to which he'd sworn them.

Together they dreamed of a day when barriers would be broken and lands connected by hours, not days or months, because of flight.

This test flight would take him in a wide loop out across the North Sea and back. December's upcoming race from Dover deep into Europe promised a hefty financial prize that interested him far less than the notoriety a win would bring him, along with the financial support he needed to make further advances to his aircraft.

He needed to be ready for that race. Nothing could go wrong today or any other day.

A marriage proposal depended on it. His life depended on it.

CHAPTER SEVEN

"Cuppa?"

Polly always knew what Harriet needed before she expressed it. This trait was especially welcome after staying later Friday night to accommodate the schedule changes for the day's knitting and alpaca-related adventures, which had been followed by another trip to Alfred's farm to check out the newly afflicted animals.

This Saturday morning, Harriet postponed the invitation until she had properly guided the office pets, Charlie and Maxwell, to their customary spots. Although a person didn't so much guide Charlie—a calico cat whose fur had been permanently damaged by a fire she'd survived as a kitten—as get out of her way.

Maxwell, who was even sweeter than most long-haired dachshunds, had grown so accustomed to the wheels that served as his back legs that Harriet had to do little more than make sure his harness was well fitted. Keeping up with the other boarding animals was no longer a challenge to him, which Harriet considered great progress for a dog who'd been paralyzed when he was hit by a car.

Many pet owners commented that the two animals did far more than set the tone "All are welcome here" and bring joy. They had a calming effect on children, adults, and even the patients. Both were examples of resilience and survival. "Look what Charlie and

Maxwell have endured and how they're so happy," Harriet often heard nervous pet owners murmur to one another.

They skillfully stayed out of trouble, especially keeping their distance from anxious or hostile animals. Pain could make even the most even-tempered creature unexpectedly hostile.

Betsy Templeton popped unbidden into her mind. Harriet tucked that away for later contemplation.

She ducked into her office and finally allowed herself to sip the tea she was growing to love almost as much as coffee. Who would have thought it? As the tea relaxed her body, another thought slipped into her mind. Was Alfred's inconsistent hostility rooted in pain? He certainly was a mystery.

And he had a genuine mystery plaguing his animals too. As off-putting as his personality appeared, he certainly was eager for her to return to his farm to see if she could decipher anything unusual in their demeanor or bedding, their food sources or—could it be parasites? She added another question mark to her notes. What else hadn't she considered?

Were the reckless teen boys who allegedly deposited the chipmunk related to her investigation? For all Harriet knew at this point, Alfred's animals' problems were unconnected. Random illnesses with no common symptoms, no common ground but timing.

She hadn't found anything of significance that would explain the symptoms in Alfred's goats. It was highly unlikely the Whitby lab would return the sample results on the weekend. That would mean waiting until Monday at least. What could she explore in the meantime? What had she missed?

Harriet could pore over veterinary journals for hours, hunting for a commonality in the cases on Alfred's farm. But that wouldn't be the most efficient use of her time. She needed more to go on than what she had, which was nothing.

Her musings were interrupted by chaos. What was happening? Noise was expected in the waiting room, but this went beyond that. Harriet hurried to the front.

The entire waiting room seemed to have exploded. Dogs barked, straining at leashes. Cats yowled from inside their crates. All attention seemed to be focused on the front door, where a woman had just stepped inside with a toddler at her side. Harriet couldn't imagine why that had caused such a ruckus, when it never had before.

"Good morning. Do you have an appointment?" Polly called over the cacophony, waving a clipboard.

The newcomer stood frozen on the threshold, apparently uncertain about the best way to navigate her way to the reception desk. "I don't, but she needs immediate medical attention."

"Which one? The monkey or the rabbit?" Polly asked.

Harriet did a double take and laughed. The "toddler" at the woman's side was a capuchin monkey, dressed in floral overalls. It cradled a tiny rabbit.

"The rabbit. Winslet's rabbit, Bunny," the woman replied. "My name is Ramona Patel, and I run a petting zoo nearby. My animals are used to Winslet, my monkey, so it didn't occur to me that bringing him to you would cause such an uproar. I'm so sorry."

Polly smiled at her. "It's not a problem. We trust our clients to be able to control their pets, so you should be safe to bring Winslet and

Bunny in here, and we can get you checked in. You could carry Winslet if you're concerned."

Ramona offered a hand to Winslet, but the monkey shrugged away from it, his bright little eyes intent on the reception desk as if he knew where he needed to go. Ramona stepped forward, and Winslet kept pace with her. The sea of rowdy dogs parted before them as owners soothed and shushed their pets.

When they reached the reception desk, Polly gave Winslet a smile. "Aren't you a clever little thing?" She looked up at Ramona. "I do need to ask if you are licensed to possess a wild animal."

Ramona nodded. "I can assure you that I am in full compliance with all the licensing and regulations, since I own a petting zoo. I can produce Winslet's papers for you if necessary."

This close, Harriet was able to catch an East Asian lilt in her accent.

"That won't be necessary, since we're not treating him today. However, if you could email the papers to me so we have them on file in case you ever do need treatment for him, I'd appreciate it." Polly was typing away at her computer, filling out the required forms to get Ramona and her pets registered. "Why don't you tell me about your petting zoo, Ramona?"

Harriet smiled as she skimmed her upcoming scheduled appointments to see if she could squeeze in an urgent rabbit issue. If anyone could calm a stressed animal owner, it was Polly.

Ramona's expression relaxed. "My petting zoo is open to all ages, and we see a lot of tourism in these months. It allows me to keep my beloved Winslet and allows him to care for his beloved Bunny. Winslet is especially popular with our younger visitors."

Harriet could believe that. It brought her joy to see the capuchin monkey in his little romper. Harriet guessed that the monkey was usually higher energy, but he seemed concerned about his rabbit, a Netherland dwarf, at the moment. The monkey cradled the little rabbit that appeared to be very much a living, breathing friend, despite their species differences. Winslet and Bunny made a curious pair.

Harriet squatted to be closer to Winslet's eye level, but the monkey toddled past her and headed to an open exam room. "Polly, is it all right if Ramona comes with me? I'd like to see what's going on with Bunny sooner rather than later."

Polly gave her a thumbs-up. "I'm all set on her paperwork. I'll get your appointments shifted, as long as our kind and considerate clients don't mind."

A chorus of agreement rose from the waiting room as Harriet headed into the exam room Winslet had claimed.

Ramona followed close behind. "He knows Bunny is ill. Don't ask me how. But he's been carrying her everywhere. It's like he's asking, 'Won't someone help my friend?' Can you, Dr. Bailey?"

Ramona picked up the pair, but Winslet wouldn't let go of his charge until Harriet laid a soft towel on the stainless-steel exam table. Then the monkey gently slid Bunny onto the towel and clasped his long-fingered hands together as if praying.

Time to figure out what was ailing this little rabbit.

Winslet watched closely while Harriet stroked his friend. "What's troubling you, little one?"

"Bunny is quite listless," Ramona offered.

"Has she been eating?"

"Not well."

Brody poked his head in. "Polly mentioned you were examining a capuchin monkey's Netherland dwarf and said I might be allowed to watch."

Harriet waved him in. "Of course. Ramona, this is my intern, Lyle Brody, one of the most skilled young veterinarians I've ever met. Brody, come take a listen."

He donned his stethoscope, warmed the disc in his hands, then laid it gently where Harriet indicated on the rabbit's chest.

"On rabbits this small," she told him, "you may need to search for the lungs."

He nodded, moving the stethoscope disc around on Bunny's chest. Then he stopped and listened. "I hear fluid," he said, his voice low.

Harriet nodded. "I concur. Winslet, I think your friend may have pneumonia."

The monkey's brow-arched expression didn't change. It remained hopeful and yet concerned.

"It's likely a round of medication will kick this," Harriet said. "I'd like to keep her here tonight and maybe the next forty-eight hours, so that I can monitor her progress. Winslet is welcome to stay with her, Ramona."

Ramona sighed in relief and nodded her gratitude. "I can't imagine the two of them separated. Thank you so much, Dr. Bailey."

From what Harriet had seen, the two animals had formed a deep friendship despite their differences. She'd seen dogs adopt abandoned kittens, horses and donkeys becoming best friends. Why not a monkey and a dwarf rabbit? Someday she'd ask Ramona to tell her the story of the beginning of their friendship.

Before Harriet realized it, she was mentally at her wedding reception, fielding similar questions while guests milled about. "When did you and Will meet? What first attracted you to each other? Was it friendship first?"

Definitely. She'd been attracted to him right away, but she'd never considered their friendship might develop into something deeper. She was more grateful than she could ever say that it had.

Ramona was talking. Harriet jerked herself back to the present.

"How much more will it cost for Winslet to stay as well? He doesn't like to admit it, but he isn't independent. He needs to be fed and cared for by a human too."

Grandad, I wish you could have lived to see a scene like this. I hope you would have approved of my deputizing Winslet as a special care nurse for the duration of Bunny's stay. Recalling the tales of how often Old Doc Bailey had accepted bartered items like a fresh ham or homemade pie in lieu of cash for services rendered, Harriet was confident he would.

"Since Winslet is an important part of Bunny's healing, I'm going to consider him working for room and board," Harriet said.

"How kind of you. Thank you," Ramona said. She gazed at the unlikely pair. "I'll miss them both for the next couple of days. But I know they're in good hands. Please call me with any updates." She said goodbye to her pets then slipped out of the room.

After Harriet supervised Brody's administration of the first injection, she scooted the towel closer to the monkey, who seemed to know it was now okay to pick up his pet bunny again. He rocked Bunny as a mother might rock an injured child while Harriet escorted the uncommon duo to the larger of the recuperation kennels. In an enclosure that size, the capuchin would have room to stretch his legs.

An hour later, the monkey was still holding Bunny. Both slept peacefully despite the rattle in the bunny's chest. Pneumonia in tiny lungs presented a compounded problem.

And speaking of compounded problems, what was it about goat anatomy that might react differently to the mysterious illness from other animals? Had Harriet made assumptions in her examination? Sheep were far more prevalent in England than goats. The population differences alone made a professional like Harriet less familiar with Alfred's animal of choice.

Anatomy. Allergies. Affinities. She added to her list of suspicions.

If a human being was behind the troubles with Alfred's goats, could it be someone acquainted with goat idiosyncrasies, or was the trouble because the perpetrator was *un*educated about goats? Or was it indeed some kind of attack against Alfred?

She added two new categories to her list of human suspects. *Familiar with or unfamiliar with goats? Vendetta against Alfred?*

When the clinic at last fell quiet after closing on Saturday afternoon, Harriet dug into her research. Will was deep into his final preparations for his sermon on Sunday, as usual, so they'd agreed to spend the day in their own pursuits.

Somehow, they'd managed through texting to decide on details for the caterer and videographer. The church organist, Mr. Snart, would of course handle the processional and recessional, although

Will and Harriet had yet to agree on a still photographer and the soloist, if they wanted one.

Will insisted his cousin Emily had a wonderful singing voice and that she sometimes played guitar too. She could accompany herself as a musical change of pace to the organ for a solo.

Will, I trust you, but...

Her ex-fiancé, Dustin, had taught her, in one of their finer moments, that if she needed to add the three-letter word *but* to a statement, it wasn't trust. She found that she agreed with the sentiment in this moment.

Still, it wasn't lack of trust but need for confirmation that sent her to the internet. She searched for his cousin's name on social media. Could the woman have recorded a video of herself singing? Yes! Several, in fact. She clicked on a video, and Emily's voice floated through the laptop speakers, enveloping Harriet in its warmth and resonance. She opened another video. Apparently, Emily often sang for weddings, in venues ranging from ancient cathedrals with pipe organ accompaniment to outdoor weddings under meringue-peaked white tents.

Harriet replayed a song she hoped Emily would agree to sing for their ceremony, if Will agreed. The more she heard it, the more she loved it. Could anything speak more clearly of their relationship and future together?

Now that I have found you
In the unexpected,
The cherished sphere
Of simple days,
I love the word forever.

Now that I have found you
In twilight's glowing heather,
In brush-stroked moors
And dew-kissed morns,
I'll honor you forever.

Now that I have found you
In firelight's warmth and wonder,
In promises kept
And cliffs windswept,
I'll cherish you forever.

Now that I have found you
And you at last have found me,
Your presence more
Than shore to shore,
Than yesterdays and 'morrows more,
Than morning new
Brings time with you,
I'll hold your heart forever.

She was delighted when her phone rang with a call from Will, and she answered it at once. "Hello there. I was just thinking about you."

"I'm glad to hear it. Are you free to eat with me later this fine evening?"

The weather report hinted at spotty showers after sunset, but any evening with Will was a fine one. "I am."

"Would it be rude of me to ask if you could meet me there?"

"Where?"

"A longtime friend of my father is in hospital in Scarborough. He's alone and nervous about a surgery tomorrow. I'd like to pay him a visit to pray with him. There also happens to be a new lobster restaurant near the beach in Scarborough. It has great reviews and an interesting menu. I know it would be a half-hour drive for you, but if you'd be willing to meet me there after I'm finished with the visit, we could try it together."

"Alternatively, if you're comfortable with it, I'd love to tag along on your pastoral visit."

"Really?" His tone had brightened. "I didn't want to presume—"

"We're in this together. And besides, I'd rather travel those miles with you than without you."

He hesitated for a moment then asked, "Are we absolutely firm on the decision that eloping, like Van and Polly did, is out of the question?"

Harriet burst out laughing. "Our families would find a dungeon somewhere to cast us into if we bailed on the wedding festivities already in the works. Speaking of which, I would love it if Emily could sing for our wedding."

"I've resisted asking if she'd be willing until you were certain. Have you heard her sing 'Now That I've Found You'?"

"I have. 'I love the word forever.'"

"As do I."

They finalized their plans to leave for Scarborough. She'd see if Brody would be willing and able to check on Winslet and Bunny plus handle the evening routine for Charlie and Maxwell in case she and Will returned late.

Polly tapped on her office door and laid an envelope on Harriet's desk. The return address said, *Royal College of Veterinary Surgeons.* The chief regulatory board in the United Kingdom. What could they want?

She wouldn't let it affect serving beside her husband-to-be, their dinner together, or her thoughts during tomorrow's sermon. Whatever it contained could wait until they were open for business next week.

Will and Harriet hadn't yet reached the outskirts of White Church Bay on their way north when something caught Harriet's attention.

In an open field on the high plateau above the sea, Betsy Templeton worked her metal detector as if searching for the Holy Grail. She stooped, picked up something, then tossed it aside. Apparently, she was determined to find more than a long-lost family treasure.

Her daughter-in-law sat behind the wheel of her car along the side of the road, engrossed in a book while her mother-in-law played detective.

Harriet didn't know who else had ventured onto Alfred's property during the series of goat illnesses. He seemed to have so few friends. But she knew one person who had—Betsy. And apparently often, at that.

Perhaps it meant nothing. Or perhaps it meant everything.

CHAPTER EIGHT

The weekend turned out to be just what Harriet needed. After a delightful time in Scarborough with Will on Saturday and a refreshing church service on Sunday, she woke up feeling reenergized and eager to work on Monday morning.

It was a good thing too. Harriet had barely gotten her English muffin in the kitchen toaster and the lights flipped on in the clinic when she heard pounding on the locked front entrance. Alfred peered through the glass at her.

She glanced at her watch, half tempted to make him wait the eight minutes before office hours began. But she heard the rear door creak, and lively chatter told her that Polly and Brody had arrived. So she unlocked the entrance and ushered Alfred inside. Concerned as she was for his animals, she admitted to herself that her attitude about him could use some polishing.

"Taste this," he said, holding out something white and smooth on a small plastic spoon.

The word *poison* crossed her mind, as did a suspicion that, despite lack of evidence, the crisis on Alfred's farm could be related to that word...or to him, for that matter. Self-sabotage was not out of the realm of possibility, though she had no idea what his motive would be.

"Don't be turning up your nose." Alfred held the spoon in front of her mouth. "Taste. Please."

She did. She might be foolish, but the way he said *please* put her oddly at ease. Rich, creamy flavor filled her mouth as she took the spoon from him. "Goat cheese?"

"Yes." He straightened.

She savored another small bite. "Alfred, that's some of the best goat cheese I've ever tasted. Is it yours?"

Alfred beamed with obvious pride. "It is."

Harriet drew a breath. "I have to say, it's delicious."

He set a small container on a nearby end table in the reception area. "Yet another of my goats took ill last night. I just wanted you to know what's at stake. This goat cheese that's providing my income and that's on every table of every high-end restaurant from here to Scotland."

"I thought you said London."

"There too. More are asking about my supplying their needs. Word gets around in those circles."

She'd envisioned Alfred's as a small operation, a tick or two above Jeb's. She hadn't realized it was so successful.

"If we don't stop that Pender-mind-yer-own-business woman—"

"Why would Arlene Pendergraf be interested in sabotaging anything, much less your goat cheese production?"

Alfred threw his arms in the air. "Who can say? She's always nosing around, peering over the wall that separates our properties. For all I know, she has one of those *drone* thingies flying over my land, dropping plagues like we used to drop leaflets during the war."

Harriet prevented herself from retorting. She couldn't think of a professional way to say she thought he was dangerously close to outright conspiracy territory.

He folded his arms over his chest. "I'm a mite miffed that I have to do my own detective work on this situation."

"What detective work have you done?"

"You mean, what detecting have I done that *you* should have? Or Detective Constable Worthington, who refuses to take my calls? I do not believe an officer of the law is allowed to block a caller."

The day was ten minutes old. Technically, the clinic wasn't even open yet. Could she drink coffee with one hand and tea with the other? "Alfred, I'm a veterinarian."

"The jury is still out on that one."

Polly dinged the bell on the reception counter. "Time out."

Alfred immediately looked abashed. "I apologize, Doc. I have a mystery that needs solving before I lose everything I have. The milk is still testing fine with the cheese maker, but I can't in good conscience sell to them until my animals stop falling ill. I'm shut down. Still milking so my nanny goats keep producing, but the product is unusable until you come up with answers. Still, that was a mite harsh."

"More than a mite," Polly said, her tone severe.

"Polly, it's okay. Tell me what you mean, Alfred. What investigative work have you been doing without me, and did you discover anything?"

"The bloke from Thirsk."

It sounded like a movie title, but Harriet wouldn't say so. The last thing the conversation needed was more sarcasm. "What man in Thirsk?"

"The goat trader. Lives in the shadow of the Chalk Horse, I hear. Raises goats purely for selling. I bought a couple of weaned kids from him a month or so ago. He volunteered to deliver them, so I didn't see his place. I didn't think anything of it at the time, but that also means I have no idea what those kids came to me with from his operation. Got me thinking the bloke could have been like Jeb's alpaca friend. You know, not on the up-and-up."

Harriet's mind spun. She didn't want to hazard a guess about what the conversation was doing to her blood pressure. *In the genes, huh, Aunt Jinny?* "Polly?"

"Yes?"

"Did you make coffee already?"

"Started the pot as soon as I came in. It'll be ready any second."

"Thank you." Harriet took a deep breath, trying to keep her tone level and free of accusation. "Alfred, I wish you'd told me you'd recently added new goats from a different farm. That's important information that would have affected my approach to the situation. You didn't physically confront the Thirsk goat trader, did you?"

He snorted. "I did not confront him. I figured that was up to you."

She was grateful for that, plus a little embarrassed. She hadn't been moving as fast as the mystery deserved. True, she was waiting on the lab results, but she could have asked more questions. If she had, she might have found out about the new additions to Alfred's farm sooner. So many major events were converging in her life that some things were falling through the cracks. A wedding in a few weeks' time with all that entailed, her day-to-day duties, and Alfred. Not to mention a new health issue her aunt wanted her to address, which was probably driven in part by everything else.

"Jeb did some hunting online for me," Alfred explained. "For reviews and the like on the bloke's business."

If she'd known about Alfred's recent purchase of goats, that would have been her first move. But it was her own fault for not asking him where his stock had come from or if he'd added to it recently. "What did you find out?"

"Mostly good reviews, although he might have planted some of them himself. Don't know if a person can do that, but if he's a dodgy goat trader, he might be tempted to."

"He'd be taking a big risk to do that," Polly said. "More likely, if he's not legit, he'd have friends or neighbors post fake reviews."

Alfred rubbed the back of his neck. "It's hard to know who to trust these days," he said. "And speaking of neighbors, I still think it's that Pendergasty woman."

Harriet had heard enough about that. "Alfred, that's a bunch of codswallop."

Alfred startled. "Where did you hear that word, Doc?" he asked.

"I first heard it from Grandad," Harriet said. "It was something he wrote on the back of one of his paintings. I thought he might have been describing an area of Britain I hadn't seen. Codswallop Hollow, perhaps? When I asked him about it, he laughed and said he didn't know of any place like that. But he wouldn't tell me what it meant. The only thing I could figure was that he didn't much care for that particular painting."

Alfred's expression shifted. He pressed trembling lips together. Eventually, he said, "I don't think I've heard that word since your grandfather used it in a tiff with me on the cricket pitch." His eyes softened. "A fine competitor, he was. In his younger years, anyway.

I learned a great deal from him. What painting are you talking about? Is it in the gallery?"

"I've seen it, or a copy at least, in my aunt's cottage. I don't know why he was so disappointed in his work on that painting. It's beautiful, if you ask me. But I suppose artists can be disappointed in their work when it doesn't reflect the vision they had for it. All we can see is what they actually produced, and we don't have their mental image to compare it to, so we don't see how it falls short for them."

Alfred dropped into a reception room chair, more disarmed than she'd ever seen him. "Was it a wash of green with light spilling in from the right? Long shadows and two wickets crossed in the foreground?"

"You've seen it before?"

Alfred opened his mouth but closed it when the bell above the front door jingled. A little girl and her mother toted a boxful of mewing kittens into the reception area.

Polly called to them, "Have a seat. Be with you in a tick."

As the kittens' family settled near the reception desk, Alfred finally spoke. "We played cricket every Wednesday. And then one day I finally won. He wasn't upset though. He was tickled. Like I'd grown to where I could beat him, and he was the proud coach. Then I told him I was leaving White Church Bay, and we got into an argument. When I walked off in a huff, he yelled, 'That's a load of codswallop!' It was the last time we ever played cricket together, but the day before I left, I went to say goodbye, and he showed me a painting he was working on. He said it was to remind him of our good times on the pitch."

Harriet was only half listening by the end of his speech because she'd gotten stuck on the words *leaving White Church Bay*. What did that mean? But it seemed like prying to ask, so instead, she sat down in the empty chair next to Alfred. Should she pat his work-worn hand? Put her arm around his shoulder?

Before she could decide, he abruptly stood, swiping at his eyes. "A working man ought not let the day get away from him like this. I've got too much to do. I just thought you might like to know about the goat trader."

"You're right. Thank you."

"He's worth investigating, is what I'm saying." Alfred turned to leave. "You can keep the rest of that goat cheese, if you want."

"Thank you," she said again. It was quite generous of him. Not to mention unexpected, considering how frustrated he seemed to be with her work thus far. She really never knew what to expect from him.

"Good day to you." With that, he was out the door.

Before she dove into her appointments, she checked on Winslet and Bunny. Both were perkier. Winslet waited patiently while Harriet listened to Bunny's lungs. They sounded appreciably better, and Harriet found no apparent side effects from the medication. If Bunny kept improving after the next injection, Polly could call Ramona to pick up the pair before the end of the workday.

At least something was going as planned.

It occurred to her that she'd found an even more mismatched friendship than a monkey and a rabbit—her beloved grandfather and Alfred. What could those two have had in common, other than an apparent enjoyment of cricket? Was the sport enough to call it a friendship? Mentorship? And for what? Certainly not veterinary medicine. It wasn't the first time she longed to ring up Grandad and ask him questions about life, love, animals and their ailments, his art, and now the mercurial Alfred.

She made a mental note to probe her network for any information about a goat trader in Thirsk. Now that Alfred had given her a lead, the least she could do was follow up on it.

Then, unable to curb her curiosity any longer, Harriet hurried to her office and opened the letter from the Royal College of Veterinary Surgeons. She sank back in her chair as she read it.

Polly knocked on the doorframe. "Harriet? I've got that boxful of kittens out in the waiting room. Want me to get Brody to take a look?"

Harriet pondered. She'd be within shouting distance if their problem involved more than what a vet usually saw in a batch of barn kittens. "Sure. I have a phone call or two to make." She paused then said, "Have we gotten any complaints about the practice lately?"

Polly frowned. "Just the usual one about vets living the high life, what with the prices they charge. But we don't pay much attention to those."

Harriet sighed. "We can't afford any more unsatisfied customers contacting the Royal College of Veterinary Surgeons."

Polly's expression fell. "Trouble?"

Harriet tossed the letter onto her desk. "I'm not sure how seriously to take it. Are you familiar with the term 'smear campaign'?"

Polly scowled. "I certainly am. But where would that be coming from? You've won the hearts of the entire White Church Bay community, Harriet. Except, like I said, for the occasional cheapskate— or Alfred. And that's no easy task."

The letter didn't require a response. It was merely a notification that the college had received some anonymous complaints. Reading between the lines, Harriet wondered if that meant someone from the RCVS might show up at the clinic undercover with a sick chicken, a sob story, and a hidden camera.

Yes, Aunt Jinny. I do recognize the need to somehow fit a dose of knitting into my routine.

CHAPTER NINE

The hour and a half drive to Thirsk on Tuesday would afford Harriet three welcome tension relievers. To clear her head and stretch tight muscles, she first allowed herself to walk along the cliffside path for about fifteen minutes then retraced her steps to where she'd parked the Beast before she started her journey. The beautifully distracting views of that coastline walk could straighten the most tightly coiled nerve.

The second grace she offered herself was to decide that driving around North York Moors National Park—which stood in the way of an as-the-crow-flies path—was not wasting time. She would enjoy every blessed sight, sound, and fragrance of the summer-lush terrain.

And then, though she'd seen it before, she took time to marvel at the physically realistic silhouette of a horse carved into the hillside in the mid-1800s to mimic and honor the prehistoric chalk horses of Southern England. The animal stood starkly white against the deep green of the hillside into which it was carved and then filled with crushed chalk. Leucipotomy, the Greek word for the art of carving white horses into chalk uplands, had always sounded to Harriet like a type of veterinary surgery.

One day she hoped she and Will could take a road trip to the Uffington White Horse—the oldest of the UK's geoglyphs, purported to be from the Bronze Age. From pictures she'd seen, Harriet knew the Uffington horse was less realistic-looking than the one before her. And, unlike its southern cousins, the one Harriet now viewed was cut into limestone rather than chalk, making its color duller than the others. But she still found it utterly fascinating.

Many of the chalk horses had completely disappeared. Without humans to tend the deeply carved trenches, undocumented carvings had been buried under soil over the centuries. The stuff of legends and lore and wonder, the silent chalk horses of England stood as testament that perhaps Harriet didn't need to solve every mystery to appreciate their beauty and significance.

That was not, however, the case with the threat to Alfred's goats. More of them were in trouble now. Some with similar symptoms of lethargy and suspected poisoning, some with neurological issues. Harriet was grateful that most had recovered on their own without her medical intervention, but she had no idea whether that would continue to be the case. It was possible that they would develop stronger reactions to whatever was causing the issue. And Harriet could never sit back and allow animals to suffer, even temporarily. She had to get to the heart of this and soon.

As she mentally recounted the theories—some wild, some logical, some intentional, and some unexplainable—about England's chalk horses, she thought about how both exceptional craftsmanship and what could never fully be known was all rolled together. And it wasn't lost on her that a community of volunteers and hired caretakers worked diligently to clear brush and overgrowth so the chalk horses would remain visible to those looking for them—in some cases from nearly forty miles away.

The result was truly awe inspiring.

"Study the science of veterinary medicine," Grandad had told her. "But never lose your sense of awe. And learn to be content that some things are not able to be explained." Harriet's thoughts wandered to her study of Scripture and what she was learning about the character of God, the delightful discoveries she couldn't fully explain. Her grandfather's words reminded her that not every mystery had to be solved.

Harriet was confident that he didn't mean this case. Grandad would have chased down an answer as stubbornly as Harriet was. Alfred's mystery, and the mystery that was Alfred himself, couldn't stay hidden without great cost.

She left the hillside with its startling equine beauty and headed off to spy on a bloke in Thirsk.

The goat trader, Bernard Trammel, wasn't hard to find. But it was hard to imagine this jovial man in his forties—seven children around his feet, counting the twins in a double pram—with anything to hide, much less brokering shady goat deals.

But Jeb's unscrupulous alpaca salesman had put her on alert for the unexpected.

She took herself out of spy mode and decided to be upfront with the man, explaining that one of his recent customers was her veterinary client and that he had experienced a rash of mysterious illnesses affecting his animals.

"The ones I sold him?"

"No. They're doing fine, as far as I know."

Mr. Trammel seemed eager to help and started listing the kinds of ailments that might be common with goats.

Knowledgeable as he was, he seemed unfazed by her questions and not at all offended that she would want to observe his operation. But he did get logged into Harriet's mental list of those who knew goats well enough to know how to harm them.

Goats of all shapes and sizes bleated and bounced in enclosures all around the tidy farm. Several smaller goats ran free in the yard.

One of Mr. Trammel's younger children, a girl of about seven, Harriet guessed, interrupted their conversation and introduced herself to Harriet.

"My name's Bevie. I guess because Dad and Mum have a bevy of children." She laughed as if she'd told a stage-worthy joke. "Watch this."

The girl called one of the goats to her side, a lovely black-and-white creature. The goat bounced closer, caught sight of Harriet, and fell over. It lay stiff and still for a few moments then scrambled to its feet and hopped off to join its friends.

Harriet, who'd seen the breed before, chuckled. She wasn't surprised that the child had shown her a fainting goat, which had the tendency to fall over as if dead, or "faint," when it was startled.

"They're the children's favorite," Mr. Trammel explained. "I've sold them to petting zoos so other children can enjoy them, but I've kept these for my own kids."

Harriet nodded. "I've heard they make good pets, in spite of that startle reflex. They're fun, and they don't need as much space as larger breeds."

"I've found that to be true," he agreed. "Their life expectancy is longer than you might expect with something that startles so much. But their muscular system makes them easy to keep corralled because they're not prone to jumping fences, like other breeds. I mean, goats always try to escape because they take fences personally, but the fainters are more likely to try crawling through a hole somewhere rather than jumping."

Jumping fences. As goats do.

As Alfred's goats likely did.

Harriet surveyed the structures within her view. As far as she could see, it was a carefully thought out and well-run operation. As glad as she was that the Trammels had happy, healthy animals, it dumped her investigation back to square one.

"You know they don't actually faint," Bevie said, holding a goat like a puppy. "They're my-o-ton-ic." She pronounced the word carefully and looked to her father for approval.

"That's right, Bevie." Her dad removed his cap and wiped his forehead. "Myotonic. They stiffen or fall over as if fainting, but they remain fully conscious. I've often wondered...well, you'd think me daft, Doc."

"What is it you've wondered? I'm a wonderer myself."

"Do you think human physicians would learn something if they studied this breed of goat? Do you think it might give them insights into panic attacks in humans?"

How could Harriet not like this "bloke," as Alfred called him? "I don't think that's daft at all, Mr. Trammel. In fact, I think it's a great idea. I can ask my aunt Jinny about it sometime. But for now, do you have time to show me around your operation?"

"It would be my pleasure."

The tour lasted half an hour. With all the evidence she saw of Mr. Trammel's level of animal care, the quality food that would keep the goats in the pink of health, an immaculate recordkeeping system that was clear and easy to use, and a beautiful acreage free of any possible dangers that she could see, she was confident she could assuage Alfred's concerns about his purchases from this man.

Besides, the two young goats Alfred had purchased from the Trammel operation hadn't been among those exhibiting any symptoms. Harriet believed it was highly unlikely they carried a disease or disorder they hadn't succumbed to themselves.

She'd done her due diligence in checking out the goat trader, observing his goats, and watching for any clues in the way he handled the animals.

Leaving with a suspicion resolved was both victory and defeat. She was no closer to having an answer. She'd added Mr. Trammel as a possible suspect on her mental list when Alfred told her about him. But now she mentally crossed him off.

Or was that premature?

She needed another look at the kids that Alfred had bought from him. Had they been shipped off this property on purpose? Maybe not because Mr. Trammel *intended* any harm, but because they weren't good for his flock? And if so, why not?

Alfred had not come to the Trammel farm to pick up the kids. They'd been delivered. A long way for a busy farmer and father to travel to deliver two young animals.

Lord, I know there's a fine line between being suspicious and discerning. Help me always to know the difference.

Then she noticed a transport trailer near one of the outbuildings. "Mr. Trammel, would you mind if I took a look at your trailer? Is that the one you use when delivering goats to your customers?"

"It's the one I've used for the past two or three years. Thinking of purchasing one yourself?" If the man was trying to disguise guilt, he was excellent at it.

"Just curious. Anything make it especially beneficial for transporting goats?"

"The size, mostly. Go ahead and take a peek. It's worked well for us, although I mostly use it for acquiring animals rather than delivery. I kind of have my hands full, as you can imagine." He indicated the spread of his farm and the children never far from their father.

She had to be even more upfront now. "The kids you sold to Alfred Ramshaw—is there a reason you delivered them to his farm rather than have him pick them up?"

He straightened. "If they're not ill, is he having some other kind of trouble with them? I can't offer a money-back guarantee on every goat I sell, but if they've been problematic for him, I could consider that."

"No. To my knowledge, they're fine. I just wonder if they might have been carrying something with them that you were unaware of. Something in the trailer, perhaps? Peeling paint the animals could have ingested, or had stuck to their hooves? I'm not accusing you at all. I'm on a hunt for possible answers for Mr. Ramshaw."

Mr. Trammel's expression didn't change. "Let's examine that trailer. Neither he nor I can afford a problem like that, although I've never noticed anything out of order. Oh, and I made the delivery to Mr. Ramshaw's farm for a good reason. Please don't think ill of me, but I wanted to make sure they were going to a good home. I hadn't dealt with the man before. He seemed a little…"

"Rough around the edges?"

"Exactly. I was heading that direction, more or less, so I volunteered to drop the kids at his farm."

Within minutes Harriet could tell the trailer was in pristine condition, like everything else about the Trammel farm. She was coming to expect it from this operation. Mr. Trammel assured her no paint was ever used on his property unless it was nontoxic for both children and animals.

Harriet scanned the interior and found nothing to spark concern.

On or off the suspect list? How could she keep the goat trader on it? Betsy Templeton was far more suspicious than this man.

But Harriet still swiped a gloved hand over the area inside the trailer where goats would be secured then turned the glove inside out and slipped it into her pocket. Evidence was evidence.

She prayed it would show nothing.

As she headed back to Cobble Hill Farm, Harriet surveyed the land from the opposite viewpoint from the trip to Thirsk and considered where she stood in the investigation—frustratingly nowhere, unless testing the glove in her pocket revealed something.

Despite the ever-present annual checkups, vaccines, and emergency farm calls, Harriet was grateful for the lighter workload that often came with mid-to-late summer, especially as the wedding drew nearer. She was particularly grateful for her competent best friend and receptionist, Polly, and now Brody, who were both capable of handling so much without her input.

Then why did guilt nag at her when she stopped at Purls of Faith for knitting club? They met Tuesday afternoons and Friday mornings. Not a typical schedule, but it happened to work out well for Harriet so far. A Tuesday afternoon breather and information-collecting session might help both her blood pressure and the investigation, even though she'd have to keep it brief this time.

Betsy was visiting her daughter and family in Manchester, so the group dynamic held a different tone.

Arlene arrived late and out of breath.

"Are you all right, Arlene?" Harriet asked. "Can I get you anything? Water? Tea?"

Arlene dropped into one of the cozy-on-their-way-to-worn chairs in the side room where the knitters met. "What I need is relief."

"From what?" Harriet asked.

"From who, actually. A certain neighbor of mine thinks my greatest ambition is to make his life miserable." Her face flushed, no doubt from frustration. "Quite the contrary," she added softly.

Flushed or blushed? Harriet could not bring herself to ask that question. But she took note.

Another woman in the circle pressed. "Alfred? Is he still at it?"

"He must be. I can't imagine anyone else stuffing my postbox with flyers that say, 'Goats rule. Sheep drool.' Can you imagine being so childish? And they do not drool. My sheep are clean and healthy. His goats are the problem."

"How so?" Harriet asked casually, keeping her gaze fixed on her knitting needles.

"You know goats," Arlene said.

"I do. But what in particular about Alfred's are a bother?"

"Oh, nothing. He's the bother. His goats are just doing what goats do—pushing boundaries. My sheep are not going over the wall to invade his pasture. But his goats are apparently training for the Olympics in dressage. They leap that wall onto my property as if they're schoolboys breaking into the playground after dark."

"He's never mentioned his animals wandering onto your land."

"The man thinks I *lure* them onto my property. I don't need to tell you that's an utterly ridiculous notion. What possible reason could I have to want to do that?"

"Codswallop," Harriet said under her breath. Someone was either lying or grossly misinformed. Or mean-spirited.

Harriet had a guess, but knowing Alfred—or rather, not knowing him at all—she couldn't begin to be certain.

Needles clicking formed the only sounds in the room for a time. Eventually talk turned to the weather, to Harriet's upcoming nuptials, to the price of wool...

It was an interesting discussion when hearing both sides—the wool purchasers knitting away and the wool producer, Arlene, trying to pay her bills from the wool and meat produced on her farm.

"How do you manage all that on your own, Arlene?" Harriet asked.

"I have help. I hire local young people. It's another expense for me, but it's worth it. I don't have to manage everything alone, and they're learning a life lesson or two in the process. I have two young brothers helping me this summer. I couldn't get away for knitting club or the grocer without them, although I do wish…never mind."

"No, go ahead, Arlene," Harriet said. "The more you talk things out, the more relief you'll find."

Arlene seemed to consider this. She blew out a breath. "Some young people keep time differently than I do, that's all. Seven a.m. my time might mean eight thirty to them."

A low chuckle circled the room.

"But for the most part, they're decent workers. They do things mostly on time and well, and they always ask questions to make sure they're handling a situation correctly. And they stay until their work is done. I do worry about their 'need for speed,' as you Americans say, Harriet. They drive like whirling dervishes."

It wasn't until Harriet returned home an hour later that she recalled the marks made in the clinic parking lot by unknown drivers who'd dropped off a sickly chipmunk.

Aunt Jinny had seen two young men in the vehicle. Could they be the hired hands who drove like whirling dervishes on the property adjacent to Alfred's?

Harriet hadn't gained more insights about the woman Alfred suspected of sabotage. But she'd returned from the knitting club with a stronger suspicion about the chipmunk dumpers.

And she returned to a phone call from Alfred. One of the new kids was no longer free of symptoms.

CHAPTER TEN

Wednesday was spent explaining what Harriet had a hard time understanding herself. The lab results they'd been waiting for were not coming. The samples had somehow gotten contaminated, and any results would be worthless. The Whitby lab admitted it had happened on their watch, not Harriet's, but that was little comfort.

Alfred didn't take the news well, and Harriet couldn't blame him. At least she now had the sick baby goat and an older goat from Alfred's farm in the kennel for observation and sources for new samples.

After handling the clinic's scheduled appointments, Harriet spent Wednesday afternoon toggling between caring for the goats and hand-delivering the samples to Whitby. Brody had volunteered, but Harriet wanted to be the one to transfer the samples into the hands of the lab coordinator. She was determined that nothing else go wrong.

Why was the goats' ailment so hard to diagnose? The saboteur, if there was one, deserved a dishonorable medal for stumping all traditional testing and diagnostic methods. Who around White Church Bay would have the medical or scientific insights to hide the source of the problem or their nefarious methods of attacking the animals?

A pharmacist? Chemist? Another vet?

Her breath caught in her throat as another suspect popped into her mind—one she didn't even want to consider.

Think, Harriet. Think carefully.

Alfred's animals' ills and Brody's arrival at the clinic had nothing to do with each other. They couldn't. Brody was an answer to prayer, not a suspect.

But what did she truly know about him? Other than what she saw during work hours—impeccable kindness and efficiency. Yes, anything was possible, but what would compel a man who'd spent so many years training to heal animals to then turn to hurting them? Unless...

His background had been thoroughly checked before Harriet took him on as an intern. But the sudden retirement of his previous mentor had always felt odd. And she had spent too little time getting to know Brody as a person.

Harriet had leaned heavily on what Brody offered the clinic rather than trying to figure out who he was behind the scenes. Did he have something to prove? Or some grudge against goats?

Harriet! Calm down, and proceed cautiously.

Brody had volunteered to deliver the samples. He'd seemed genuinely disappointed when she insisted on doing it herself. What could that mean?

It could simply mean he wanted to help.

Or not.

She would stay alert but keep a tight rein on her accusatory thoughts.

By Thursday, both the goats in the kennel—old and young—were faring much better and were able to return home. Brody had taken the lead in their care. Did he have a hero complex, tormenting the goats so that he could later swoop in and heal them? Or was Harriet completely off her rocker?

The timing of Brody's arrival with the arrival of Alfred's troubles pestered her late into the night and popped up frequently all day Thursday and much of Friday. She double-checked the locks on the medication cabinets far more often than necessary and monitored the inventory of supplies as if Brody was guilty, hoping beyond hope that she was wrong.

It was unsettling that someone she'd thought was a godsend could possibly be the exact opposite.

Saturday's noon closing time for the clinic couldn't have come soon enough. It was a day for tourists and their pets. And that came on the heels of a late-night conversation with Harriet's parents.

She hoped she'd finally convinced them it would not be necessary for them to fly across the pond for the wedding with Barkley, the offspring of a homeless mutt she'd rescued as a child. They suggested Barkley could serve as ring bearer for the ceremony, but he was a dog her parents loved, not a dog she'd grown close to. Barkley's mom, Lucky, had passed long ago, while Harriet was still in college. Harriet and Barkley had never connected, but her parents absolutely doted on him.

She loved her parents dearly, but she felt as if that suggestion had been more for their benefit than for hers.

Besides, she had no idea how well Barkley would get along with Maxwell and Charlie. Her parents would be staying with her for the wedding so they could watch the animals while she and Will were on their honeymoon. She knew her pets could get along with just about anything, but Barkley wasn't always the most social animal. She had gotten through to them, hadn't she? All she needed was a jet-lagged ball of fluff snarling at her as she walked down the aisle.

This morning, she at least was able to think of more ammunition for the next conversation they'd have. Saturday morning offered her more than enough experience with the influx of international tourists whose traveling pets hadn't managed the trip well.

One family's dog was now quarantined for the rest of their vacation. Another couple's nervous cat had been forbidden to fly home on the airline that brought it to Yorkshire. Harriet offered nerve-settling medicine but couldn't intervene with the airline.

Another pet—someone had actually brought a snake on vacation, which was mind-boggling—rested comfortably in a reptile cage in the kennel after laying five eggs, which she was now incubating. The owners had been completely unaware of the snake's condition.

In her occupation, she'd learned that animals were curious and their humans even more so.

Polly left early for a family reunion while Harriet finished some surgical sutures. She'd had to remove two abscessed teeth from a beloved Munchkin cat. Harriet suspected the owners traveled with the Munchkin for the attention its stubby legs brought the humans.

When she locked up the clinic, Maxwell and Charlie were waiting for her. She slumped into a chair. Maxwell laid his front paws on her tired feet as if to say, "I get it, Mom." Charlie jumped to the back of the chair and kneaded her shoulders.

"You two are the best."

Will was working on his sermon for the next day, his traditional use of Saturday afternoons. She had some hours to read or take a walk, if she could find a spot not occupied by people taking selfies with ancient historical artifacts or centuries-old buildings.

When had she become so cynical? She herself still stood in awe of the beautiful history all around her new home. She groaned and put her head in her hands. Maybe Aunt Jinny was right about her blood pressure.

The phone rang. Harriet groaned again and picked it up. "Hello?"

"Hello, Harriet, this is Arlene Pendergraf."

"Hi, Arlene. How are you? Is anything wrong?"

"I'm not calling officially, exactly. I know I've asked you to tea in the past and it hasn't worked with your schedule, but I wondered if you were free this afternoon. I've made a batch of my famous sticky toffee pudding. I know it's not quite a summery treat, but I am so fond of it."

Harriet had hoped for another invitation, and was delighted. "I've heard rumors about your sticky toffee pudding, and I'm happy for the opportunity to try it. What time would you like me there?"

"If you're not busy, you could come right now."

She was already heading to her bedroom to change out of her work clothes. This could be an opportunity for great tea and conversation. She might even have a chance to peek over a stone wall.

Arlene's tiny cottage looked as old as Hadrian's Wall, but far more friendly and inviting. The ceilings were so low that both women had to duck through doorways from room to room, but Harriet was growing used to such things in White Church Bay's ancient houses.

"Easier to keep warm in the winter," Arlene explained when Harriet commented on it. "But there's no escaping the heat in summer. I count on those breezes blowing through the windows, since I never was able to buy the air conditioner I'd hope to gift myself when I received my LLB."

"LLB?"

"Bachelor of Laws degree."

"You're a lawyer?"

"Oh no, dear. The LLB is the first step in the training. By then, I'd fallen in love with a man who cared about farming and raising animals. We made plans, which changed my plans."

"So, you married and moved to this property? Wait, scratch that question. You told me you never married. I'm sorry I forgot that detail."

"I'll explain over tea."

Arlene steered Harriet to a cozy table for two by a window with a gauzy curtain that danced in the air currents. The table was set with a typical four-o'clock-tea spread—dainty cucumber sandwiches, cream cheese and herb fingerling sandwiches, tartlets and mini-scones—and a cottage-shaped teapot befitting the home in which it sat. Arlene tucked the flowing skirts of the dancing curtains behind glass knobs affixed on either side of the open window.

"To answer your question," she said, "we did not marry. I delayed further studies and licensing toward practicing law, believing a proposal was imminent." She ran a finger along the rim of her empty teacup. "It was not."

Harriet could well imagine the struggle the woman had faced.

"Some would say it was my folly to purchase this property after my disappointment. A home suitable for one, and land suitable for a family—of animals of my choosing. Perhaps it was. Folly, I mean."

"Did you ever return to your studies?"

"No. I lost my passion for more than just a man I had believed loved me. I suppose I could lecture at colleges about all the ways *not* to weather despair."

Harriet accepted the tea her hostess offered, its aroma perfuming the air as potently as the sweet peas and late peonies in a small vase on the table. "I doubt anyone would call this charming cottage or your beautiful property a folly, Arlene. Not with any accuracy, anyway."

Arlene faced the scene out the window as Harriet did, the older woman seeming to view with fresh eyes the gentle slope of land toward the slowly flowing stream, where Harriet assumed the property ended. The infamous stone wall to the right was dotted in four spots by oaks that formed sentinel points down the length of it. Brambles along Arlene's side of the wall made it seem all the more formidable.

Sheep like grass, not brambles. She needs some goats to take care of those...

Harriet pulled her errant musings back and admired the low-clipped pastureland. Arlene's sheep were efficient lawn mowers. Harriet also noticed fruit trees in the garden that held vegetables and flowers growing in raised beds. A delightful blend of symmetry and serendipity.

"I've never called the cottage a folly," Arlene murmured. "It was a refuge for me, and that feeling has only grown over the years. It's my sanctuary of sorts. I chose solitude over heartbreak, although they still compete for my attention."

Her voice held the timbre of cello music. Harriet could listen to her storytelling style as long as Arlene would allow. And Harriet had once embraced the same—solitude over heartbreak. Until Will, anyway. "Tell me about your animals."

Arlene leaned back with a light chuckle, careful not to spill her tea. "Now that may well have been genuine folly."

"How so?"

"At first, I merely collected a few pets for companionship. But as you know, pastureland can quickly grow from a carpet of green to a suffocating carpet of weeds. Someone suggested I buy a few sheep, purely to keep the grass clipped."

Harriet could predict the results.

"You know how that goes," Arlene said, offering Harriet the small china plate of cucumber sandwiches. "The sheep needed more than grass. They needed shearing. And milking. And inoculations. Then along came the babies. All of a sudden, I wasn't using the sheep for my purposes. They were using me for theirs, and I found that I didn't mind at all."

Harriet grinned as she reached for a miniature berry tart.

"And then we fell in love with each other."

Harriet startled with the tart halfway to her mouth. "Your man wised up?"

"No. He was out of the picture. I mean I fell in love with those darling, silly, endearing sheep. And their wool is magnificent. I can't describe the satisfaction of giving someone a scarf I knit out of wool that I spun myself, from my own sheep."

"Forgive me for asking, Arlene, but can your flock provide enough wool for you to live on? I'm sorry if I'm getting too personal."

"I take no offense. I know you're asking because you're as caring as your grandfather and grandmother were, although I knew your grandmother too short a time. My parents provided well for me. And then I've been frugal in many ways and uncommonly blessed in others. The wool simply helps make ends meet. Much is at stake in keeping my sheep healthy and well-tended. And keeping myself healthy in body, mind, and spirit."

"It's a good approach to life."

"More tea?"

"Yes, please." Harriet extended her cup. If Polly was her younger, high-energy friend, perhaps Arlene could become her older, wiser, calming friend. "And may I have another of those berry tarts?"

Arlene finished filling her cup. "You certainly may, but you might want to reconsider filling up on those. I do want to introduce you to my sticky toffee pudding. Which we will then need to walk off with a ramble around the gardens and property and a visit to my flock, if you are of a mind."

"Nothing would please me more." And Harriet meant it.

She was glad she'd followed her hostess's recommendation. Arlene's sticky toffee pudding was the richest and best she'd ever tasted. Even the way the sauce clung to her silver spoon was a work of art. She told Arlene as much.

"Thank you, my dear. I try not to take undue pride in it," Arlene said as they savored their last bites. "I found the original recipe in a ladies' magazine from the 1940s, and I've merely added some touches of my own throughout the years, as one might expect. Although I must say using Medjool dates may have been a genius move on my part, hard as they once were to find in the market. They're not called 'the fruit of kings' for nothing, and their taste lends itself so perfectly to this pudding."

Harriet watched for any eye twitch, any "tell" that would give away insincerity or subterfuge in this gracious woman. She found nothing in Arlene's expression but wisdom and peace. Except perhaps the remnants of a heartache Harriet had known herself. "So far, this afternoon has been just what I needed."

"Are you ready, Dr. Bailey, to be reminded of your life's work?"

"With a visit to your flock? Absolutely." She idly thought of how Will spent much of his life visiting his flock too.

"Oh," Arlene added, "did you bring—well, I wouldn't want your nice shoes to get all mucky."

"My wellies are always with me."

Arlene placed her hand over Harriet's with an approving smile.

Harriet was pleased with the exceptional health of Arlene's flock. Her border collie appeared to be a fine guardian and aid to Arlene.

"This is Hamlet," Arlene said, stroking the dog's twitching ears.

Hamlet's ears never stopped. His eyes always on the alert, he paused for human attention only briefly then returned to his duties overseeing the flock. Once assured they were in no danger, he dropped to a crouched position, head still erect.

"Is Hamlet muzzled at times?" Harriet asked as they neared the stone wall.

"Never. He only barks when sheep are misbehaving or danger is near. Why do you ask?"

"I noticed a small abrasion on the top of his nose, an arch like one might expect if a leather or plastic strap was rubbing against his skin."

"Thanks for mentioning that, Harriet. I'll check into it later. I expect Hamlet may have taken a shortcut through the brambles and picked up a scratch. He'd give his life for those sheep. If they listened to him, they wouldn't go near that tangle. I must have the boys trim it back again. Lots of work, but what can you do?"

"Let me know if you need a salve for the scratch," Harriet said. "If you had goats rather than sheep, your pasture wouldn't be as neatly trimmed, but the brambles would be gone. Brambles are a goat's sticky toffee pudding."

"Goats!" Arlene said, casting a glance toward the wall and the property on the other side.

They both laughed as they drew nearer to the enemy camp.

Harriet could do little more than gain a quick assessment of Alfred's property from this angle. She didn't want to alert him to the fact that that she was investigating him, or rather, the situation. Nothing seemed amiss. There were no breaches in the stone wall. No foul odors, except the faint smell of diesel, likely from the tractor idling as Alfred checked his furrow of fresh-cut hay.

Harriet ducked back farther to keep from being noticed. That was all she needed in her dealings with the crotchety farmer—suspicion that she was somehow in cahoots with Arlene.

They had quickened their pace to leave the scene when something caught Harriet's eye. "Don't look now," she whispered to her companion, "but it appears Alfred has installed a security camera in the branches of that tree. And it's aimed at us."

"Of all the paranoid nonsense." As they walked briskly toward the cottage, Arlene said, "I suspect Alfred may be his own worst enemy. He seems incapable of allowing himself a moment of happiness. It's one crisis after another with him. Always someone else to blame."

There was more vitriol in her tone than Harriet had believed her capable of.

Arlene stopped herself. "Forgive me. I really did believe I'd conquered the urge to gossip. And it's a genuine shame that his goats are doing so poorly. I'm sure I'd be a terror too with a mystery malady attacking my sheep."

Harriet laid her hand on Arlene's arm. "Do you think he might stoop so low as to make his own goats sick? For sympathy, do you think? Is he just lonely and in need of attention?"

"Alfred is fully invested in those animals of his," Arlene said. "And isn't he always going on about the 'fortune' he's making with his goat cheese? I can't imagine him risking all of that for some drummed-up sympathy."

"Forget I suggested it. I'm grabbing at straws to make sense of what might be happening."

"Have you been to his place? I mean, closer than looking over the fence line?"

"Yes, but too briefly, I'm afraid. It's high time for a much deeper examination."

CHAPTER ELEVEN

Conrad Stokes took a deeper look at the damage from his abrupt landing—it hadn't quite been a crash, but it had been more sudden than he might have liked—in the pasture high above White Church Bay. Repairs and delays would always be part of an aviator's life. Mechanical difficulties had interfered with yet another flight.

To others, Conrad's aircraft might look like an exaggerated children's plaything, not unlike the bamboo toy the Wright brothers' father had given his sons, no doubt unaware it would inspire their life's work.

But curious as its soaring height and delicate wings might appear, Conrad had invested all he had into this endeavor. Failure was not an option. A prize awaited him at the end of the year, and he would be the one to claim it. The repairs now required were a minor setback. That and finances. He should budget for a compass and other navigation aids. Somehow.

As expected, Elizabeth had found another excuse not to attend the day's test flight. She hadn't attempted to hide her disappointment that the weather perfect for a picnic was also perfect for flying. But she believed in him, didn't she? She'd get over it. By tomorrow, she'd be apologizing for throwing a fit.

Or he would.

How could two magnificent things—Elizabeth and flying—always stand in opposition despite how much they both meant to him? Even though Elizabeth said she supported him, she and flying seemed always to be leading him in opposite directions.

Hadn't King George VII visited the Wright brothers in Paris? Conrad himself would soon be counted among the leaders in the field, if he had his way. Aviation is not a pipe dream, Elizabeth.

One day he would soar high above what had kept his feet, and his longings, tethered to the ground. Not for brief stretches but exploring from above lands he could only imagine now.

He addressed the damage to the wheel assembly with fervor. Maybe Elizabeth would agree to travel with him by train to Dover and the Isle of Sheppey aviation training grounds, so that she could see for herself what was possible.

And perhaps she would agree to marry him before it made sense.

CHAPTER TWELVE

A moving sermon, Pastor Will." Harriet slid her hand into Will's as he stood outside the church to greet the exiting congregation.

"I assume you were willing to ignore the moments I was distracted by the sight of the future Mrs. Knight in the congregation," he said.

"Future Mrs. *Bailey*-Knight," she corrected playfully.

"Move it along, Doc," grumbled a coarse and familiar voice behind her.

"Good morning to you as well, Alfred." Harriet was in too good a mood to let the cranky farmer bring her down.

"Sunday morning's no time to be flirting with the reverend."

Will spoke up. "My fiancée is welcome to flirt with this reverend any time she pleases, Alfred."

Alfred lifted his face to the sky. "Good Lord in heaven, are ya' hearin' this...this...?"

Harriet slipped her hand through Will's bent arm. "This *codswallop*, Alfred?"

"He hears it," Will said. "And I do believe He highly approves."

Alfred scoffed then tugged on Harriet's sleeve. "If you're done with this foolishness, I need to speak with you privately."

She followed him off the path into the churchyard.

"Doc, I want you to open your clinic so I can show you the latest evidence."

"Unfortunately, I can't open the clinic on Sunday for a non-emergency."

"This *is* an emergency."

Harriet brushed away an insect. "Is it truly an emergency, Alfred?" It wasn't unusual for Harriet to be called away from various engagements, including hers for that afternoon—discussing her honeymoon with Will. They were planning to enjoy the sights in Wales, Ireland, and France for a week. It sounded ideal to Harriet, and holding the space for such a peaceful afternoon felt like a necessity in the midst of her crazy life season.

She'd been called to a veterinary emergency midmeal, midhike, and even mid-teeth-brushing. Maybe with Alfred she'd try the "I'm committed to help you but not right this minute" approach. If she didn't set boundaries around her personal time, she would never achieve work/life balance.

Alfred hesitated then said uncertainly, "Well, it is urgent."

"I'm sorry, I can't open the clinic this afternoon," Harriet replied. "But I haven't forgotten you, Alfred. I've been doing a lot of research about goat illnesses this last week. I really think our next step is for me to see your animals and walk your property to collect other investigative materials or observations that might prove vital in resolving your mystery."

Alfred huffed. "So first thing tomorrow morning then?"

Harriet managed a smile and said, "I'll look on my schedule as soon as I get to the clinic in the morning and let you know when I can come. I promise, it's a priority for me." She should ask Brody to accompany her. Not because she wasn't fully capable of handling Alfred and his ire but because it might be good for her young assistant to get experience in dealing with a difficult client.

Besides, taking Brody might provide an opportunity to judge his reactions to being so close to the scene of whatever crime was happening, if there indeed was a crime.

Why was it not a surprise that Monday dawned thick with fog? Harriet peeked out her bedroom window as she dressed in her workout clothes. The sea was reduced to a sliver. The moors were smothered under a quilt of mist. And Alfred was on the day's agenda. As if she didn't have enough factors obscuring whatever the truth was in his case.

Walking the Cobble Hill property before her workday in the fog wouldn't provide the views she normally craved, but the quiet would be good for her soul, and the mist would provide a natural moisturizer. Or so she told herself.

She took the familiar trail along the cliff. It struck her as eerie that, in places, the fog was so thick she could get completely lost if she veered off the path a few feet.

No wonder so many British mystery novels were swathed in fog.

All too soon, it was time to open Cobble Hill Veterinary Clinic for a new day, a new week.

Her first patient was a lame lizard. A bearded dragon, to be more precise.

The dragon's owner, a teenage boy named Lennon Knox, was mortified that he'd caught the dragon's leg in its enclosure door. She assuaged his fears with her confidence that Camelot's leg would heal just fine and both could return to their happy demeanors.

"It'll look a little bizarre for a while," Harriet told him. "I'll need to pull the fractured leg straight back and secure it to Camelot's body and tail."

"Will that hurt her?" The teen tried to play tough, but Harriet could see fear in his eyes.

"I don't think the procedure itself will be fun for her, but she'll be fine after that. It'll look like she has three legs and a very fat tail. That position will allow the muscles to pull the bones naturally into alignment and will provide stability for healing. No surgery. The splint will be all that's needed."

"Whatever you think's best, Doc." Lennon eyed his pet anxiously.

Harriet decided to follow a hunch while she worked. "Lennon, by any chance do you know the two young men, a little older than you, who are working as hired hands at Arlene Pendergraf's this summer?"

"Gregory and Heath Adamson? Sure, I know 'em. They're a lot smellier now that they're working with sheep instead of gaming with the rest of us."

"Video gaming?"

"Yeah. They're tough to beat. Seems to me they should have chosen some technology gig for their summer job. They know a lot about computers and game systems and other electronic stuff."

Harriet kept the boy talking while she set the bearded dragon's leg. "What kind of electronic stuff?"

"They're into robotics, drones, things like that. They even build their own."

From that description the brothers didn't sound like the kind of young people who would thrive as farmhands or even consider spending their time devising nefarious ailment-inducing products to sabotage an older man's goat farm.

"How come you're wanting to know about them?" Lennon asked.

"I just like to know about the people who are working around the animals I care for. I want to know how they treat the animals, how knowledgeable they are, things like that."

Lennon seemed to consider this. "Makes sense," he said.

Almost instantly, the procedure appeared to relieve any discomfort Camelot felt, although it was hard to judge a lizard's feelings from its facial expression. Even before leaving the clinic, Camelot was navigating well on three legs and a megatail.

Monday mornings at a vet clinic were not unlike Mondays at a people clinic. Suddenly everything tolerable during the weekend seemed a higher priority. After a rash of examinations, Harriet checked with Polly. They agreed that she could get away for an hour or so around eleven. Charting and paperwork would have to wait until after her visit to Alfred's place.

She knew the route to his farm well now, after her journey to and from the adjacent property for tea with Arlene and her previous visits to his place. She calculated she'd need about fifteen minutes to navigate the back roads and wood-canopied lanes. Although the fog had not lifted, which could add time to her short journey. She'd need to plan a buffer for the trip.

Harriet carefully went over the equipment she wanted to take with her. This was a much-needed visit. She'd been researching viruses that might present the symptoms Alfred's goats were experiencing—goat pox, perhaps? Or bluetongue virus, also known as BTV? She'd examined every inch of the ailing animals she'd seen. But she hadn't scoured the affected goats or Alfred's farm for parasites and insects. She was no entomologist, but she could collect specimens for an expert to examine.

Although, why would an insect-borne disease not have affected the neighboring sheep? No bubble of protection surrounded Arlene's property. It seemed unlikely that any environmental factors at Alfred's wouldn't also be present at Arlene's.

But Alfred had what he claimed was a point of interest in solving his mystery.

A little past ten, Harriet set an alarm on her phone to allow an extra five minutes of back-road navigation to Alfred's. She'd just poured herself a cup of tea in the kitchen when Polly joined her.

"Who's our next patient?" Harriet asked.

"Two dogs, a cat, and a ferret are waiting," Polly replied promptly. "None of them urgent." She filled her own mug and added a little milk.

"We should be able to stay right on schedule then." Harriet followed Polly to the waiting room to greet the first client.

The cat's flea situation was quickly addressed. The dogs needed only their immunization updates. The ferret's rash was more concerning, but Harriet administered an ointment and strapped on a small surgical cone of shame to keep him from making matters worse. She gave care instructions and the ointment to the ferret's owner and saw both to the front door.

To her surprise, Polly wasn't at the front desk. Instead, Brody sat there, a textbook open in front of him.

"Where's Polly?" Harriet asked.

"She asked me to tell you she headed home. She wasn't feeling well. Want me to fill in at the desk?"

Harriet checked the time and shut off the alarm on her phone. A few days ago, she would have trusted Brody to be alone in the clinic and at least answer the phone or explain her absence. But suddenly she wasn't at all sure about it. Right or wrong, she thought about the medications and chemicals accessible. Some of them were dangerous if not used properly. And unfortunately, Brody had the knowledge to use them improperly.

She wanted to be wrong about Brody, but nevertheless she slipped the kennel keys into her pocket as well as the drug cabinet keys. "If you could, that would be helpful. I'll be gone for the next hour or so. You can flip the sign to Closed, and hopefully there won't be any emergencies. If you can just answer the phone, that would be great."

"Will do." He shooed her toward the side exit, like he couldn't wait to be alone.

That didn't make her feel any better.

As it turned out, Harriet's feelings had very little impact on how the situation unfolded. Fifteen minutes later, she was on the phone with Brody.

"The Beast has a flat, and I don't mind telling you that fog and flat tires are not compatible."

"Where are you?"

Harriet switched her cell phone to the other ear. "I don't know. I have my hazard lights on, but even I can't see them, and I'm standing right here. I think I missed a turn. With the sun nowhere to be seen and no compass—not to mention my navigation app insisting I've already arrived at my destination—I have exactly no idea where I am."

Brody chuckled. "That's not really helpful."

"Tell me about it. And remind me to update the app when I get back to the clinic. If I ever do."

"What can I do?" Brody asked. "Want me to come looking?"

"No, we need someone at the clinic. Will you call Alfred and tell him the situation? My phone battery's running low."

"I'm on it. Then you want me to call Pastor Will to change the tire for you?"

"I can change the tire myself, so I'm not totally stranded. And the flat is on the passenger side, so it's a little safer. But you know these roads. They're treacherous at the best of times. Once I get the tire changed, I'll try to reorient myself and see if I can find Alfred's farm. Who knows? Once I get rolling again, I might end up in Whitby."

"Or the North Sea."

Harriet groaned. "You're so comforting. I'm going to hang up now so you can call Alfred. And I suppose it wouldn't hurt if I texted Will before my phone dies."

Fog and flats made poor companions. Fog and lug nuts were even worse. Her fingers damp and her vision blurred, Harriet dropped not one but two of the nuts into the long grass that edged the road.

Oh, she'd searched. She had scratches from the thorny blackberry bushes to prove it. Surely they'd heal before the wedding. Or she'd find herself a long-sleeved sweater to wear over the tulle and lace and satin. That wouldn't look absolutely absurd at all.

What was the minimum number of lug nuts needed to keep a wheel in place while driving the backroads? She considered searching online for the answer, but her phone battery had reached the end of its energy.

Aunt Jinny, it's a good thing you can't see me now, and that there's no blood pressure cuff anywhere nearby. But you'll be happy to find out that changing a tire is indeed an aerobic workout. That has to count for something.

She heard the familiar sound of hoofbeats. A horse? Who was out for a trail ride on a day like today?

She had her answer in another handful of *clop-clops.* "Alfred? I didn't know you owned horses."

"I just have this fine steed," he said. "I didn't know you had an interest in berry picking in this kind of weather."

Harriet grimaced. So much for the scratches on her arms not being noticeable. "Flat tire."

"Yes, that's what your intern said. Climb on."

"What?" Harriet eyed the horse dubiously.

"You'd rather brave the creatures that hang out in ditches in the misty fog than accept a nice ride to your next appointment?"

Harriet laughed for the first time in the ordeal. "I'm sorry. I didn't mean it like that. I have the tire changed, but I've…misplaced two lug nuts."

Even in the thick fog, she could see him rubbing his chin. "Have you now? That explains a lot."

"If you have a flashlight, I think I could find them." She said the words, hoping they came across as confidence.

"Glad to hear it, but there's no reason for you to do that right now. Now hop on up here."

Something in the weeds tickled her ankle. She scooted out of the ditch and looked for foot and handholds to use to climb onto Alfred's "mighty steed."

"Can your horse see in the fog?" She gripped the back of the saddle and held tight as the horse made a U-turn.

"He's blind, so it doesn't matter much to him. Trust me. He knows his way home."

Not more than half a minute had passed when Harriet ventured, "How far are we from your place?"

The horse turned its head then its body to the right.

"And there we be," Alfred said.

She'd gotten stuck no more than thirty yards from Alfred's farm. Her navigation app had been right after all. She *had* reached her destination.

"Why'd you bring the horse?" she asked.

"Two reasons. My Porsche is in the shop. And this horse doesn't move fast enough to miss his turn."

Harriet wished she knew Alfred well enough to know whether he was joking about owning a Porsche. No wonder she was stumped on this case. She couldn't understand the sick animals' owner any more than she could puzzle out the malady itself.

CHAPTER THIRTEEN

This would prove interesting. She'd be viewing Alfred's property and hunting for more clues in dense fog. Checking his animals when she couldn't see more than a few feet in front of her. Looking for insects in proverbial pea soup, and without a detective's handy magnifying glass.

Alfred's house was enormous compared to Arlene's. Harriet wondered if at one time the two properties had been joined and Arlene's was the gardener's cottage. But she dismissed the idea. The stone wall had been there for hundreds of years, if moss and lichen told the story.

To Harriet's surprise, Alfred's house was not lifted from the set of a horror movie. It was an elegant pale-stone Georgian, from what she could see through the haze and remember from her first visit, when she hadn't approached the house. This time, Alfred led her straight there. The back door through which they entered had a fresh coat of paint in a color that reminded Harriet of glacial rivers.

Beyond a mudroom, the space opened to a well-appointed kitchen. The area was open, airy, and neat as a pin. Somehow, Harriet had imagined Alfred cooking in a pot over an open fire—if he cooked at all. She thought he would be more likely to subsist on prepackaged freezer meals or bread and butter with the occasional treat of cold cuts. She'd wondered if takeout boxes overwhelmed his trash can.

She couldn't have been more wrong. This was the kitchen of someone who enjoyed food preparation and took pride in caring for the space dedicated to it. She could tell the difference between a kitchen that was spick-and-span from lack of use and one that was lovingly tidied after being put through its paces. This was definitely the latter.

"This is a beautiful kitchen, Alfred." She spotted a phone charger plugged into an outlet above the counter. Pointing to it, she asked, "Is that for an android phone?"

"It is," Alfred said. "Do you need to charge your cell?"

Harriet held up her dead phone. "I would really appreciate it," she said.

"Help yourself. Then wash those tire marks off your hands and have a seat at the island. I'll get some tea going to chase the fog out of our bones." He washed his hands at the sink, filled a large teakettle, and set it to boil on the sparkling industrial-size stove. "I cook some. Studied to be a chef for a while and worked in a kitchen or two."

Suddenly she better understood his fondness for fancy foods like his specialty goat cheese for high-end restaurants.

She was flummoxed but in a pleasant way. She was also beginning to be a little ashamed that she'd assumed so much about him incorrectly, unfairly. How else had she misjudged him?

"Don't suppose you're a biscuit person, skinny as you are."

Harriet considered herself of average build. But she was beginning to understand his gruffness a little better now, so instead of taking offense, she smiled at him. "I happen to love a good biscuit, Alfred. I don't suppose yours are homemade, are they?"

"I won't say. Can't have rumors spreading." She caught a glimpse of a grin at the corner of his mouth as he turned away. He opened an antique tin on the counter and took out a handful of what sure looked like homemade shortbread. He arranged the cookies on a plate and pulled a small bowl of chicken salad from the double-door stainless steel fridge. Had she even seen one of those since leaving the States?

"I'm sorry. I didn't mean to interrupt your lunch," she said.

He waved away her concern as he cut two thick slices from a loaf of hearty-looking bread. "You didn't. I already ate. I was thinking you may have missed your midday meal."

She glanced at her watch. Indeed, she had. "Thank you. That's very generous." There was a good chance that Brody had let Will know she was stranded, so she should text Will to let him know her abandoned car, if he found it, did not mean she'd been abducted by ne'er-do-wells. "Alfred, I need to call off the bloodhounds looking for me."

"You do that. And tell them about the value of a blind horse while you're at it."

She chuckled. "I will."

While she updated Will and Brody, Alfred set out the rest of the spread. A platter of fresh vegetables and fruit, a sleek pot of tea, and a glass jar of herbed goat cheese.

She told Brody to call her with any emergencies and to keep records of other phone calls until she returned. With Polly gone, Brody requiring her supervision for investigative as well as internship reasons, the flat-tire delay, and this stop at Alfred's stretching out far longer than she'd anticipated, the day was growing more complicated by the minute.

If she hadn't entertained the possibility that Brody might somehow be involved in Alfred's dilemma, she wouldn't have thought twice about admitting she wouldn't be back in the office until much later than planned. She was probably imagining the worst—that Brody was not who he said he was.

She returned her attention to the meal and the kitchen in which she sat. "I'm sorry for holding you up, Alfred."

"I respect your wanting to be responsible. It gave me time to pull this together." He set another plate before her.

"Are these candied walnuts?"

"Yes. I like to fiddle with things like that once in a while. They're good dipped in the goat cheese. But the cheese is the best bit."

"Between candied walnuts and Arlene's sticky toffee pudding, I'll need to let out the seams of my wedding gown."

Alfred stiffened. "She made sticky toffee pudding for you?"

"Well, not for me, especially, but I've had it, yes." What was she thinking? How far would Alfred retreat into his normal rough-as-sandpaper status with a slip like her mentioning Arlene?

He picked at something invisible on the island surface. Had he known about Arlene's dessert specialty? Well, the whole community likely knew. That had to be it. But why the downcast eyes? Downcast, not hostile.

She tried to recover the conversation. "Your chicken salad is delicious, Alfred. Some of the best I've tasted. Is that tarragon?"

He nodded. "The stuff grows like weeds in my kitchen garden. It's surprisingly good with goat chops too."

"I'm not—"

"Let me guess," Alfred said. "You're not a fan of goat meat." He snorted. "Americans."

"We have our admirable qualities," she said and then winced. Even she could hear a tinge of defensiveness in her tone.

"I'm sure you must. Probably haven't even tried quality goat but think you know everything anyway." His single overall strap bounced on his chest when he rose and walked to the fridge again. She focused on the meal before her, and the tea she hoped wasn't laced with arsenic.

No true Brit would mess with good tea. That could be her saving grace.

Within minutes, he had cooked up something that smelled divine in a cast-iron skillet. "Here. Taste this."

His command had worked well the last time. She took the fork he offered and selected a chunk of steaming, fragrant meat.

The morsel melted in her mouth. She dropped the fork onto her plate.

His expression reminded her of a schoolmaster waiting on an explanation for a student's tardiness.

"Alfred, you've made me a fan of goat meat."

His smile stretched from molar to molar. "You should taste it with roasted baby potatoes from my garden."

"You're a phenomenal chef."

He brushed it off. "That's too fancy a word for a bloke like me."

"I disagree," she said.

He and Arlene would make a great team.

If only they weren't mortal enemies, at least from Alfred's perspective. Arlene called it a one-sided feud. But neighbors who shared a property line had been the fodder for feuds time out of mind.

Thus part of the reason for her visit.

After lunch, he loaded the dishwasher while she wiped the island with a hand-knitted dishcloth that had clearly been used for years. It was a true incongruity in this modern kitchen. Maybe the cloth had belonged to his mother. She tried to imagine a woman raising a child like the little boy Alfred must have been. She couldn't even picture it.

"Do you mind if I get a peek beyond those double doors?" she asked. "I'd love to see what else you've done with renovations to this fine old home."

He leaned against the sink. "It's not what you'd expect."

Nothing about Alfred was what she expected. Was he hiding something beyond the boundary of the kitchen? Then again, it wasn't as if she had a right to poke around his home. "If you'd rather I didn't, I understand."

"No. It's fine." He drew a deep breath. "Come on through here." He crossed to the doors that separated the kitchen from the rest of the grand house.

Or not so grand. Apparently, all of Alfred's creative genius and money had been poured into the kitchen. The rest resembled the day after demolition on a home-improvement show. Adding to the ambiance was a setup that seemed to serve as living quarters. The furniture, a small bed, a table and two chairs, was old, bare, and sparse. Interior walls were framed, but that was all.

"It's a work in progress," he said, a touch of chagrin in his tone. "A work in long progress. But it will be grand again one day, if my money and energy hold out and I don't meet my maker first."

"It's not hard to envision what you plan for this place," Harriet assured him. "If it turns out anything like your kitchen, it'll be magnificent."

He seemed taken aback by the compliment. "One step at a time, as they say. Although I don't have a set of steps to the upper level at the moment. That'll come. Eventually."

"Do you have someone helping with the restoration?" Her voice echoed in the open space.

"No. It's just me." He paused. "It's always been just me."

He held the double doors as if he expected her to walk back through the kitchen and forget the hollowness.

She tried to forget. But the sense of emptiness lingered no matter where her steps took her.

"Fog's lifting," he said, pointing out the window over the sink. "We'd better get to what you came here for. Investigating."

"You said you had more evidence?"

His expression shuttered. "I'll save that until after you've seen the goat that went to his knees this morning," he began, his voice gruff again. "I got him separated from the others. But he doesn't look good. He's not one of my milkers, of course, but he's a favorite, and, well…"

"Let's go take a look, Alfred. Oh!" She smacked a hand to her forehead.

"What is it?"

"My wellies are in my Land Rover."

"Let's go saddle up then. We'll take the Lamborghini this time, otherwise known as my pickup. We'd better get moving. We've got all that road to travel." This time, Harriet caught the twinkle of amusement in his eyes.

She snorted. "All thirty yards of it."

They'd only made it a few feet beyond the back door when he stopped abruptly, forcing Harriet to do the same. "Let's see if we can find a couple of lug nuts in the machine shed. I think I saw an old jug full of miscellaneous nuts and bolts in there. Maybe we can get your wheels secured so you can drive yourself here first, then to the clinic. You do have petrol in the vehicle, don't you?"

"Plenty." She might actually make it out of this adventure alive.

She followed him to the shed and waited while he struggled to open the door. "I haven't been in here for a few months," he said, breathless from the effort. "It's a real mess. I keep trying to find the time to clean it out, but you know how that goes." The hinges creaked and the door dragged on the ground when he finally wrestled it open.

Alfred hadn't been kidding. Every flat surface in the shed—every bench, every table, was covered in what looked like junk. But Harriet knew enough about Yorkshire farmers by now to know that an item that looked like junk to her was something a resourceful farmer could find a use for as it was or refurbish for whatever the need might be at the moment.

High above them was a small skylight so covered in spider webs and dust, it was a wonder any of the sun's rays filtered into the shed. Alfred made his way to a workbench by the light that spilled in the open door.

She waited while he found what he wanted, and then they exited the building, the door once again scraping the ground as Alfred closed it.

"Your veggies are doing well, Alfred." Harriet stepped closer to the garden, wondering whether she was about to cross a line with him. When he didn't panic, she continued toward his potato plants. "Oh. That's interesting."

"What is?"

"Must have been the weather conditions last fall when you planted. Your potatoes have little clusters of what look like small green tomatoes. That doesn't happen all the time."

"Huh," Alfred said, bending to look for himself. "Thought I had a volunteer tomato plant in there."

"It's a part of the potato itself, connected right here," Harriet said, pointing. "It's the fruit, actually, or the seed of a potato plant. Aunt Jinny taught me that when I was much, much younger. They only appear when growing and weather conditions are just right."

"Don't know that I've seen them before. I suppose I should harvest them."

It was Harriet's turn to be alarmed. "No! I don't know what evidence you wanted to show me, but this might be your problem. The green potato berries can be toxic to humans, and to goats. Are your animals allowed near the garden?"

"Well, what kind of garden would I have left if I permitted that? What a question."

Harriet looked toward the fenced area several yards from where they stood. "Couldn't they wander this way if they escaped?"

"Anything's possible. Goats are ruthless when they want something. But we'd know they'd been here. They wouldn't daintily tiptoe up and nibble on these potato berries. They'd trample the plants—every last bit they didn't eat, that is."

"The plant itself is also toxic for goats," Harriet said. "Can I take a branch of these berries back to my office? It might help us be more specific in our toxicology investigation."

"I doubt it's as simple a solution as that, Doc, but be my guest. Plus, as I say, I have irrefutable evidence to show you."

Harriet decided to reserve judgment until she saw it for herself.

CHAPTER FOURTEEN

White Church Bay

July 1910

There was nothing else for it. If Conrad could eliminate more of the comforts on his bi-wing plane—like the padding for his pilot seat—he would reduce more weight and drag. Once he drew more attention and more support for his work, he could afford to invest in lighter-weight materials for the construction of the craft itself. All of England should be behind him, but it wasn't.

Yet.

Eating seemed less important than perfecting his techniques and understanding wind currents. His trousers and shirt now fit too loosely. But, he reasoned, his physical bulk would be less of an issue in takeoff now.

He tied his trouser legs tight at his ankles to prevent the winds from ballooning the fabric. What more could he do?

If he could trim away his concern for Elizabeth so easily, it would at least lighten his mind. Her parents—stoic and "sensible," according to them—claimed it was not their distrust of Conrad, but their protection of their daughter that motivated them to object to their being engaged. He could not make Elizabeth see otherwise. With Elizabeth in the middle and Conrad and her parents on opposite sides of a growing rift, she grew more wan and strained by the day.

"Love makes sacrifices," her parents had said.

"So does progress," he'd told them.

They hadn't spoken again since.

He checked the wind again. He'd show them. All of them. This would be worth it.

CHAPTER FIFTEEN

Harriet returned to Cobble Hill with a small branch of potato berries, another sick goat, and a sincere prayer she could restore it to health, for everyone's sake.

She also came home with her proverbial tail between her legs. After he'd led her to the ailing goat, Alfred had taken her back to the house to show her video footage of Arlene and Harriet gazing over the wall into his property. He realized they had been up to no mischief—at that moment, anyway—but Alfred demonstrated all the signs of having been betrayed. Not by the two women, necessarily, but by the additional footage he showed Harriet.

Arlene's two hired hands were caught on camera, fighting through a bare spot in the brambles to lower a goat over the wall onto Alfred's property.

Just when Harriet had begun to believe the boys couldn't be involved.

She would talk to Arlene about that later. For now, she had some serious goat recovery to address.

Brody was still stationed at the reception desk, watching the door as if royalty might walk through any moment. He jumped at the chance for some hands-on veterinary assistance work.

And Harriet was happy that, should the goat not make it, she'd have a witness it wasn't her doing. Provided she could trust Brody.

"Speak to me, sir," she murmured.

"What would you like me to say, Dr. Bailey?" Brody asked.

"I was talking to the goat."

"Oh, of course." She caught a hint of amusement in his voice.

"What is this? I don't understand what's going on. What are you observing, Brody?"

The young man bent over the animal on the exam table. "Respiratory distress."

"Yes."

"Airways seem irritated."

"That could indicate an allergic reaction or having ingested something that caused the irritation. But you know goats. Who knows what they're getting into?"

The young man bent even lower over the animal. "This is interesting."

"What is?"

"He's not reacting in any way to the restraints. Wouldn't he naturally buck and resist?"

"He's lethargic, as several of the others have been. Let's start an IV—electrolytes and hydration. We may need to give him oxygen."

"Noted."

"We'll need typical labs. And toxicology, including an additional test we haven't considered before. I'll explain more later, but Alfred may have been inadvertently poisoning his own goats with potato berries."

Brody's eyebrows rose. "I didn't even know there was such a thing. I'll get the IV started."

Harriet sighed. "Thank you, Brody. Let's see if we can find some answers."

Harriet sent Brody home when it got dark. This was one of the times she especially appreciated living on the premises. It might be a very long night. But Charlie and Maxwell and her own home were mere steps away. And all three called to her.

She'd processed the lab work she could do at the clinic. One of the curious readings was a low blood glucose level. That could explain the lethargy, but not the rest of the symptoms. She added glucose solution as well as the electrolytes. If this illness or disease or toxic reaction or whatever it was had hit a mama goat shortly after giving birth, it was no wonder the symptoms had affected her so fast. Here was a strong goat fighting for his life with apparently nothing wrong with him except what had caused these random, seemingly unrelated symptoms.

Harriet had insisted she'd be okay on her own, but Will stopped by anyway with takeout fish and chips from Cliffside Chippy. They shared the meal and Harriet's observations about Alfred's farm.

"I wonder how much of Alfred's gruffness is an act," she said.

Will sprinkled more salt and vinegar on his chips. "What makes you say that?"

"For a while, I wondered if he had some kind of mental disorder, and that's not my field. But I see glimpses of what I think is the real

Alfred. That person is generous, talented, a fine businessman, innovative, and..." She trailed off.

"And what?" Will pressed.

"Heartbroken, I think."

Will nodded. "I wouldn't be surprised. Heartbreak often shows up in ways that hurt others, intentionally or unintentionally."

Harriet forked up a bite of flaky fish. "Maybe that's it. Or fear. I wonder if he's afraid of being as alone and empty as the unfinished part of his house."

"There's a way to cure that. He could be nicer to people."

"I think he's trying. He fed me goat meat."

Will widened his eyes in mock alarm. "Harriet! Should we have your stomach pumped?"

She laughed. "No. If he was going to poison me, he would have put it in the chicken salad. He wouldn't want his goats' reputation to be tainted. But thank you for your concern, Will."

He smiled warmly. "I will never tire of hearing you speak my name with such tenderness, Harriet."

The moment shattered when the goat's heart monitor beeped loud enough to be heard down the hall. Harriet took off on a run with Will at her heels.

Not a trace of fog blurred the dawn of the new day. But someone already waited outside the clinic door when Harriet unlocked it Tuesday morning.

"Alfred? How long have you been sitting there?"

He staggered to his feet, rubbing his eyes. Had he fallen asleep leaning against the building? "What did you say?"

"How long have you been out here?"

"A fair bit of time."

"I was going to call you at a reasonable hour, as opposed to this one."

"Saw the light was on."

"And you happened to be passing by?" Weariness prevented her from a full laugh. "Come on back."

"Is he—"

Harriet smiled at him. "Believe it or not, that goat is even more stubborn than you are."

Relief washed over Alfred's features. "The old goat."

"Exactly. He tried to die on us."

"But he didn't?"

"Come see for yourself." Harriet ushered Alfred into the treatment room.

The goat wasn't back on his feet by any stretch of the imagination yet. But he rested comfortably on a blanket on the exam room floor, Charlie kneading his side and Maxwell dodging the goat's attempts to chew on his prosthesis straps.

A major part of this mystery was how the afflicted animals recovered to near normal so quickly. So many possible causes would have left permanent damage or taken them far longer to recover.

Alfred knelt in front of his animal and rubbed the top of the goat's knobby head. "Oh, Ferdinand." The goat leaned into Alfred's touch.

"Ferdinand? Is that the Spanish word for stubborn?" Harriet joked.

"It's German for 'brave in journey,' actually, and I think he's wearing it especially well today. Thanks, Harriet."

Harriet's heart warmed. She hoped his more familiar address to her meant he wouldn't be so hard to get along with now and they could be friends.

Alfred peered into the goat's large eyes. "Ferdinand, whatever Arlene's hired hands did to you, they will pay for it. Mark my words."

Harriet's heart sank. She was too tired for this conversation, but it had to happen. "Alfred, you know, you don't have any proof those boys did anything to him."

"I've got the video footage. And I have the right good detective constable on his way to arrest the two of them when they show up at the Pretendergrass estate this morning."

"You can't be serious." Minutes before, her compassion had taken over. Now she was back to irritation over Alfred's endless suspicion, which bordered on paranoia.

"I've never been more serious in my life. What kind of poison did they use, Doc? The DC will want to know."

Harriet clenched her jaw. "I don't even know that it was poison, and there's no evidence Gregory and Heath are responsible. It could just as reasonably have been the potato berries, Alfred."

"You saw the video."

"I saw the brothers putting a goat back where it belonged. On your side of the wall."

"Sure, after they poisoned him. Or that woman did."

It was time to put an end to this. "Alfred, Arlene is my friend, and I can't let you keep spreading nasty lies like that and threatening her reputation." Harriet met his eyes squarely. "And I know you care about that. I have a feeling she might have been your friend too, at one time."

His chin quivered. "I don't want to hear anything about that ever again. I'm beholden to you for saving Ferdinand. But this is not over, and justice will be served."

A racket sounded from the front of the office. Who was trying to kick the door in?

"Excuse me, Alfred. Someone is trying to get my attention."

"Can I take Ferdinand home?"

"Just wait here until I get back, and I'll explain."

As if she hadn't spoken, he followed her from the exam room to the reception area where they found "the right good" Detective Constable Worthington.

"I didn't expect to see you here this morning, Van," Harriet said, removing her exam gloves and tossing them in the bin near the reception counter.

"I have a report for Alfred, who said I could find him here. And from the way he talked, you'll likely be interested to know this information as well."

Alfred stepped forward. "Where are the boys? In your vehicle?"

"No, Alfred," Van said. "I have no reason to detain them, much less arrest them."

"I sent you video evidence," Alfred said, hands waving. "What more do you need?"

"The law needs more than what I saw on the video you emailed to me." Van kept his tone even and measured.

Harriet's stomach clenched. "Alfred, there's a lot of accusations flying around. I have a feeling most of it is unfounded."

Yes, the boys had been caught with a goat…just prior to the animal taking ill.

She knew better than to stack coincidence on top of coincidence. What she'd seen showed them putting the goat back on Alfred's land. But before they returned him, could they have—?

If so, that was no harmless, youthful prank.

Alfred huffed. "What did the boys have to say for themselves?"

"They're teens who took a summer job helping Arlene Pendergraf, Alfred," Van said. "According to them, your goats have been hopping that wall regularly, lured by the thorny blackberry bushes on Ms. Pendergraf's side. The brothers were simply returning one of them."

"I can't keep goats from being goats," Alfred said. "But if Arlene was upset about it, she could have told me."

It took all of Harriet's self-control to keep her mouth shut.

"There was no reason for her to hire those boys to make the goats ill before sending them back over." At least Alfred had lowered his voice to a normal level.

Van took a notebook from the breast pocket of his uniform. "They claim Ms. Pendergraf hired them for weeding, clearing away brush, cleaning up after the shearers are done, cleaning out water troughs, and helping with lambing—"

"Well of course that's what they'd tell you!" Alfred's ears turned red, and he'd raised his voice again. "You didn't find anything on them? No trace of suspicious materials on their hands or clothes?"

Harriet doubted they were wearing the same clothes now as they were in the video. But she resisted pointing that out to Alfred.

"Listen," Van said, "I've dealt with these two brothers before. Had them in my Sunday school class a few years ago. They're harmless, Alfred. And more than a little scared of a visit from me this early in the morning. They said it was the first day they've shown up to work on time. Guess that'll teach them."

Harriet spoke up. "Van isn't trying to make light of the situation, Alfred. He has nothing to go on other than the video, which only shows them returning your goat."

Van nodded. "I'll keep my eyes open, Alfred. And if I see anything out of order with those two, I won't be shy about digging deeper."

After caring for Ferdinand all night, Harriet was operating on too little sleep, no shower, no breakfast, and no time to change her clothes. And now the first real client of the day was peering through the door at this circus. Thankfully, Harriet heard Polly's and Brody's voices coming from the kitchen.

"Can we move this discussion to another location, or disband it altogether?" Harriet asked the two men. "I have patients to see. Alfred, you can come back to visit Ferdinand when we're not busy. He won't be discharged until I'm satisfied he's ready."

Van peered at Harriet. "You okay, Doc?"

"Sleep deprived."

"Alfred?" Van waited for the man to speak.

Alfred spluttered for a moment before saying, "I have chores waiting for me back at my place."

After he left, Harriet had the distinct feeling that she hadn't done anything more than kick the can down the road, but that couldn't be helped at the moment. For now, she had other animals to care for.

CHAPTER SIXTEEN

The fog in Harriet's brain on Tuesday had been thicker than that in the air on Monday. But somehow, she made it to the glorious moment when she could drop into bed.

On Wednesday morning, she awoke feeling refreshed and ready to face the day, aside from a crick in her neck, probably from sleeping so soundly.

Ferdinand was a little stiff too but making great strides in his recovery. Another day at Cobble Hill, and the old goat could return home.

Alfred had brought over a container of chicken soup fragrant with lemon and tarragon around midmorning. Harriet had accepted the peace offering and allowed him to check on his goat. He and Ferdinand seemed to enjoy their visit together. Alfred even ruffled Maxwell's ears when he left and said, "Thanks, kiddo."

During a lull between clients, Polly caught up on paperwork and Harriet ran through her checklist.

Reply to Mom's email about their flight arrangements? Check.

Call about toxicology report? Check. No results yet. The lab was short-staffed, but because of the previous sample contamination, they promised to expedite as best they could. She couldn't fault them, as she knew the panicky feeling of being shorthanded.

Work on her half of the wedding vows? Harriet had tried but came up empty. Maybe one more good night's sleep would benefit that project. How could she possibly communicate all that was in her heart regarding Will and their future together?

Just as she released a satisfied sigh that things were quieting down, the door burst open followed by a frantic, "Please help us, Doc!"

An adorable Labrador puppy lay limp in the woman's arms.

"Back this way," Harriet said. "Exam Room Two."

"There's something horribly wrong with her," the woman said.

Harriet recognized the face from the community but not the name. "Let's see what we can figure out. I'm Dr. Bailey."

"Oh, I'm Linda Granville. I work at the Happy Cup part-time. My husband and I own a hobby farm a little north of here. Mostly chickens and heirloom vegetables."

The pup's head lolled to the side.

"Lay her down here on the exam table. Are you okay to stay here while I examine what's going on? I need to ask you some questions."

"Yes, of course. Oh, precious baby. We've only had her a few weeks. She's the dearest thing. I don't know what's happening."

Harriet checked the animal's pupils. Her eyeballs rolled disconcertingly, but the pup didn't seem to be in pain. "When did the limpness start?" She hoped what she was witnessing had nothing to do with what had affected Alfred's goats. Some of the symptoms were too familiar.

"She had a spell like this two days ago, but then she was better yesterday. So I thought it was a fluke."

"Has she been snippy or irritable?"

"No, not at all. Content, happy, a bit lazier than usual."

"Something is going on neurologically," Harriet said. "She seems to have lost muscle tone, and her reflexes are quite a bit slower than they should be."

"She was fine until that first spell she had."

"Was it a seizure?" Harriet opened the dog's mouth to check the color of her gumline. The dog didn't resist at all. Even well-trained dogs who easily allowed her to peek into their mouths were startled by the initial attempt, so the fact that the puppy didn't even try to pull away was alarming. "Have you seen a seizure in an animal before?"

"On the telly, but it was nothing like that. She'd been outside like normal, just exploring and enjoying the day. When I called her to come, she took the longest time responding and then walked toward me crooked, if that makes sense. Slow, and as if she was dizzy or disoriented."

"How long did that last?"

"Maybe three hours. I kept her inside with me. She just lay in her bed, her head flopping once in a while like you just saw, sighing. I'm not sure I've ever heard a dog sigh like that before."

"But she could breathe okay? Nothing obstructing her airway?"

"She was breathing fine. Nice and easy. I looked for that in particular. I have young children, you see."

"So you know how to check for an obstruction." Harriet tried to let her facial expression offer Linda a measure of comfort, small as it might seem with the disconcerting symptoms.

The woman sniffed but couldn't hold back the tears.

Harriet leaned closer to the puppy's face. "What is going on with you, sweet girl? Oh!"

"What is it?"

"Bend down here. Can you smell it?"

Linda obliged then frowned. "Smells like alcohol. Nobody in our family drinks, Dr. Bailey."

Harriet straightened and stroked the animal's chestnut-colored fur. "I don't want to alarm you prematurely."

"What is it?"

"Could be several things. Diabetic ketosis. Kidney disease. Possibly even an insect-borne virus." If so, this was enormously serious for the community as a whole.

"Oh dear."

"We won't know anything for certain without blood work and a more thorough examination. I would give her something for pain, but if anything, she seems euphoric. I see no signs that any of this has been painful for her."

"I found that curious too," Linda said.

"Are you comfortable leaving her here for the night?"

"Yes. Please do whatever you have to. The children will be worried."

"I wish I could tell you more than that we don't know anything yet. We can save our effort for worrying until we discover something to worry about. If we do, that is. Whatever this is could be utterly treatable."

"Look at that. She fell asleep. She's never snored before. Is that a sign of anything?"

Harriet checked the dog's airway again. The odor was strong. But her airway didn't seem obstructed by anything other than her normal anatomy and her lolling tongue. "I'd say snoring is a sign she might be related to my grandad."

"Or mine."

"Go on home," Harriet said. "Leave your information with Polly at the front desk. I'll contact you as soon as I know anything. But perhaps sleep is what this pup needs right now. Who knows what she's been through or what her body is trying to fight off?"

"Thank you, Dr. Bailey. Everyone says you're the best. For our animals and for those of us who love them."

"I'm glad to hear it, Linda. We'll do everything we can to get to the bottom of this. There are no guarantees with animals, or people either. But we'll try our best. What's this beauty's name?"

"It's…it's been an ongoing debate in our house. Three kids, two parents, and my elderly aunt who lives with us—that makes six opinions. Two months is too long to have a family member without a name. We've had some major distractions, but that's no excuse. We've gone round and round about it. My husband and I vetoed several options the kids came up with, like 'Lazy' and 'Goofy.' I wouldn't want her carrying a name like that around her whole life." She paused to sniff. "We planned to vote on a name for her tonight—a naming party. I can't bear to pull that off right now."

Harriet was determined not to leave Linda without hope. "Maybe we'll let her pick her own name in a few days. We could write different names on pieces of paper and let her draw one out of a hat, or scatter several papers on the floor and let her pounce on one. I think she deserves a say."

Linda managed a watery smile. "That would be lovely. Thank you, Dr. Bailey."

"That's what I'm here for."

The puppy perked up within an hour, whether from her nap or her IV, Harriet had no idea. The tests she could do on-site, including preliminary blood work, were still processing. If this was related to the goat illnesses, it could cause panic in White Church Bay and the surrounding area. An illness that affected any animal regardless of species was frightening, especially when there was no way to know how the individual animals would be affected or how long it would take for them to recover.

Harriet also prayed the dog's issue wasn't a brain bleed or any number of seizure-like anomalies. This pup deserved a chance. And she had already wriggled her way into her family's hearts.

She was quickly doing the same at the clinic. Polly and Harriet fell in love with her instantly, as did Maxwell, although once back to normal, the pup ran circles around him.

Nothing about the dog seemed out of the ordinary for a puppy that age. Into everything. Curious about all things moving or still. Hungry. Rambunctious.

Nothing in the lab work showed anything definitive—except, strangely, a slightly elevated blood alcohol level. Harriet had played a hunch based on what she'd smelled from the puppy's mouth. But the kidney malfunction she fully expected to find connected to the blood result was not there. The puppy was discharged with a clean bill of health and a new bow attached to her collar.

Harriet suggested Linda and her family check their garage for an open container of antifreeze. Or maybe the pup was on a particularly high-protein, low-carb diet? Silly as the question seemed,

Harriet knew that in humans, the combination could cause a falsely high blood alcohol level. But no. Linda was feeding the little dog normal puppy food from the local pet store.

The pup was back the following day, loopier than ever. Linda left her at the clinic before going to her part-time work at the Happy Cup.

After another thorough examination and another puppy nap, Harriet called Linda's cell phone. "I don't know what to tell you. She's right as rain again now. I did more blood work and X-rays. I'm wondering if we should try a neurological specialist at this point. She can't go on like this. And you can't either. But she's just fine right now. We can keep her longer this time, but I don't know what that would tell us. Intermittent mysteries are the hardest to solve."

She was becoming all too familiar with that truth when it came to Alfred's goats.

"Thanks, Doc. I'll come get her after I'm done here. It's unnerving when it happens. Poor thing."

"I agree. It must be so difficult for you. If I didn't know better, I'd think the little thing was tipsy and simply needed to sleep it off."

"She can't be. She doesn't have access to anything like that in our home."

"Linda, please don't take this the wrong way, but is it possible your aunt is dipping into your cooking wine and sharing it with your pup?"

Linda shook her head. "We don't have any cooking wine, but I see what you mean. I hate the thought of spying on my aunt, but if she's doing something that could be dangerous for the puppy, we need to know."

"We do indeed. I don't advocate invading your aunt's privacy, but I've grown pretty fond of this puppy. She keeps coming up fine in her lab tests, so I don't have any answers, which means we need to look elsewhere for them. Do check the garage, please. And do you happen to grow potatoes in your garden?"

"Not this year. None sprouted. It was the oddest thing."

"That may be good. Potato berries and potato plants themselves can be toxic to some animals. I'd be surprised if the symptoms presented this way though. We'll pray this is the last of your dog's issues, whatever they are."

Harriet hadn't heard from Alfred since his Wednesday visit with Ferdinand. It was now Friday morning. Had he gone three days without any other animal falling ill? Could the crisis be over for him?

Interestingly, Arlene's hired hands had quit the day Van questioned them. The boys were gone, and there were no new goat ailments. How could that not seem suspicious?

Harriet walked toward the reception area, pondering how she might find out where the boys were now so she could interrogate them herself. But she was interrupted by Polly's cheerful, "Linda, how nice to see you. What brings you in today?"

Oh, no. Harriet rushed into the reception area to find out how the nameless puppy was afflicted today then stopped short in confusion.

"Hi, Doc. Meet the no-longer-unnamed puppy."

Bright eyes, bouncing, bounding, curious, whole body wriggling with joy. What a relief.

"She's doing well, Linda?"

"Right as rain, as you can see."

"I'm glad to hear it."

"And we named her Bailey, after you. It was unanimous."

"I'm honored." Harriet crouched to let Bailey express her gratitude with her puppy version of hugs and kisses. "This is one healthy dog," she said. *And I am one grateful doc.*

"She is, now that she's no longer tipsy. We discovered the source of the problem last night."

"Oh?" Harriet straightened and lowered her voice. "Not your aunt, I hope."

Linda's laughter filled the room. "No, it was our broken freezer."

"What?"

"We lost a bunch of food when our deep freezer died on us. Frozen vegetables, some premade meals, and a ton of frozen bread dough, which we tossed behind one of the outbuildings far from the house. Do you know what happens to frozen bread dough in the heat of summer?"

"The yeast turns into—"

"That's right. This little rascal was chowing down on that fermented bread dough. Caught her red-handed, or rather, red-pawed, right before I planned to confront my dear aunt."

"Wonderful timing."

"Couldn't have been better. I can assure you, we'll never make the mistake of disposing of anything fermentable in a similar way again."

Harriet laughed. "I think in the long run you'll be very happy with that decision. Problem solved."

"It's nice to know you can do that for someone, anyway." Alfred Ramshaw entered the clinic, wearing his usual storm-cloud expression.

Jeb the would-be alpaca farmer followed him in.

Harriet braced herself. What now?

CHAPTER SEVENTEEN

What can I do for you two gentlemen? Oh, I have the toxicology reports back for you, Alfred. I was about to call you. Unfortunately, they reveal nothing we didn't already know."

Alfred lowered his gaze a moment then drew a deep breath. "And it wasn't the potato berries?"

"No. But I would still fence off the garden more completely to keep your animals away."

"I see," Alfred said.

"Is that what brought you in?" Harriet asked, aware that Linda and Bailey were watching this exchange with open confusion.

"Not quite." Jeb removed his cap, which was hardly recognizable under a layer of dust and cobwebs. In fact, all his clothing was in a similar condition.

When the younger man seemed to have trouble verbalizing his needs, Alfred jumped in. "Jeb needs a mouser, Doc."

"A mouser?" Harriet replied.

"Absolutely." Alfred turned to Jeb. "I mean no offense by this, but son, you could well use a regiment of them for your property."

A rodent problem on Jeb's farm. Harriet should have guessed. "How can the vet clinic help you?"

Alfred brushed dust from the front of his overalls. "You're likely to find a stray cat wandering in here, aren't you?" He eyed Charlie as if she were for hire.

"We do. But perhaps you should try the animal shelter in one of the larger villages, if you're looking to adopt."

"More like borrow," Jeb said. "I'm allergic to cats, but I could use several for a while, to get ahead of the problem. You know what happens when a house and barns are abandoned, Doc." He scuffed the toe of his boot on the linoleum.

"I do." She'd seen it often. "But if you intend to return the cats to the shelter after they've performed that service for you, it's rather cruel to the animals, isn't it?"

"They'll go back considerably fatter," Alfred said with a grin.

"Have you considered an exterminator?" Harriet asked. "Their services are meant to be temporary."

"I'd rather sneeze for a few weeks," Jeb said, pulling out the lining of his trouser pockets as explanation. A cloud of dust settled from the pockets onto the floor. "Besides, I worry that an exterminator might use chemicals that would be harmful to Lovie and any other alpacas I end up with."

By the end of the conversation, they'd decided what would work best was a poster for the bulletin board near the front door of the clinic.

WANTED

SEVERAL VIGOROUS AND ADVENTURESOME BARN

CATS FOR TEMPORARY DUTY AS MOUSERS.

MEALS AND HOUSING FURNISHED.

Alfred's number followed, as Jeb had yet to purchase a cell phone. Alfred's dedication to helping the younger man simply added another layer to his mysteriousness. Every time Harriet thought she had him figured out, he went and proved her wrong.

Alfred's brows tented. "Oh, one more thing, Doc. Despite my better judgment, I ordered a couple more goats from that trader in Thirsk."

"And how are they doing?"

"So far, so good."

"Glad to hear it."

"Time will tell. It always does," Alfred said, a hint of wistfulness in his statement.

Within a few minutes, the two left Harriet's reception room in search of scrap lumber, in spite of, it seemed, Alfred's "considerable means."

Another layer to the mystery.

If she didn't love her aunt Jinny so much, Harriet would have ditched the knit-for-your-health idea after one week of the experiment. A lovely pair of mittens from one of her clients would have sufficed for her appreciation of the wonders of knitting, at least until winter's chill. But it was Friday morning, and Aunt Jinny had never steered her wrong in the past.

The wedding plans were mostly done, including the flowers in shades of both deep and light lavender, pink, and blush—the colors of the blossoming heather that would soon carpet the moors. But she was convinced she must have forgotten something, so the wedding continued to take up space in her mind. Her clinic schedule was still hectic, and her parents were soon to arrive on British soil. Yet here she sat, needles in hand, trying not to let knitting raise rather than lower her blood pressure.

"Crafting yourself a wedding garter, Doc?" Betsy Templeton asked.

"That's one tradition I'm happy has faded in popularity." Harriet's brow furrowed as she focused on the stitches slowly growing on her needles.

Betsy harrumphed. "Looks like a garter to me."

Harriet had to admit the resemblance. "It's supposed to be the cuff of a mitten. I didn't intend for it to look so frilly."

"Not frilly. Posh, I'd say," Arlene said. "However did you manage to do that?"

"Happy accident?" Harriet said.

Betsy wrinkled her nose. "I doubt an accident can ever be considered happy."

Harriet opened her mouth to apologize, but Arlene laid a hand on Harriet's arm and whispered, "Betsy lost her husband, Philip, in a plane crash, Doc." Arlene leaned closer. "It was quite a few years ago, and she doesn't like to talk about it."

"Oh, the poor thing," Harriet said. "How sad."

"Do you see what she's knitting?"

Harriet looked more closely at the elderly woman's work. She had taken it for granted that everyone else in the room was advanced in the craft of knitting, but now she could see that Betsy was making something that could turn into a simple scarf. Harriet looked at the bag next to Betsy's feet and saw a stack of knitted squares inside.

"They look like potholders," Harriet said to Arlene.

"They're squares for blankets," Arlene said. "Philip was the financial director for a missionary organization headquartered in London. One of their missions is to provide warm blankets for vulnerable and orphaned children. People from many different countries knit squares that are sent all over the world and then sewn together and distributed to the children. Betsy's made thousands of squares by now. One right after another. Says she intends to do that until she can't hold the needles anymore. I think her persistence is a beautiful tribute to her husband and keeps his memory alive."

"Grief doesn't have an expiration date," Betsy said, as if she'd heard every word. "But helping others is a way to keep it bearable."

"That's right and true, Betsy," Arlene said, a unique softness in her voice that made Harriet wonder if Arlene didn't know that truth better than most.

Arlene nodded toward the half-formed square in Betsy's hands. "You're doing fine work there."

An idea popped into Harriet's head. "Betsy, I'd love to make squares for the children," she said. "Could you please help me know what I need to do?"

Betsy's face lit up like the proverbial Christmas tree. "Really, Harriet? You would do that?"

"Of course I would," Harriet said. "I'm knitting to lower my blood pressure, and I can't think of anything I could knit that would make me happier and therefore calmer."

Arlene smiled. "Maybe we can all take a leaf out of Harriet's book and knit squares for a couple of weeks. What do you think, Betsy? Should we send a huge box to London at the end of the month?"

Betsy looked around the circle, and tears came to her eyes. "I can't tell you how much that would mean to me," she said. "And to the children."

The women returned to their knitting after Betsy provided the name of the organization so each woman could look it up on the internet and follow the instructions for knitting the squares.

After a few minutes, when conversations were humming around the room again, Harriet leaned close to Arlene and asked, "Do you know where your hired hands landed after they quit? I heard they haven't been around since their run-in with Van Worthington."

"I don't know what those lads were so jumpy about. Last I heard, they both signed up for the navy. I hope they do well there. I think the discipline will do them good. Their mother said they're staying close to home in Ramsdell until they have to report, next month sometime. She's keeping them too busy to get rambunctious."

Ramsdale. A bit too far to still be causing more trouble at Alfred's—if they ever had. Harriet crossed them off the suspect list. For now.

"Have you decided what to do now for hired help?"

"I'm flummoxed, actually. This late in summer is a rather awkward time to hire. University students will head back soon. Most other young people have found summer occupations or don't want one."

Harriet's needles stopped moving of their own accord. "Arlene, I might have an idea for you," she said. "I know a young man with a good work ethic, but he's in need of some farm education and experience. I doubt he could offer you more than a few hours here and there, and he'd need to be taught every step of the way. But I think he'd be an eager student and a hard worker. His name is Jeb."

"Anything would help at this point, Harriet." Arlene's posture straightened.

"He's a friend of Alfred's," Harriet said.

"Oh." She tilted her head as if contemplating. "Do you think that would be an issue?"

Harriet tried to make light of the concern, though it was one she shared. "I don't know. Alfred might appreciate having a spy on your premises."

Arlene scoffed. "Rubbish!"

Harriet warmed to the idea. "Stay with me, Arlene. The truth is there's nothing to spy on. I know that as well as you do. Hiring Jeb to work for you, if he's interested, will put some much-needed money in his pocket, give him a crash course in farming, and quiet the unfounded suspicions in your neighbor's imagination."

Betsy seemed oblivious to their conversation, engaged as she was in perusing the bargain bin of odd-lot bits of wool.

Arlene turned her face away. "Do I want to help a friend of Alfred?" she said quietly. "No. Is it likely God would look kindly on the act if I did? Yes."

"'Pray for your enemies,'" Harriet said, pulling out a scripture verse she knew Arlene would find appropriate.

"That's just it," Arlene said. "Alfred wasn't always my enemy. He isn't now. He just thinks he is."

"He wasn't?" Some days it felt as if Alfred considered all of humanity his enemy.

But Arlene seemed unwilling to expound. "Can you put me in touch with that young man? Jeb, did you say?"

"I'll try, Arlene. He has no phone at the moment." Harriet realized that the only way she had of getting in touch with Jeb was through Alfred. She didn't think that would be an option for Arlene.

"I may need to correct that for him, if he's to work for me. I would need to be able to get ahold of him when I needed to."

Arlene and Alfred, both intent on rescuing the mysterious Jeb Hawks, a relative stranger to them both. But could they be any more disparate in their approaches? Could Jeb form a bridge between them? Or would he intensify the feud? The one-sided feud, Arlene would remind her.

Time would tell.

Lightning cracked the sky, and thunder followed soon after.

Betsy bolted back to where the other women sat, her eyes wild. "Was anyone struck?" The woman tested all limbs and heads for signs of electrocution.

"Betsy, we're not likely to be struck inside a building like this." Harriet's words appeared to do nothing to reassure her.

"It's happened before. Happened before," Betsy muttered, her eyes wild and haunted.

Arlene stood and directed her friend to a waiting chair. "We're all fine. It's a simple summer storm. Imagine the good it'll do the plants—all those fruits, vegetables, flowers, and crops."

Another crack of lightning seared the air, and its companion thunder rattled the windows of the yarn shop. Betsy grabbed at anything to stabilize herself for the next blow—a fistful of Arlene's summer apron in one hand and her bulging knitting bag in the other. "This is no trifle. Them that thinks so'll be the first to perish. Put your affairs in order, mates."

"Let's pray," Harriet suggested.

Arlene picked up on her idea at once. "Yes, let's."

Betsy already sat with her hands folded in her lap, head bowed and eyes closed.

"Lord of wind and sea," Harriet began, "You calm the waves and bring peace to our hearts when storms rage. You bring us to the harbor we long for. Lend us Your peace that passes all understanding, and remind us that our hope lies in You. Calm our minds and hearts in this storm, and in all others we weather in this life."

"Amen," Betsy said reverently.

The door to the side room opened, and Will dashed inside, dripping with evidence of the downpour. What an unusual July it was turning out to be. Harriet wondered if the month's extra bouts of rain meant August would be especially lovely.

Will stashed his umbrella in a corner where puddles wouldn't be noticed. "Good afternoon, ladies. What a fine summer we're having." Rain dripped from the tip of his nose and eyelashes.

The women chuckled at his joke.

"What brings you here, Pastor Will? Are you thinking of taking up the fine art of knitting?" Arlene asked.

"Don't be silly, Arlene," Betsy said. "He's here for her." She nodded toward Harriet.

Will sidled up to Harriet, keeping his distance so as not to drip rain on her. "Enjoying your knitting therapy?"

"Ever so much." She winked at him. "What brings you here?"

"I suspected you'd walked to knitting club today. The tempest is subsiding soon according to the weather forecast, but I thought you might want to share a brolly for the trip up the hill." He gestured to his umbrella.

Betsy's eyes widened in alarm once more. "Pastor, I would not venture out into this fray. Your very life could be in danger."

"We'll be careful, Betsy," Will assured her. "It's starting to lighten up already."

"At least give the woman her own brolly then," Betsy huffed. "Purls of Faith keeps a few by the exit."

Harriet had finished packing her knitting supplies in her bag. "If it's all the same to you, I'd rather share an umbrella with Will, as we'll soon be sharing every aspect of our lives."

Arlene smiled. "How sweet."

"Tomfoolery is what it is." Betsy sank back into her chair to wait for the last drop of rain to complete its journey from the clouds.

CHAPTER EIGHTEEN

At least it wasn't raining. Conrad adjusted his goggles so the leather strap didn't bend his ears. This was it. One final chance to prove his worth as an aviator. He had investors interested in supporting him, but they were uncommitted as yet. Winning this endurance and distance race as deep into Europe as possible would make them commit. He was sure of it.

The December weather made it even riskier. But with the Channel-crossing record broken little more than a week ago, he had no choice.

The lovely Mrs. Elizabeth Stokes had cried as expected when he kissed her goodbye at the door of their flat. If only he could lend her his confidence. Risk was an inevitable part of any early venture, as he'd often assured her. But he was good at what he did. She should trust his skills.

And she would, after this race. After all, she'd finally defied her parents and agreed to marry him.

She'd chosen not to accompany him to the field for takeoff, however. Other men's wives or girlfriends preferred to watch.

Then again, far too many of them had seen their man tumble over the cliff rather than catch the updraft to soar.

Elizabeth had her reasons. One of them an especially good one. But Conrad couldn't let concern for her distract him from his goal.

He'd thought her parents would acquiesce and stand by her this day. But they were likely preparing for a heart-warming family Christmas without their daughter and new son-in-law, who hadn't been invited to the table. Maybe they'd change their minds once they learned they were going to become grandparents.

Just wait. When the world takes notice of a man in a simple machine flying over all obstacles, farther and faster than all others, we will be invited.

He didn't miss the hint of fog. But at least it wasn't raining.

CHAPTER NINETEEN

"Polly?"

Polly poked her head around the corner. "Yes, boss?"

"How full is tomorrow morning's schedule?"

"I just added an appointment for all four of Blanche's sheepdogs to get their nails trimmed. You know the groomer refuses because they're so high energy. But otherwise, the schedule is fairly open right now. What did you have in mind?"

"Skiving off," Harriet said. "I think that's how you'd say it."

Polly gaped. "You're planning to play hooky? *You*?"

"I was hoping to. Can we reschedule all our Saturday appointments if they're not dire or urgent? I'd like to make the most of the day."

"*Carpe omnia* and all that." Polly nodded in approval.

"Isn't it *carpe diem*? Seize the day?"

"Why stop at day?" Polly called over her shoulder as she turned toward the reception desk. "Carpe omnia. Seize everything!"

Within minutes, Polly had crafted a poster for the entrance and a brief message for the clinic's answering machine.

"Thank you for calling Cobble Hill Veterinary Clinic. We'll be closed this Saturday for the Dog Days of Summer Festival, which is entirely fictional, but our hardworking Doc Bailey needs a break. For emergencies, please press one to be connected to Dr. Barry

Tweedy, a trusted colleague. Otherwise, stay on the line and leave a message, and we'll get back to you on Monday. Thank you, and have a great weekend. We recommend celebrating with your own Dog Days of Summer Festival."

"That sounds great," Harriet said after she'd listened. "I really appreciate Barry filling in for me. I would have been okay with getting emergency calls forwarded to my cell phone as usual."

Polly rolled her eyes. "I know you would have. It's because you don't have healthy boundaries or balance between your work and your personal life. Dr. Tweedy is happy to fill in for you if you need him to. He said it was the least he could do after you helped him figure out what was wrong with that cattle herd last month."

Harriet waved a dismissive hand. "That was nothing, considering all the help he's given me since I moved here." Dr. Barry Tweedy had known her grandfather well and taken her under his wing when she'd moved to the area. He'd also put her in touch with other colleagues, and she quickly became part of a healthy and active support network.

If Alfred had any more sick goats, perhaps Harriet should try consulting them.

The promise of a free Saturday lightened every task leading toward it the rest of Friday afternoon and into early evening. A steady flow of broken bones to set, immunizations to administer, and teeth or beaks to clean made every day full but rewarding. Fortunately, Polly had been able to squeeze in the nail trims for Blanche's sheepdog quartet.

"I don't know how you do it," Blanche told Harriet admiringly as the third dog offered his front paw for her attention. "These dogs are always well-behaved, but that's usually about their job. When I take them away from their flock, they panic until they realize we're coming here. Then they're delighted to see you. You just have a way with them."

Harriet chuckled as she clipped the last nail of one paw and switched to another. "I don't know about that. I suspect it's more about how Polly sneaks them treats every time they're here."

"That would make sense, except that I've trained these dogs not to accept bribes. Otherwise, any thief with dog biscuits could make off with my entire flock." Blanche shook her head. "No, Dr. Bailey. It's you they like."

Harriet laughed and rubbed the sheepdog's ears affectionately.

The good feeling buoyed her until just before closing, when Brody announced that a dire need awaited her in the parking lot. She took the side door, which was nearest, and as she came around the building, saw Alfred walking toward the clinic's front door.

"Good afternoon, Alfred," she called. "Can I help you?"

"You certainly can." He stepped back. "Your man Brody said we should wait out here, but I don't have time for all this tomfoolery."

"What seems to be the problem?"

Alfred planted his hands on his hips. "Other than 'Isn't it mysterious that all of a sudden my goats aren't falling over one by one?' you mean? The problem is that there's a thievery happening in our very midst."

Jeb piped up from behind him. "He's a bit miffed because I talked to Ms. Pendergraf about work she needs doing."

"Stealing the boy right out from under my nose." Alfred huffed. "Can you believe that?"

"You don't own Jeb, Alfred." *Careful, Harriet. Tiptoe through this, don't trample.* "If he's willing to help out a person in need, that's a good thing, right?"

"You mean when he's a person in need himself? I'm over there day and night helping the boy bring some order to his sorry excuse for barns and living quarters—"

"Hey!" Jeb's exclamation was the loudest Harriet had heard him speak.

She couldn't blame him. Alfred's statement wasn't fair. Jeb was doing the best he could with the dilapidated farm he'd naively bought from "a friend."

Then an idea struck her. If Alfred was at Jeb's "day and night," who was looking after Alfred's place?

"The point is," Alfred said with an apologetic grin at Jeb, "that we have plenty of work to do at Jeb's. Now this person is threatening to abscond with him."

Harriet leaned against the exterior wall of the clinic, arms folded across her chest. "Alfred, Jeb is a grown man. He's got the right to make his own decisions. And Arlene isn't just 'this person.' She's a lovely woman, and my friend. She doesn't deserve your unkindness."

"Yeah," Jeb added.

"Jeb is free to work wherever he chooses," Harriet repeated. "I would think you'd be grateful he's found a source of part-time income that will also give him experience and knowledge in running his own farm. Don't you want what's best for him?"

"Yes," Alfred said, ducking his head. "I do want what's best for him."

Harriet didn't back down. "Then what's the problem? I don't believe you really think he's not grateful for everything you've done for him." She paused then said, "Are you afraid Jeb won't have time to spend with you anymore if he works for Arlene?"

"That's rubbish," Alfred said.

Jeb put an arm around Alfred's shoulders. "You'll always be the one who rescued me, Mr. Ramshaw. You and Doc Bailey here. And every penny I make lending Ms. Pendergraf a hand will help me build up my 'sorry excuse' for a farm."

Alfred cleared his throat. "That's not it," he said. "I don't have a problem with Jeb working for someone else. If he's going to buy more alpacas, he needs a job."

Harriet decided to confront him with what was fast becoming obvious. "It's Arlene, isn't it? It's not that Jeb is ungrateful. His working for Arlene is the real issue, isn't it?"

"It's a conflict of interest," Alfred insisted with a scowl. "Consorting with the enemy."

Even in her wildest imagination, Harriet couldn't imagine Arlene being described by anyone else in all the world as an enemy. Gruff as he was, could Alfred truly believe that about her? So far she'd had no luck convincing him otherwise.

But the whole point of Jeb working for Arlene—besides it helping him—was that somehow Harriet could prove Arlene's innocence and Alfred would have to admit his neighbor wasn't trying to sabotage his operation. Arlene could get the help she needed on her farm, and Alfred could hear from Jeb's own lips that she wasn't the vile person he claimed she was.

But the longer this conversation went on, the less sure Harriet was that Alfred could be convinced of anything that wasn't his own idea. "Alfred, I imagine you'll get an earful from Jeb about Arlene if he works part-time for her, won't you? You'll have an eyewitness account of what happens on the Pendergraf farm. He might even be able to catch her in the act of doing something to one of your goats."

Alfred's eyes lit up at the prospect. "Well…"

Harriet would have been ashamed of herself for suggesting Jeb "report" to Alfred if she wasn't hopeful it would break down the relationship wall rather than build it higher.

Alfred looked away, as if he could see his farm from where he stood. Eventually, he said, "My boy, why don't you take Ms. Pretendability up on her offer? You could use the coin, and I could use a few hours without you underfoot."

Smooth, Alfred.

"No offense meant," he added.

Jeb beamed at his mentor. "None taken."

And still, Harriet's Friday wasn't over. *How does a dog with wheels for back legs limp?* Somehow, Maxwell managed to pull it off.

Earlier in the day, Polly and Brody had both commented about his favoring his front right leg. Harriet was hoping that Maxwell had simply slept on it wrong and it was a little stiff but would work itself out.

No such luck. His limp had persisted, making his normal gait— smoother than most long-haired dachshunds because of his high-tech back leg contraption—decidedly pathetic.

She couldn't ignore his need, no matter how tired she was. "Let's take a look, Maxwell." Harriet carefully unstrapped Maxwell's prosthetic harness, lifted him onto the exam table, focused the overhead beam of light toward his right leg, and felt for tender spots.

Nothing registered in joints, bone, or skin. Gratitude coursed through her. Harriet adjusted the light and studied his right paw more closely. Ah. An ingrown nail. Such a relatively small and simple problem, uncomfortable as it must be for him.

"You, my dear Maxwell, will likely recuperate much more quickly than many of my other patients. That's the hope, anyway."

Maxwell's dark eyes searched hers. He lay as still as the best of her patients while Harriet attended to his ingrown nail. Perhaps it was his years of experience as the clinic dog, but he seemed to understand that she was helping him. His cooperation ensured that the procedure went quickly and easily. Because of Maxwell's dependence on his two front legs, she was especially attentive to her method of bandaging the injury after applying a triple antibiotic salve.

Harriet reattached the harness and watched Maxwell pad around the exam room. Soon, his pronounced limp had shrunk to a barely noticeable one, caused more by the bandage than actual discomfort. She knew that once the injury in his paw pad was healed, he'd be back to his normal self.

If only all our concerns had as simple a solution.

In that moment, Harriet became profoundly aware of the history in which she stood. In this very exam room, her grandad had bent over patients not so unlike hers, and in many cases the same ones. He'd performed surgeries with less high-tech equipment than Cobble Hill now boasted. He'd truly walked alongside his patients and their owners in every sense of the phrase.

A revelation struck. Was that why he'd developed his artistic talents while also running the clinic? Was painting his knitting? Did he step away from the sterility of the surgical suite to exchange his vet jacket for an artist's smock as often as he could?

Aunt Jinny said high blood pressure ran in the family. Who had first suggested Grandad pick up a paintbrush? His doctor? Was it a school hobby he'd carried with him into adulthood?

She'd thought him a superhero, able to do so much so well. What would he tell her if she could ask him now?

And what would he say about Alfred? Harriet had a hard time believing that what had plagued so many of Alfred's goats was over merely because they'd had a couple of days with nothing new to report. Would Grandad agree with her? Arlene's hired hands were off to join the navy, but that had the feeling of coincidence rather than resolution. Besides, they had no motive. And from all accounts, as "teen" as they were, they weren't mean-spirited, as evidenced by their dropping off a sick chipmunk at the clinic. No one had a bad word to say about them, other than their natural immaturity.

What would Grandad have to say about ailments so hard to pin down? "If looking in the expected places yields no results, look to the unexpected." She remembered him saying that time and time again.

Where had she not looked? What had she not addressed? What assumptions had she made that might have been ill-informed?

One was that it couldn't be Arlene's doing.

Another was that she had done no follow-up lab work or exams on those animals that had been returned to the herd, those who had supposedly recovered. What if a chronic illness was lying dormant in them? What a tragedy that might turn out to be. Alfred's operation was at a standstill until she could reassure him the current lull in symptoms was more than temporary.

The lights in the gallery cast a warm glow on the stones of the parking lot. Summer hours meant more day's-end visitors. How often had Harriet passed the gallery with little more than a nod to its connection to the heart of her grandfather? Had she grown too accustomed to his paintings to notice the finer details, the soul of the art beyond its artistry? Or even to notice where his brush might have slipped as his hand, weary from a day of caregiving for animals and their people, drifted?

What is close is too often ignored. She'd been the last, apparently, to notice Maxwell's limp. That was not a pattern she wanted to repeat. No matter the workload, no matter life's circumstances, no matter the time it took, no matter what hour of the day or night, she was determined to pay attention to the brushstrokes of what God had given her, including her motley collection of friends, her clients, a loving church family, and soon—oh so soon—a new future with Will.

Especially when it came to her marriage, she vowed not to let the overarching mysteries lead her to neglect the day-to-day.

Harriet was surprised to feel renewed energy in her legs as she climbed the stairs to her bedroom. A long Friday well-spent before a day off. What a sweet feeling. The day had offered an abundance of opportunities to connect with God and to hear or feel Him answer as she spoke or worked with those who crossed her path at Cobble Hill Farm.

Including Alfred. She had no other explanation for why she would have patience with that man except that God must have her on assignment with the curmudgeon. Her empathy for him grew rather than diminished. *Curious, that.*

The phrase sounded like something Grandad would have said. She reached for a notebook and jotted herself a reminder to take another look at the painting in Aunt Jinny's kitchen, the one that somehow connected her grandfather as a mentor for the surly Alfred. What a unique friendship they must have shared. Or maybe it was more rivalry than friendship.

Harriet allowed herself the gift of putting Alfred out of her mind so she could sleep well and fully enjoy the weekend to come.

CHAPTER TWENTY

A whole Saturday to herself. Not a half-day of work. One of her final alone days as a single woman. And how did she intend to spend it? Over a leisurely breakfast in the garden, she opened her wedding planning folder and marked off all that had been accomplished. Then she created a new list of the few remaining responsibilities.

The battery-operated tea candles had arrived, enough to line the front of the church for the ceremony and to illuminate the castle for the reception. The spare room brimmed with supplies.

Harriet had yet to select a matron-of-honor gift for Polly. She'd take care of that today.

Will had said he would handle the rehearsal dinner arrangements, which meant engaging the women's group from the church to provide food for their small wedding party and family members. Will's best man and groomsman, Van and a friend from college, and Polly and Ashley Fiske—Harriet's friend from the States— were their only attendants. That simplified some of the arrangements, allowing Will and Harriet to devote more time and finances to decorating the church and making the reception a warm, welcoming affair.

A week earlier, they'd agreed on their top choice for a photographer, knowing full well from the late date that they were unlikely to secure his services. But wonder of wonders, another wedding had canceled, and Will and Harriet's request filled what would have been a loss for the photographer.

As the sun rose higher, Harriet checked off specific photos they would want from the photographer's emailed list. Then she added some other shots not on the list and sent the document to Will for confirmation or additions.

Her heart was encouraged by the feasibility of carrying out the remaining items. What had seemed such a daunting list had been whittled down, little by little, as Will and Harriet shared responsibilities and accepted help from friends and family.

She marveled at how much could be accomplished in the nooks and crannies of life over a few weeks, and in this glorious morning of uninterrupted time.

A jet high in the sky above her left a trail that resembled pulled taffy. She watched it until it dissipated into a cloudless blue.

She straightened with a start. "Something old, something new, something borrowed, something blue." How could Harriet adhere to the classic saying?

Something old. Her grandma Helen's diamond earrings. Something new. The dainty gold bracelet Aunt Jinny had given her for her birthday was new enough. Something borrowed. The pearl wrist clutch her mother was loaning her. And something blue. She would tuck a sprig of the garden's forget-me-nots into her bouquet. A symbol of fidelity and faithfulness.

Yes, she would treasure that age-old tradition with those four items.

She hadn't yet made a packing list for their honeymoon but did so in short order.

Harriet leaned back in the patio chair, contentment spreading over her with the sun's warmth.

A purring sound near her ear startled her awake as Charlie settled on her shoulder. Harriet was surprised that she'd fallen asleep for—she checked her watch—almost an hour. That was not her typical pattern.

She pushed to her feet just as her phone rang on the table beside her.

"Come on, you two," she said to Charlie and Maxwell as she collected her wedding planner, laptop, and breakfast dishes. "We're going to…let the answering machine take that call."

She could do it. She could resist looking at who was calling.

But what if it was Will? Or her mom?

She checked the display. Neither. It was the caterer, and she couldn't let that go to voice mail. She scooped up the phone right before it stopped ringing.

The caterer's meat supplier had introduced a radical price increase. Did they still want two options—chicken and beef for the reception? And did they want sparkling water at each table?

Harriet thanked the caterer for the heads-up then said she'd consult with Will and get back to her on Monday.

It's always something.

Water.

Before the day was over, she needed to conduct water testing on Alfred's farm.

This mystery had to be solved before her wedding day.

The rest of Saturday flew by with catch-up work, largely focused on more research in her veterinary journals regarding goats and any recent waves of maladies. She'd called Dr. Gavin Witty, another colleague she'd "inherited" from her grandfather, to tap into his wisdom. He was only about ten years older than Harriet, but he'd been serving in the area long enough to have seen much more than she had.

He listened attentively to the list of symptoms, her analyses to date, and the ever-growing list of what was discovered to be *not* the cause of the threat to Alfred's herd. Gavin also wondered if it might be viral in nature, which would not make her investigation any easier.

After a few more minutes of discussion, he said, "Is there any possibility this could be an intentional poisoning?"

"Oh, I hope not," she said. "But I'm checking into that as well."

Harriet could picture Dr. Witty's curly red hair and fair skin as he added, "Let me know if I can be of any assistance. Hey, how's Lyle Brody working out for you?"

"You know him?"

"I know of him. He and my nephew were roommates at the University of Surrey, both in the School of Veterinary Medicine. I put in a good word for him when he was seeking internships. Never dreamed he'd wind up interning at your practice. But I'm glad he did. He'll get a well-rounded experience in rural medicine with you."

Harriet was relieved to have more information on Brody's background. "He's quick and efficient," she said. "And thoughtful."

"Doesn't surprise me. My nephew said he excelled in chemistry before settling on veterinary medicine. He'd create some very interesting mixtures in the lab until he was warned he might lose his scholarship if he kept devising ways to make things explode." Dr. Witty laughed heartily.

Harriet wasn't laughing. But she pulled herself together enough to finish their conversation and jot down *good at chemistry*.

Brody, please tell me you gave up that kind of experimenting years ago.

Harriet used every spare minute of the rest of the afternoon to study her growing collection of lab results, office notes, and research.

She examined the extensive imaging she'd done on Ferdinand. No visible brain swelling. No lesions or heart malformations or aneurysms.

But Harriet recalled from the endoscope that the lining of the first section of Ferdinand's four-chambered stomach was notably scoured-looking, as if it had been scrubbed clean.

If Alfred's poison theory was legitimate, why wasn't anything showing up on toxicology reports? Were they not testing for the right substances? Had the substance, whether ingested or injected, passed through the animals' systems more quickly than testing could reveal?

Harriet sent yet more samples to the regional lab in Whitby from what she'd reserved in refrigeration as a backup. What she wouldn't give for a fuller array of equipment and testing facilities, especially lab equipment. But the Cobble Hill Farm Veterinary Clinic was hundreds of thousands of dollars away from that.

And in the meantime, what other evidence could she gather? There was a stream that flowed across both Arlene's and Alfred's land. The water hadn't yet been tested, to her knowledge. If she could acquire samples without Alfred or Arlene knowing about it, she could avoid stirring either's suspicions about each other. The stream itself was considered public property. All she had to do was reach it.

And if that netted nothing helpful, she'd have to step up her investigation into the possibility of foul play by someone with evil intentions.

As a vet, Harriet had often collected samples from water supplies for toxin or chemical testing, mineral levels, and other potentially animal-harming elements. She'd been the reason one farmer had to dig a new well for his livestock when she'd detected copper levels far above normal. She'd helped direct another farmer to keep his cows away from a pond fed from a hot spring with high sulfite levels.

The fact that Arlene's sheep seemed unaffected by whatever was wrong with Alfred's goats had made Harriet dismiss the water source earlier, since the animals likely drank from the same stream. But she could leave no stone unturned at this point.

Wait. *Did* they drink from the same waterway? Sheep liked their water all but handed to them, calm and still. But if their trough supply originated from the creek…

It could be another copper issue. No, sheep could only tolerate a small amount. Goats could handle much more. Arlene's sheep would have suffered long before Alfred's goats if they were getting too much copper from the same water source.

Still, she couldn't bypass the possibility that the water, or something placed in the water, was to blame.

Logically, she'd need to take samples from the brook where it flowed through each neighbor's property, as well as where it flowed through property neither owned. If any of the samplings showed differing levels of naturally occurring substances, runoff, or chemicals, it might provide a clearer picture of what could be happening. But would she be able to manage all that before sunset? She decided to give it the old college try...whatever that was.

As shadows deepened late Saturday, Harriet started with the land that bordered Alfred's, which appeared long abandoned.

Somehow, that gave her hope. Perhaps something from the neglected farm leaked into the creek before it flowed onto Alfred's property and then dissipated enough before it reached Arlene's.

Even to her own mind, that seemed too easy a solution, and about as logical as saying a screen door could keep the wind out. Arlene's sheep would likely prefer still water—a spring-fed pond or a diversion from the brook where the water was quiet. Or had Arlene's sheep gotten their water from troughs? She'd have to ask if the troughs were filled from a well or from the flowing water. Hadn't she seen wooden fencing and brambles too thick for the sheep to reach the shared creek?

She drove along the abandoned lane as far as she could, pulled on her wellies, and grabbed a flashlight to navigate through the tangles that separated her from the stream she assumed traversed the far edge of this piece of land as it did on Alfred's. If she had a drone, the task could be much simpler.

A drone and a watchdog. Or an officer of the law, like Van.

It occurred to her, albeit a little late in the process, that the farm being abandoned didn't mean she wasn't trespassing. However, if she followed the stone wall that separated that land from Alfred's farm, it would lead her directly to the creek.

She tromped through grasses that had been left to run wild until she reached the stone wall. She let her hand run along its cool, rough surface until she could hear then see the creek through the overgrowth. Sunset was still an hour away, but the encroaching dark quickened her pulse.

"Let's get this over with," she told herself as she bent with her screw-top test bottle to catch the first of several samples of the clear, cold water.

Was that the crack of a tree branch? No. Only one thing made a sound like that. Someone had cocked a rifle.

She'd been caught trespassing. Just what she needed.

"Hello," she called. "It's just me, Dr. Harriet Bailey."

She aimed her flashlight beam behind her. Something glinted to the right.

"Well, if it isn't the good Doc Bailey, poisoning my water supply. Mystery solved." Alfred lowered his rifle an inch or two.

"Surely you don't believe that, Alfred."

"I should have known you and Arlene were in on this together from the start."

"We weren't. We aren't. No one is in on anything. Well, they might be. But not me or Arlene."

He sneered. "A mite nervous, are ya?"

"Anyone would be nervous with a weapon trained on them. Please put the gun down. Let me explain."

He pointed the barrel at the ground and stepped closer. "Aim that torch somewhere other than my eyes, if you don't mind."

She obeyed. If Aunt Jinny could see her now, she'd most definitely not suggest the answer to Harriet's stress was a pair of knitting needles. "I'm not dumping anything into the water, Alfred. I'm removing samples for testing."

"Are you now?"

"Come see for yourself."

"I—unlike some people I could mention—do not make a habit of trespassing on other people's land."

"Who does own this land? I'd be happy to ask permission officially. Do you know the owner?"

"I might. It doesn't matter. What is of most importance is why you would traipse through here in the middle of the night—"

"The sun hasn't even set yet, Alfred."

"To my point, what are you doing?"

"As I said, I'm collecting samples of water upstream and downstream from your property, and, if you'll let me, from where the stream runs through your land and Arlene Pendergraf's."

He snorted. "Americans."

"Excuse me?"

"It's all the same water. Here, five meters that way, and five meters farther downstream. That sort of thing doesn't happen where you come from?"

"Of course it does. I'm investigating all the possibilities."

"Except the possibility you refuse to acknowledge, Doc. The possibility that it might be that Arlene woman after all."

The words almost died in her tight throat, but she said, "I'm considering even that one, Alfred."

In the dimming light, she could see his countenance shift, and not with pride or "I told you so," as she would have expected. With something else. Pain?

"Alfred, are you feeling well?"

He seemed to gather himself. "How could it be something in the water but not affecting her sheep?"

"I don't know. But I'm running out of clues. Still awaiting—"

"I know. I know. Results from the lab."

"I'd like to believe we'll have more answers then, not more questions. Please, tell me who owns this land so I can obtain a permit or something to test the water that flows toward your place."

"It's mine."

"It's abandoned."

"Temporarily. But I own it. I have plans. Don't you worry about that. My dad would be ashamed if he knew I'd let it get this run down. Maybe…"

"Maybe what, Alfred?" she pressed.

"Maybe that's part of why I'm spending so much time at Jeb's. Making up for what I haven't done here."

"But you're 'a man of considerable means,' Alfred. Couldn't you hire someone to fix this place up? Use it to expand your herd or rent it out?"

"Won't rent it. I can't believe you fell for that 'considerable means' line. It's been a saying in our family since my great-grandfather's time. I remember both my grandfather and my father quoting him. 'Look to the sky and it will light your way. We're a family of considerable means.'"

Harriet eyed the rifle now draped over his arm. "I was waiting for the day when you admitted 'considerable means' meant you're mean in the morning, and then there's a different kind of mean in the afternoon, and there's a carry-a-rifle-and-point-it-at-a-friend mean at twilight."

She wasn't sure how he'd take it, but he bent double with laughter, removing his cap and slapping it against his knee. When he'd composed himself again, he said, "I just knew I'd find something to like about you, Doc Bailey." He put his cap back on. "More than just your relation to *Old* Doc Bailey."

She raised an eyebrow, keeping her dry gratitude to herself. "Are you going to let me finish sampling here? I don't see any debris or rusted farm equipment or any obvious source of a toxin in this section of the stream, but I'd like to do my due diligence with the process. Shortly after I moved here, there was a farmer whose animals were getting sick and we couldn't figure out why. Not until we discovered a pile of old batteries and paint cans on a nearby abandoned farm. Could be something as simple as that. But as I say, due diligence."

"Be my guest," he said. "I hope you weren't thinking you have to drive farther along the beck to get your samples. You've got your wellies on, so you might as well just wade to the other side of whatever invisible line you're thinking of and get the water that way. It'd be a sight easier." He started to retreat then said, "Unless you'd like me and my horse to give you a ride to your vehicle."

"Thank you, no," she said. He laughed, waved, and headed back to wherever he'd come from. She could still hear him laughing as she took his advice and waded in the water to collect another sample.

The rifle incident and the return to her vehicle used up all the daylight. It was then it occurred to her that if the two samples she'd collected were clean, she wouldn't need additional water testing. But just in case, before she headed home, she stopped at Alfred's back door.

Lights glowed from the kitchen. She knocked less tentatively than she felt.

"You selling something?" he asked when he opened the door. He chuckled.

"I have another question, if you don't mind."

"Come on in. Do you have a nose for garlic too?"

Harriet slipped off her wellies in the entry. "Garlic?"

"Garlic pesto lamb. Interested?"

"Alfred, where do you buy your lamb?"

"Lady next door sells it."

Her mouth fell open.

Alfred gave a hearty laugh. "Doc, you are so gullible."

Harriet closed her mouth and worked as hard as she had all day to compose herself. She'd been elbow-deep in an overgrown pasture, standing at the wrong end of a rifle. And now she was all but choking on the sense of humor of a man she'd long ago deemed humorless.

"You had a question?" he asked, doctoring mashed potatoes with butter, salt and pepper, and cream.

"Yes, I did. I don't want to run into a trespassing incident again."

"Wise of you."

"And it's late for me to bother Arlene. Do you have the phone number of the people who own the property on the other side of hers? I've never heard her mention them." She pulled out her cell phone to punch in the contact info.

He chewed his lip. Eventually, he recited a number.

She punched in the numbers, and before she reached the last one, she said, "Alfred, that's your number. You own that property too?"

"That's the extent of my vast holdings. Taste this. Too much salt?"

She accepted the spoonful of potatoes he held to her lips, "No. Best mashed potatoes I've had in a while. Can we get back to the subject at hand? You own three of four strips of land from the road to the creek?"

"I do. My inheritance, such as it is."

"And Arlene Pendergraf owns one of the middle ones?"

"That would also be true."

"How did that happen?"

"I ask myself the same question every day."

"Can you tell me the story?"

He stirred the potatoes until they were well mixed, beyond creamy and heading toward soupy. "It's not mine to tell."

Let's just add that little mystery to the puzzle. Because the whole scenario wasn't complicated enough.

CHAPTER TWENTY-ONE

Another week had begun. As wild as her Saturday had been, Sunday had been serene—sorely needed after her day "off" had been more "on." However, Mondays came by their reputation honestly. She showered quickly and dressed even more quickly.

"Come on," she called to Charlie and Maxwell. "Let's get some breakfast. And then we have work to do."

The first order of the day was a call to Alfred.

For once, she felt no hesitation. She might have the beginnings of a solution for him.

The clinic phone rang before Polly arrived, so Harriet answered, recognizing the caller ID. "Alfred, what a coincidence. I was just about to call you."

"I can't talk long. Another goat went down."

Even though Harriet had been sure the goats' issue wasn't solved, her heart still sank at the news of another case. "I'm so sorry to hear that. I'd hoped—"

"Hope solves nothing," he snapped. "Action does. I'm hauling my herd over to Jeb's property this morning. Arlene can't reach them there."

"I was actually going to suggest something far simpler—moving some of them to Arlene's."

"Are you daft?" he blurted "No offense. I'm befuddled and a bit on the ornery side this morning."

"A bit?" Harriet managed not to add, *and only this morning?*

"But still, how could you even suggest such a thing? Arlene's would be the last place I'd choose. I know you don't believe me, but I'm sure she's behind all of this somehow. You can't expect me to put my herd directly in danger like that." Alfred cleared his throat. "My mind's made up. I'm transporting my goats to Jeb's. He needs his brambles dealt with, and I need distance from that woman and her shenanigans."

"Has Jeb started working for her already? Did he see something suspicious?" Harriet doubted it, but if something had happened, she needed to know.

"No. He starts tomorrow. But I can't afford for any more of my animals to take ill."

"Of course you can't, Alfred. That's the reason behind my suggestion. I'm talking about a diplomatic exchange, if you will. If my suspicions are correct, we could reach a solution to more than one problem."

Alfred was quiet for a long time. Finally, he said, "What do you have in mind?"

"No animals other than goats on your farm have taken ill, correct? Not your dog, your horse, or any cats?"

"There was the chipmunk in your car park. Heard all about it."

"Would you have any way of proving that particular chipmunk came from your property?"

"No other animals," he admitted with clear reluctance. "Just the goats. And those crazy squirrels. Hey. I haven't seen them around lately."

"And Arlene's sheep, within just a few feet of your land, have not suffered any similar maladies."

He sniffed. "I wouldn't know, and I don't care."

"I find that sad and not particularly neighborly of you, Alfred. But that's beside the point for the moment." Harriet checked the day's schedule as she spoke. "I can get out to your place by nine thirty this morning to examine the new victim. But if we can talk Arlene into it, I'd like to suggest that you send a few of your goats to her place rather than Jeb's. His land and even his fencing need a lot of work, as we both know. His buildings aren't yet equipped even for keeping your herd's additional feed dry, are they? Plus, at Arlene's, they'll be closer to where they're used to being, and it'll be easier for you to check on them."

"You're not wrong. But you said 'exchange.'"

"I did. If Arlene agrees, I'd like to send some of her sheep to your property temporarily. I suspect that they won't be troubled by whatever is ailing your goats. Yes, it's a risk for her—"

"And a risk for me!" he interrupted.

"How can your animals be worse off on her land?"

"She'll have easier access to mess with them."

"Please don't mention the word 'poison' again, Alfred. If we had any viable evidence of a recognizable poison or any physical evidence of her tampering with something, that word would still be on the table. But all the tests have come back clean, so it must be something else. It affects older goats, younger ones, some who have wandered onto Arlene's land, others that haven't, male and female. There's no pattern, even in their specific symptoms."

"That's true," Alfred said.

Harriet slumped into the receptionist chair. "Alfred, I've tested the water and examined it under the microscope. All samples are clear of anything other than what one would normally find in a rural stream that's safe for livestock. Additional samples are on their way to Whitby, but I doubt they'll find anything different than I have. I think our animal exchange option is a trial we can't afford to skip."

"I don't see this turning out well," he said. Before she could protest, he went on. "But I see the rationale. If her sheep get sick on my property, then that makes her less of a suspect, right? She'd have to be daft to poison her own animals."

"We are not hoping for an outcome like that."

"I'd need you to check my goats' vitals before they leave my place. And her sheep. I don't want her bringing any infected animals over here and depositing more trouble than I already have."

"That would be the scientific way to handle it, so I agree." Harriet's brainstorm idea had been to remove the goats to see how they fared elsewhere, so she and Alfred were more or less on the same page. The experiment would narrow the culprit to someone or something with access to Alfred's herd at home.

But it could have a downside. If it riled up the feud Arlene insisted was one-sided, her brainstorm might turn into a storm of another kind.

"Let me propose the idea to Arlene," Harriet said. "It's no small risk for her given your open animosity toward her, but she is genuinely concerned about the mystery with your animals."

Alfred snorted. "Yeah, I'll just bet she is."

Later that morning, with Brody and Polly holding down the fort at the clinic, Harriet grabbed her medical bag and headed for the Beast.

All of Alfred's goats appeared healthy except the latest case, and he was already improving from his rough night. Another was a bit gassier than normal, but when a goat's diet consisted primarily of brush that others would consider worthless, a little gas wasn't abnormal.

According to Harriet's almost daily dive into as much as she could learn about goats, azaleas could be toxic for them. Chocolate as well. But there were no rapscallion azaleas or stray chocolates on Alfred's property. Not even behind his outbuildings. A certain puppy had taught her to check there.

She quickly deemed the chosen animals fit for transport.

Alfred waited as patiently as he seemed able for Harriet to carry out the same process for Arlene and her sheep. Jeb assisted. He waved at Alfred, who watched the examination as best he could from his side of the wall. He'd no doubt check his security camera footage as well, knowing Alfred.

Before noon, the exchange was complete. A dozen of Arlene's sheep grazed at Alfred's, and a dozen of Alfred's goats made their presence known at Arlene's, heading straight for the clutch of brambles on her side of the wall.

The tension between the two animal owners remained high, but Alfred seemed to realize that there was nothing in this arrangement to benefit Arlene. She was the one sacrificing for the sake of helping find a resolution for his goats. He still grumbled about sending his goats into "enemy territory," but a smidge of gratitude emerged with his two-word comment to Arlene.

"Thank you."

Despite everything, Alfred really did care. Harriet had to give him that.

After the transfer, Harriet stood beside Alfred on his side of the wall, observing both his remaining goats and Arlene's visiting sheep. As expected, it took a while for both animals and humans to adjust. Arlene remained near the enormous tree, on her side of the stone wall, as leaves drifted to the ground between them. Three more trees stood like sentinels along that wall. Only this tree—an oak right in the center of the length of wall—had any leaves dropping. A leaf falling in summer always seemed like such a waste of a short season.

At the moment, Harriet saw them as representing the waste of a potential friendship too.

Those two people needed each other. Arlene needed Alfred's strength. He needed her wisdom and kindness. They needed a signed and sealed peace treaty. Witnessed. Notarized. Possibly maintained by a Royal Guard.

Every other animal crisis seemed minor that day after Harriet returned.

A suture here. A splint there. An ear cleaning, dietary change, and thorn removal or two. Typical day in the life of a country vet. A molting budgie scared her owner until Harriet reassured the child and his mother that parakeets were supposed to molt.

She examined the bird carefully. No bald patches. No seeming physical distress, which would have been unusual with molting. The bird's low energy levels were part of the process of replacing feathers, given the accompanying hormonal and immune system changes during the process. Harriet went through the explanation and care recommendations on autopilot, her mind still mostly on Arlene and Alfred.

She found herself reflecting that every first-time pet owner should have an experienced pet-owner friend to walk them through what was normal and what was worth a call to the vet.

Harriet caught herself. As good an idea as that might be, she was often that experienced friend. That fact gave her patience with owners who simply didn't know what they didn't know. She resolved to keep her mind on the tasks at hand. After all, her other patients deserved her full attention too.

A review of the situation on Wednesday revealed no sheep on Alfred's side had taken ill. No goats on Arlene's side had succumbed either. And the water sample results from Whitby were ready.

She'd thought there must be something in the water. She'd hoped that was the explanation. But the water tests came back negative for anything out of the ordinary. It was unfit for human consumption because of field and pasture runoff, but it was a good source of water for Alfred's animals.

The detective instincts in her had to ask again: What was she missing?

A weapon. A motive. Opportunity. Irrefutable evidence. That was what she needed, and she didn't have any of it. What she did have was a growing list of animals who had taken ill but recovered.

And one goat farmer getting more unhappy with her by the day.

The oak leaves drifting to the ground. Why did she keep returning to that scene in her mind? An oak tree shouldn't lose its leaves in summer. Green oak leaves could be toxic for goats. She hadn't recalled noticing them in her visits to the farm before, even when she was searching for clues, for anything out of place. But the goats could have been consuming them as fast as they fell.

Harriet texted Alfred, asking him to keep the animals away from that tree until she could collect some of the leaves and investigate. If she could, she'd try to make it yet that afternoon. If those leaves were the source, time was of the essence.

CHAPTER TWENTY-TWO

Tea with Aunt Jinny late on Wednesday was a welcome invitation for processing Harriet's jumbled thoughts. A break in both of their schedules meant they could linger over shortbread and whatever other delicacy Aunt Jinny had concocted for them.

They made quite a pair. Aunt Jinny hung her white lab coat over the back of her kitchen chair, and Harriet hung her teal version over the opposite chair. The women sank into comfortable conversation over strong tea and pastel macarons in addition to the melt-in-your-mouth shortbread and open-faced egg salad sandwiches.

"Can we breathe for a moment and leave our individual office concerns for another time?" Aunt Jinny asked.

"Couldn't agree more," Harriet said. Although Alfred's mysteries—both that of his goats and the mystery of Alfred himself—wormed their way into her thoughts far too often. How long could she manage to distance herself from it all?

Not even a full minute, as she learned when her gaze fell on a particular painting.

"Aunt Jinny, would you mind if I looked at the back of that painting Grandad did?"

"The cricket green? Sure, no problem. Knock yourself out. Another art mystery to solve?"

"No, thank goodness. There have been plenty of those this past year. I'm curious about a dedication or perhaps a note from Grandad written on it. For a relationship reason this time, not an art theft or other crime."

Aunt Jinny laughed. "You do find yourself in the thick of problem-solving, don't you?"

"Both of us chose problem-solving professions." Harriet bit into a sandwich and hummed with delight at the watercress layer between the pillowy slice of bread and the egg salad. "Nice touch with the watercress."

"Thank you. It's late in the season to harvest it from the brooks and rills, but the farmers market had a hydroponic grower's booth this week. A nice peppery touch for the eggs."

Harriet paused. She would like to make stopping at the farmers market a habit this summer. But she'd have to quit a job she loved if she tried to fit in all the things she wished she could do. Her priorities needed a better management system. "The next time you're on your way to the farmers market, would you text me? If I can get free, I'd like to tag along. Even if it can't be until after the wedding."

"I'm so pleased you and Will are making Cobble Hill Farm your home. It would be my pleasure to have a tagalong like you on farmers market days." Aunt Jinny pressed her lips together.

Harriet recognized the expression. "What?"

"I think the best way for me to inquire is, 'How is your knitting project progressing?'" She tilted her head in a sign of motherly concern.

Harriet exhaled a sigh. "Aunt Jinny…"

"Few times are more stressful in a woman's life than when she's planning a wedding," her aunt said. "Add to that running a business, managing employees, and solving mysteries at the same time, and you've got a recipe for some kind of a breakdown. Although that doesn't describe most brides-to-be. The mystery part especially." She sipped her tea and gazed at Harriet over the rim of the cup.

"You think I've become excessively involved in Alfred's conundrum, don't you?"

Aunt Jinny's teacup *tinked* as she set it on its matching morning glory saucer. "Conundrums, plural."

"Plural. Yes."

"Are you trying to save his goats or save him from himself? Save his reputation? His future? His ability to build meaningful friendships? Are you his veterinarian, or his therapist?"

Harriet winced. "Ouch."

Her aunt sat back, clearly pleased with herself. "Ah. A sore subject, perhaps?"

"Maybe a bit. I appreciate your concern for me. And I won't pretend that Alfred hasn't taken more of my time than I should give him. But there's something about him that keeps drawing me in. Did you know Grandad mentored him years ago?"

"While I was at university and medical school, I heard."

Harriet studied the painting on the wall beside the small table where they sat. "Doesn't that seem like an unusual pairing— a veterinarian and artist playing cricket with an overall-wearing curmudgeon?"

"Alfred would have been younger than a curmudgeon when your grandad mentored him the first time. Before Alfred took off for parts unknown." Aunt Jinny stood and removed the painting from its hook.

Harriet pushed back from the table and took the painting from her, careful to keep it well away from the egg salad and watercress.

"I don't know what you'll find there," Aunt Jinny said. "That's just a print. The original is in the gallery, to my knowledge."

Harriet looked up. "I thought Grandad left this for you personally. He wouldn't have bequeathed his daughter an imitation of the real thing, would he?"

Her aunt chuckled. "It's a print, Harriet, not a fake. I'm content with it. His fans deserve to have the real thing in the gallery, and I have others he painted that I like better. I much prefer his animal portraits. Besides, the original of this one would overwhelm this small space. Did you want it for your own collection?"

"No." After turning it over and examining the back, Harriet announced, "There's nothing here. No message."

"Ooh!" Aunt Jinny said, rubbing her hands together. "You expected a secret message? Perhaps a clue to sick goats?"

"No, but there's been quite a number of them. All recovered, it appears, but it's still troubling. And until this is over, Alfred's livelihood is at a standstill."

Aunt Jinny sobered. "I am sorry to hear that. Well, if anyone can put a stop to the trend, it's you. If I can help in any way, just let me know."

"I can always use your help, Aunt Jinny. I depend on it. That and your shortbread biscuits. And your thimbleberry jam. And the golden raspberries that grow behind the cottage."

"That's it? No mention of the tea?"

"Well, I am still an American at heart."

Both women dissolved into giggles.

"Is it true what they say?" Harriet asked, wiping tears of mirth from her eyes. "That laughter releases powerful endorphins?"

"So much more than that, my dear. Laughter stimulates circulation and aids muscle relaxation. It is a potent pain and stress reliever, and over time strengthens the immune system."

"Then I may need time with you more than I need knitting."

Aunt Jinny clapped her palms together. "I believe I prescribed both."

Harriet winced at the beep that sounded from her phone. She thought she'd silenced her text message alerts.

"Who would be so rude as to interrupt tea?" Aunt Jinny demanded.

"Guess."

"Alfred? What does he want now?"

Harriet read the message a second time. "Another goat is ill. Arlene's sheep are fine. I need to get out there, Aunt Jinny."

"Understood."

If green oak leaves were the culprit, a slew of innocent people would have all suspicion removed from them.

The tree might have to come down, which would be costly both financially and emotionally. That tree was likely several hundred years old. No one would want to see it felled.

Instead, maybe both Arlene and Alfred could construct strong internal fences to keep their flocks far from the tree. But that still wouldn't solve the mystery of why green oak leaves would be falling midsummer. Besides, was it even possible to keep fallen leaves from blowing past any fencing?

Harriet pulled herself back to the task at hand with a reminder that she shouldn't try to solve a problem before she knew the particulars.

One silver lining remained in all this, and she would cling to it for all she was worth. Alfred's mystery could be solved before her wedding day. A second silver lining lay in the potential for Alfred and Arlene to work together and lay aside the nonsensical feud.

The hope in both possibilities would carry her straight to Alfred's farm in a few minutes. No fog. No missed turns. No flat tires—or so she hoped.

Right before she left the clinic, Van stopped by to bring Polly the new work shoes she'd ordered. He barely got in the door before Harriet gave in to a sudden urge to ask if he had time to follow her to Alfred's. He had his own evidence collecting equipment in his vehicle. Some of it might prove useful.

Always game for an adventure, he was happy to comply.

When they arrived at the property, Alfred directed them to the small pen in which he'd quarantined the sick doe as he had done temporarily with all the others. The goat had a mixture of familiar symptoms—lethargy, labored breathing, general malaise. Her heart rate was only slightly elevated. But she wasn't herself. That was a certainty.

While Van made small talk with Alfred, Harriet took a blood sample from the animal and administered a medication she hoped would help with her breathing.

Then Harriet invited the men to accompany her to the tree that she'd seen losing leaves.

"What's the detective constable supposed to do?" Alfred asked.

"Pat the tree down for hidden weapons?"

He might have been joking, but as serious as the mysterious illnesses were, Harriet felt suddenly foolish for involving Van in leaf collection.

Van did help to remove the makeshift fencing around the base of the tree on Alfred's side. They pulled it back enough for the three of them to slip through, fighting goats eager to get to what was apparently their favorite location on the property.

Harriet gloved up and collected a handful of the green oak leaves that had fallen. When she stood, hopeful that she finally held the answer to Alfred's dilemma, her attention was caught by a curious sight high above her head.

"Alfred, look at that! These leaves are drifting from one or two specific branches. The rest of the tree seems perfectly normal. Isn't that odd?"

"Why would that matter?" Van asked.

Harriet said, "I'm not sure yet, but I really need to investigate every possibility. Anything out of the ordinary is worth looking into. A tree should not be dropping leaves this time of year, much less from just a couple of branches. The rest of the tree seems to be perfectly fine."

Arlene approached them on the other side of the wall. "What are you all up to?"

"Not sure yet," Harriet told her. "Are all the animals on your side doing well?"

"Not a single problem. My sheep over there? Are they okay?"

"They're well. Come on over and see for yourself, if you want," Alfred said. His words shocked Harriet, but she was careful not to react.

"It looks like they're keeping to themselves," Harriet said as Arlene joined them. "Plenty of grass and space. And they appear to be in good health."

"And you, Harriet? You seem troubled, dear."

Harriet swallowed hard. *I've got a list of suspects with no motives, no means, and opportunities that no longer hold water. I've no definitive solution to what's troubling Alfred's goats yet, and what could be causing green oak leaves to fall in July? Oh, and I have a wedding right around the corner.* "I'm right as rain."

As if her words had summoned it, the heavens opened, releasing a torrent of precipitation.

"Arlene," Alfred said, "get yourself to my house. You'll catch your death at your age."

She called back through the torrent, "I'll take that as your way of being neighborly, you old grump." She made her way to the house faster than Harriet knew she could move.

"Come with me, Doc." Alfred grabbed Harriet's hand and tugged her toward the house. "DC Worthington, you're welcome as well."

"I'm right behind you."

Moments later, the four of them huddled, dripping, in Alfred's mudroom.

"Towels, Alfred?" Arlene asked.

"There's some old ones in the cupboard behind you there. I use them to dry the dog's muddy feet when I let him in. But don't you worry. I wash them."

"Wonderful. Thank you."

They toweled off as well as they could then filed into the kitchen, where Alfred put on the kettle for tea.

Harriet groaned as she remembered something.

"What is it, dear? Did you twist your ankle running in the rain?" Arlene asked.

"No, but thank you for asking. Alfred, can I borrow a handful of towels when I leave? My driver's side window on my vehicle is open. I didn't expect rain this afternoon. We've had an unusual rash of pop-up rain incidents for July, haven't we?"

"Certainly." Alfred stared out the kitchen window above his sink. "It's not letting up. Usually, summer storms don't hang around long. This one seems more stubborn than most."

"There's a lot of that going around," Harriet said pointedly.

"I'll get our tea ready," Alfred said as if she hadn't spoken. "And then I suppose we better get back out there. An investigator's worst enemy is rain that washes evidence away, right, DC Worthington?"

Harriet folded her arms over her chest. "Alfred, we all want to find out what's going on, but there's no use getting waterlogged in the process."

Van poked at the bottom of his shoes that were drip-drying on the rug in Alfred's mudroom.

"Why are you nosing about?" Alfred skirted around Harriet and joined Van. Harriet followed, with Arlene on her trail.

"Is it evidence of some kind, Detective?" Arlene asked, teacup still cradled in her hands.

"No. It's just a leaf."

"Another of the green oak leaves that fell." Harriet pulled gloves from her pocket. "I already have several collected, but I'll take this one too. Perhaps it's the unusual rain we've had that's knocked them loose, rather than something more sinister."

"Sinister?" Arlene asked.

"Something's causing that tree to lose its leaves at the wrong time. Let me get my test kits and microscope involved before we speculate anymore."

"If the tree was diseased," Van said, "wouldn't the others in line with it show similar signs?"

"That's the curiosity. One among many," Harriet said. "The other trees on the property are not dropping leaves, from what I've observed. Do you concur, Alfred?"

"That's true."

"Technically," Arlene said, "all the oaks along the stone wall straddle both our properties. But no leaves are falling on my side."

Alfred's generous eyebrows lifted higher on his scrunched forehead.

"Fascinating," Harriet said.

Van stepped forward. "I need to head out, rain or no rain. I take it there's no crime I have to worry about here?"

There might be, Harriet thought to herself. *I just don't know what kind yet.*

The sea mimicked Wednesday's late-afternoon mood, pewter gray waves restless with the rain's agitation. Gardens and flower beds nodded their gratitude, but the sea seemed to consider the rain competition for watery domination.

Harriet stopped at the office to write her observations in a journal she kept for her racing thoughts. Did every bride-to-be experience a similar issue, where her brain gave her no peace? She was either hyperfocused on leaf anatomy or seating charts, or she was completely unfocused, with her attention hopping from goats to sheep to tweaks to the caterer's menu to ordering more supplies for the clinic to collecting treats to welcome her parents after their plane landed.

And now this new tidbit of research.

Green oak leaves could be dangerous for both sheep and goats.

Why was it then, that Arlene's sheep were not ill and Alfred's goats were still affected by something that would not reveal itself? Could it be that the problem was caused not by the leaves but by whatever was causing them to fall from the tree?

Could a tree that straddled both their properties serve as a dispute dissolver for Alfred and Arlene if Harriet could solve the mystery? It had already succeeded in getting them both on the same side of the wall.

"Your next patient is here, Harriet."

Harriet thanked Polly and headed to the exam room. It was unlikely she would ever know boredom. Something new every day, and her wedding so close she could almost taste the Earl Grey cupcakes.

And here was her new Wednesday afternoon veterinary adventure—a rooster whose larynx had been bruised by an unfortunate interaction with an unsuccessful fox.

"He sounds pathetic, doesn't he, Doc?" asked the farmer who owned him. "I mean, I'm glad he's alive, but a rooster with laryngitis has lost one of his main reasons for living, hasn't he?"

Rooster surgery was written into Harriet's schedule for Thursday. Until she could see the internal damage, she couldn't predict whether there was hope of improvement. As hoarse as a rooster sounded on his best day, his larynx was a delicate mechanism.

Harriet returned to her oak-leaf investigation. She'd studied the leaves she'd collected, but they offered no clues. The internet suggested the cause could be a fungal infection called oak wilt. But the leaf didn't match typical oak-wilt presentation, at least not to Harriet's untrained eye.

Before the Alfred conundrum, she could go a week or more without a major illness in a large animal. Ah, the good old days, with a kitten ear infection here, a dog giving birth there, annual shots, flea-and-tick treatments...

But the past year had held so much more than what might be considered ordinary. A jewel thief, a missing baron, art thefts, animal kidnappings. To say nothing of her best friend's elopement. Her own engagement. Wedding planning.

If she added the move to England and still grieving the loss of her grandfather to the list, Harriet figured she must have crossed some threshold of major life stressors. She'd certainly like to reduce some of those, but if she couldn't solve this case, she doubted that would happen.

CHAPTER TWENTY-THREE

E arly Thursday, Arlene Pendergraf stood in the reception area with a lamb on a leash. It was a wonder her border collie, Hamlet, had let it out of his sight. But there Arlene stood, wearing her typical floral-print apron.

"How can I help you, Arlene?" Harriet asked.

The lamb tugging at the leash seemed full of energy, bright-eyed. What could be troubling it?

"It's a private matter," Arlene said, shortening the leash. The lamb bleated—surprisingly loud for one so small—but then seemed to smile up at Arlene.

"Oh?"

Arlene nodded toward the exam rooms, her lips pressed together.

"I see. What's her name?"

"Who?"

"The lamb?"

"Ah. Aesop."

As Aesop pranced down the short hallway, Harriet smiled at her antics. No signs of illness in this one.

Once behind the door of the exam room, Arlene remained standing despite the chair Harriet offered her. She tugged at the collar of her blouse. "Is it warm in here?"

Harriet switched on the oscillating fan in the corner. "Better?"

"Oh, thank you. I'm sorry. This is hard for me," Arlene said. "I'm not often dishonest." She wrung the end of the leash in her hands.

"There's nothing wrong with Aesop, is there?"

"Well, no. You're as good as they say, Harriet. You could tell she was fine without even examining her."

"I could tell by your facial expression that Aesop isn't the reason you're here."

Arlene wrung the leash more furiously, until the lamb bleated in protest. She immediately dropped the leash and let Aesop wander the exam room. "I felt as if I needed an excuse to see you. Aesop was the best I could find."

"Arlene, you never need an excuse to see me."

"Not even on a workday?"

"Certainly not."

Moisture formed in Arlene's eyes. She blinked it away. "As touching as that is, I still wish to pay for your valuable time, which is why I brought Aesop."

Harriet could understand that mindset and appreciated being on the receiving end of it. She picked up the lamb, set it on the table, and examined its ears and teeth while they talked. "She's about a month old, I see."

"That's right." Arlene stuck her hands in her apron pockets. "Harriet, I have a conundrum."

"We have plenty of those around here. Let me guess. Yours is named Alfred."

When Arlene didn't respond but her eyes watered even more, Harriet stuck her head into the hall. "Brody? Would you come here, please?"

Within seconds, he stood before her.

"Would you kindly take Aesop here for a routine health check in the other room? I need to discuss a few things with her owner."

"Of course, Dr. Bailey."

"Thank you."

After Brody disappeared with Aesop, Harriet again offered Arlene a chair.

This time Arlene sank into it. "I'm not quite sure what to do."

"About Alfred?" Harriet scooted her wheeled exam stool closer.

"Tuesday this week, I took him a batch of my sticky toffee pudding, to be neighborly. I'd, um, made extra."

"That was kind of you. Especially considering how accusatory he's been toward you."

"It hasn't exactly been a secret, has it? I hoped to have a conversation that's long overdue."

Harriet took her hand. "It didn't go well?"

"On the contrary." She swiped at a stray tear. "He didn't chase me off his property. He invited me in for a few minutes. I consider that a step forward."

"I find that encouraging too," Harriet said.

"But did you notice?"

"Notice what?"

"Yesterday when you and Van and I were there, he didn't offer any of us the sticky toffee pudding I'd given him the day before. He either kept the entire batch for himself or had already tossed it in the dustbin."

Harriet couldn't help thinking Arlene was reading far too much into the situation. After all, they'd only been in Alfred's house for a few minutes. He might simply not have thought to share the pudding. "And that means?"

"I'm not sure." Arlene dropped her hands in her aproned lap. "This feud of his has been so many years in the making."

"Are you looking for me to provide clues as to what Alfred is thinking, Arlene? If so, I can't help you. I once asked him about what happened to cause the rift between you."

"What did he say?"

Harriet took in her pained expression. She wasn't certain any answer could soothe it. "He said it wasn't his story to tell."

Arlene sank against the back of the chair again. "Well, it's certainly not mine."

"Whose is it, then?" Harriet asked.

The woman's lips worked as if she wanted to say something but couldn't find the words. Eventually, she murmured, "His father's, I suppose."

"Aunt Jinny told me his father died a few years ago. Is that right?"

"He died a year ago last month." Her brow creased, and her exhales became noisy, like small puffs.

"Arlene, are you feeling okay?"

"No, Harriet. I may never feel okay. Not with this lump in my throat and this hole in my heart." She stood abruptly. "It was rude of me to disturb you at work, even under the pretense of having Aesop examined. My apologies. Do you suppose your intern is finished with the exam?" She opened the door to reveal Brody with Aesop. "Ah, hello. All is well?"

"She's as fit as can be," Brody assured her. "A fine animal."

Harriet studied her intern through new eyes. She had invited Brody to care for the lamb, the same as he had done with several of Alfred's goats when they were kenneled at the clinic. If he'd been a true suspect for whatever reason, wouldn't he have taken advantage of the opportunity to inflict more damage? He wasn't helping them heal to gain praise for himself. He hadn't given Harriet any reason to suspect him of anything, not even overextending a break or accidentally leaving a light on somewhere. His work was utterly above reproach.

"Thank you for the care you took. Never hurts to be sure." Arlene's words seemed to fizzle at the end, but she gathered herself. "It's time to go home, my little one."

Harriet would have stopped her from leaving, but the woman had clearly exhausted all the conversation she intended to have. And a reception room full of animals with various concerns waited for her attention.

As she donned a fresh pair of disposable gloves, Harriet entertained a mental picture of Alfred sitting in his pristine kitchen even now, eating an entire batch of sticky toffee pudding one spoonful at a time, savoring every sweet bite.

Or he may have fed it to his goats.

She had interacted with him more times than she could count over recent weeks, and yet she still didn't know him well enough to guess.

"I'm here for answers," Harriet said at the end of a very long Thursday.

"Kind of expected you'd be dropping by now that the weather is more to your liking," Alfred said, joining her on his front porch.

She found herself wondering if the stain on his overall bib was from toffee sauce. "Let's have another look at that tree."

"You want me to call Arlene over?"

"That's the other set of answers I'm looking for, Alfred. Can you two somehow patch up this rift between you? It's like a fault line in the community."

"What business is it of yours?" he demanded, tromping determinedly down the porch steps and toward the tree.

"Alfred, I care about both of you."

He stopped walking.

"Do you doubt what I just said?" she asked.

"No. I'm not a fool. I know you mean it." He started for the tree again, gently shoving curious goats aside as they walked.

"Arlene said the story isn't hers to tell either." Harriet dodged goats and sheep on her way into a conversation territory she hadn't ventured into before.

"Did she now?"

"She mentioned that if it was anyone's story, it was your father's. The way I figure, you're the closest person in this part of Yorkshire to him. That makes you the spokesperson for the family."

He snorted.

"How did Arlene come to possess that particular plot of land?" Harriet pressed. "I find it curious."

He was silent for several steps. "My father sold it to her, as a consolation prize for my stupidity. Gave it to her for less than the price of a pig, if you can imagine."

Of all the things she'd expected him to say, that hadn't been it. She stopped in her tracks. "Your stupidity? How? Why? I don't understand."

Before he could answer, something else drew her attention. "Alfred?"

He faced her. "What?"

"I thought you said you fixed the fence around the tree that was dropping its leaves."

"I did. As soon as the rain stopped and you all left yesterday."

"Then what is that goat nibbling on?"

They took off at a quicker pace now, shouting and waving their arms in an attempt to shoo the animal back over the fence and into the larger space.

"Stop it, you daft animal!" Alfred yelled.

"What's going on?" Arlene hollered over the wall.

Huffing, Harriet said, "A goat got into the leaves." She waved at Alfred. "We have to keep it from the rest of the herd," she told him.

"Good point," Alfred said. With a swoop of his beefy arms, he captured the animal. "Now what?"

Harriet caught up with him. "I'll have to examine her. Where can we put her where she'll be safe while we see what's up with the tree?"

"Hoist her over here," Arlene said from her side of the stone wall. "I'll keep her separate from the others and away from the tree."

Alfred hesitated for a moment but finally gave in. "Okay. Fine. The goat'll jump over on her own if I give her a little boost."

Arlene received the visitor with a "How're you doing, girl? No, you just stay with me for a bit." She scratched the goat's neck, and the goat leaned against her legs, clearly enjoying the attention.

Her sheep were nosy about the newcomer, but at a short command from Arlene, Hamlet kept them at bay.

Jeb was soon on the scene too. "Any way I can help?" He was covered in dust from head to toe but was a welcome sight nevertheless. After all, he was a point of possible connection between Alfred and Arlene.

"Can you keep that goat from crossing back over, Jeb?" Harriet asked.

"I'll do my best," he promised.

"He really is a good sort," Alfred grumbled so only Harriet could hear. She suppressed a smile.

Harriet moved closer to the tree so she could examine it. Her gaze roamed from treetop to roots. She'd expected by now that green leaves would lie in piles at its base, but only a few were there. Her steps did, however, crunch noisily. "How long have green acorns been falling too, Alfred?"

"I didn't notice them before now. Much as I've traveled over this spot, setting up the fencing and all, you'd think I would have. Can't have the goats eating green acorns or they'll—"

"Have stomach and respiratory issues."

"Doc, is that the answer?"

"It might well be."

Alfred rubbed his hands together. "So what do we do now?"

"I've enlisted the aid of a couple of boys I believe can give us a hand here. Do you have a ladder close by? The branches we need to see are pretty high."

"A couple of boys? You don't mean—"

Harriet knew better by now than to let him launch into another of his paranoid rants. "I do. They have a story to tell as well as a drone we can borrow to see the tree from above. We need all the help we can get at this point."

"You can't be serious."

"Alfred, trust me, please. They'll be here soon. We need their help."

"How low must I stoop to get my goat cheese production back in business?" he mumbled as he headed toward his garage. Moments later, he returned with a ladder. He leaned it against the tree trunk as a car pulled onto the property.

Harriet jogged to greet the brothers, Alfred trudging behind her.

Gregory and Heath stepped from the vehicle. They waved at Harriet as she approached then Gregory retrieved a drone and remote from the trunk of their car.

"Can't believe you invited those two hooligans onto my land," Alfred grumbled.

Harriet shot him a warning glare.

"Mr. Ramshaw, Doc Bailey," said Heath, the older brother, "we'd better start with our apologies first."

Harriet focused her gaze on their faces rather than the flying machine in their hands. "We're both ready to listen," she said with a pointed look at Alfred.

"Mostly to you, Doc," Gregory said.

Harriet waved a hand. "I forgave you over the phone, boys. You know that."

"Still, here in front of you, and in front of Mr. Ramshaw, we want to tell you how sorry we are for not being more honest right away."

Alfred huffed. "What are they talking about, Doc?"

Heath took over again. "We're the ones who dropped that chipmunk off in the car park and tore out of there when we saw the doc coming out of the woods," he said. "But we didn't mean to cause a fuss."

Harriet couldn't wait for Alfred to hear the rest. She nodded to encourage the boys to continue.

"The reason is a mite embarrassing."

Alfred's eyebrows shot up. "So spill it already," he growled.

"How that chipmunk got into Greg's car in the first place, we don't know. Must have been when we bailed out of the car to get away from the bee."

"The bee," Alfred echoed, emotionless.

Gregory looked sheepish. "Yeah. We left the doors open so the bee could get out but never thought about what might get *in*. Thought we were in the clear when we came back to the car."

"Next thing we know, we've got a chipmunk about as scared as we were climbing over the seats and scooting under our feet," Heath added.

"We weren't far from the vet clinic. On the road that runs right past it," Gregory said. "So I pulled into the car park and we shooed it out onto the cobblestones. It must have landed on its head or something, because it wasn't moving. We panicked and took off."

"We didn't mean the little guy any harm," Heath concluded.

Alfred took a step closer, skepticism etched on his face. "Why didn't you tell the truth to the detective constable when he questioned you?"

Heath sighed. "It'd be bad enough to have to admit we were scared of a bee in the car. What would people think if they found out we got all panicky over a chipmunk?"

"We know we should have told the truth," Gregory added. "We're really very sorry. We're not cut out for country life, obviously. We haven't apologized yet to Ms. Pendergraf for leaving her high and dry, but that's next on our list."

"I hope she's been managing all right," Heath said.

Alfred turned to Harriet. "Do you believe their story?"

"I do. I've seen what fear of losing a reputation can do to an otherwise reasonable individual."

Alfred's eyebrow quirked. "And you never messed with my goats or did anything Ms. Pendergraf asked you to do that might harm them?"

Harriet startled. He'd used Arlene's *real* last name.

"No sir. Only thing we ever did was return them when they jumped the wall."

Alfred held out his hand to the boys, and they shook it. "I understand what it's like to be scared when you want to be strong," he said. "And now you think you can help?"

Harriet said, "I asked if they'd be willing to lend a hand. Or rather, a drone."

"I guess that'll be okay," Alfred said.

Harriet pointed upward. "Boys, we need a view of what's happening in that oak tree near the middle of the stone wall. A couple of the branches are almost bare. And I suspect there's something making them drop their leaves."

"And green acorns too," Alfred added.

"Do you drive a drone better than you drive a car, Gregory?" Harriet smiled at him to soften her words and let him know she was joking.

The two boys glanced at each other. "Yes, ma'am. I do," Gregory said. "Although we won't be able to get too close to the tree without getting tangled in the branches. But we'll do the best we can."

Soon the drone buzzed through the air, surveying Alfred's acreage and flying as close as Gregory could get it to the tree.

Then Heath took over navigating the drone while Gregory showed Harriet and Alfred the images the drone sent to their laptop.

Harriet asked if the attached camera could zoom in closer. "There," she said.

"What are you seeing, Doc?" Alfred squinted at the screen.

"There's something in that cavity in the tree, something shiny. And it's dripping onto the branches that are nearly bare."

"Dripping? What could that be?"

"We're about to find out," Harriet said.

Despite the boys' offers to do the climbing, Harriet insisted on seeing for herself what might be at the heart of Alfred's goats' illnesses.

The first ladder Alfred had retrieved wasn't tall enough, so he enlisted the brothers to help him haul a roofing ladder to the base of the tree.

By that time, Arlene and Jeb had joined the spectators, which included a fine collection of goats. The animals had lined up, noses in the air, eyes trained on Arlene, who held a bowlful of what looked like kitchen scraps.

"May I, Alfred? They're being so good. And it might keep them out of the danger zone." Arlene patted the nearest goat's head. "I'm also in charge of beverages. Iced tea, Harriet?"

Harriet gave her a grateful smile. "Not right now, but thank you."

Alfred waved a hand in the air. "Kitchen scraps? Sure, go ahead. They could stand a bit of spoiling. Happy goats make better milk after all."

Arlene tossed scraps toward the goats as if she were a kid at a petting zoo.

And Alfred had let her. Arlene, the woman he'd once suspected of poisoning his animals. Harriet would have shaken her head, but standing at the base of such a tall ladder made her dizzy as it was.

Veterinary medicine rarely required her to climb that high. And it didn't escape her that a misstep might put a major crimp in her wedding plans. But she'd take every precaution as she climbed toward the tree cavity in question.

Had a squirrel stashed something there that had affected the tree? With every step up, she grew closer to knowing.

When she reached her destination, her heart pounded faster than if she were running a marathon. What was that?

With a gloved hand, Harriet swiped at what oozed from the metal container lodged in the opening in the trunk. She took a tentative whiff of the fluid on her gloved finger.

"What is it?" Alfred asked.

She thought back to the day she and Arlene had gotten close to the tree and smelled what Harriet thought was fumes from Alfred's idling tractor. "Unless I miss my guess, it's some kind of fuel."

She'd treated a cat drenched in gasoline before, but never imagined Alfred's goats being poisoned with it, and never from a spot this high in a tree.

Harriet traced the path of the drizzle down the trunk to the affected branches beneath. The slow dripping and affected branches were only on Alfred's side of the stone wall, not on Arlene's. If Alfred's goats had been feeding on green leaves and acorns from those branches, they could have been ingesting traces of gasoline in addition to the natural toxins those leaves and acorns contained.

But how did a tree suddenly start leaking fuel?

CHAPTER TWENTY-FOUR

Harriet hadn't fathomed having to climb the ladder a second time that day, but there was only one thing to be done.

"I'll need a long rope, a bucket, and something protective, like a cloth bag for the other items," Harriet said with her feet firmly on the ground.

"What did you find up there, Doc?" Alfred asked.

"The bucket is for what I think is an old fuel tank of some kind. The cloth bag is for the smaller items in the tree cavity. Not sure yet what all is in there, but there are a bunch of things I don't want affected by the leaking fuel tank."

"You'll need something more protective for your hands if you're letting that rope down," Arlene said.

"I'll get her some leather gloves." Alfred hurried away.

Within five minutes, Harriet was up the ladder again. The second time wasn't as scary as the first. She carefully set the fuel tank into the bucket, collected the items in the cloth bag, tied both bag and bucket to the rope, and carefully lowered them to the ground. The tank was unlike any she'd ever seen on a modern farm. It looked truly antique and still had fuel in it. What would have made it suddenly start leaking now after apparently being in the tree for years? And speaking of being in the tree, how in the world did a fuel tank get up there in the first place?

She'd used the flashlight Alfred had insisted she take up the ladder with her this time. The tree's cavity was full of evidence of a human's handiwork, and its contents were on their way to the ground to the gathering of people who had been instructed not to touch anything until she got down there.

Harriet wondered how well they'd follow her request.

She descended the ladder as securely as she could, grateful to feel grass and dirt under her feet again.

"This beats all," Alfred said, peering into the bucket.

"I'm afraid those damaged limbs will have to be removed," Harriet told him. "I don't think they'll recover. But it didn't appear that any other branches were dropping leaves or unripe acorns. We may have reached the real cause of our goat ailments."

"That would be a blessed relief." Alfred swiped at his forehead. "But"—he poked the bucket with his toe—"there's still *this* mystery to solve."

"What do you make of it?" Jeb asked later, when he, Harriet, Alfred, and Arlene were seated around the items scattered on an old canvas tarp draped over the island in Alfred's normally immaculate kitchen.

Harriet removed her leather gloves and pulled on a fresh pair of disposable ones so she could better judge the texture of the items. "That's obviously a container for fuel."

"But who would put it in a tree?" Alfred rubbed the stubble on his chin. "Even those boys Arlene had working for her couldn't have managed that without getting noticed."

Would Alfred never stop looking for a culprit—or two—to blame? Then again, Harriet had to admit that at least the brothers seemed to be exonerated in his mind. "This can looks really old. I can't read the markings on it, but I'd venture it's been in that tree for decades. One thing we do know though."

"What's that?" Arlene asked as she stood and moved from the island to the counter along the far wall. Raspberry tarts and other delicacies had made their way from her side of the stone wall to Alfred's kitchen, along with the iced tea.

"We know your troubles with sick animals may well have come to an end, Alfred. Once those branches are removed and any remaining fuel is washed off that tree, you shouldn't have trouble with it anymore. It seems clear this has been the source of their ailments. Your goats will be able to roam freely again."

"As if a goat ever obeys a boundary," Arlene said with a grin, taking her seat again.

"Maybe it'd be best if there weren't a boundary at all," Harriet said before she realized she was talking aloud.

"Meaning what?" Alfred gave her the expression she'd come to know as suspicion mixed with a dash of mischief.

Jeb grinned. "Maybe what the good doctor means is that your land could use a trim like Arlene's sheep would offer, and her land could use the brambles chewed off like your goats could. The sheep eat the low material and the goats like what's higher up."

"Jeb," Harriet said. "You're a genius."

He ducked his head. "Never been called that before."

Harriet nodded. "And you're absolutely right. Sheep keep their heads low while eating, which is why the grasses on Arlene's side of the wall are clipped close and tidy while she fights a battle with the brambles."

"I do," Arlene said.

"Meanwhile, your goats love roughage, Alfred. Goats don't like to eat with their heads down if they don't have to."

"I know all that," Alfred groused.

Harriet smiled. "You're a smart man. Smarter than someone who would let old grudges stand in the way of what would be best for both of you."

The room was silent for a few moments before Alfred said, "It isn't a grudge. It's shame."

All the artifacts scattered on the canvas seemed far less important than what Alfred had just laid bare on the table.

Arlene turned to face him. "You're ashamed of me?"

"Not you, Arlene," Alfred said. "Of me."

Arlene's cheeks flushed. "For the longest time, I didn't understand any of it. Why you would leave town so suddenly. Why you would leave me. Why you'd abandon your family. I couldn't imagine what I'd done to push you away."

"You did nothing wrong, Arlene. That's the point. It was me and my foolishness."

Jeb gestured to Harriet that he was going to head outside.

Harriet nodded but stayed where she was. The two might need a referee. She'd seen the damage a couple of stubborn goats could do to each other in her career as a vet. Her skills might be needed here.

"But if you loved me like you said…" Arlene's next words seemed to catch in her throat.

Love? They'd been in love? With a start, Harriet remembered Arlene's story of a broken engagement in her youth. She was talking about Alfred?

"I was scared. That's at the heart of most foolishness, isn't it? Fear?"

"Alfred, you were afraid of loving me?"

Harriet realized her time in the room would be better served if she focused on praying for a peace treaty to develop out of the conversation. *Lord, please keep this conversation productive and healing.*

"I was. In those days, I wasn't the easiest bloke to get along with," he said.

Harriet managed not to snort out loud. That was hardly a thing of the past.

"Alfred, that's always been true," Arlene told him. "But did that stop me from saying yes when you proposed?"

"The minute the words were out of my mouth, I regretted them."

Arlene grabbed a fistful of apron near her heart. "I didn't know it was that soon you knew I was a mistake."

"I just told you, Arlene. It wasn't *you* that was the mistake. It was me. Who did I think I was, asking a fine woman like you, a beauty like you, a kindhearted, lovely soul like you, to commit to spending her life with someone like me?"

"I loved you, you old fool," Arlene said, as close to annoyed as Harriet had ever heard her.

"I figured you'd get that sorted out in your mind soon enough. My dad told me almost every day that I wasn't worth the nappies I was kept in as a babe. Wasn't worth the time it would have taken him to teach me things. You hear that often enough, you start to believe it."

Arlene leaned closer to him. "Did you think I was stupid, Alfred?"

"No. Never. You bested all of us in grammar school. To say nothing of how far you went toward becoming a lawyer and everything. That's nothing to sneeze at."

"What I mean is," she said slowly, "did you think I wasn't smart enough to know my own mind, my own heart? I fell in love with *you*, not your occupation or your education."

He was silent.

"Did you think the words I said to you thirty years ago were lies? I know that's how you've acted since you came back from your wandering. But do you really believe I would have lied to you about wanting to be with you forever?"

"Alfred, you left Arlene at the altar?" Harriet blurted.

"So to speak," he said quietly. "It was a week before our wedding. I took off without a word to anyone. Wandered around for a while. Found myself in some unsavory situations, I must say. I guess regret only knows how to make more of itself."

"Pain begets pain," Arlene said. "I don't have any children—"

"That weighs on me too," Alfred said hoarsely.

"So I knew I'd have to make do somehow. I clung to Jesus. And it pained me even more that I didn't know where you were, what you were doing or facing, or if you knew to cling to Him too."

Alfred's chest rose and fell. "I'm glad my dad sold you the farm. That you had something of your own."

"It wasn't your dad's idea at first. It was your mother's. And it was both a gift and a curse. For so many years I looked at the stone walls that surrounded me, knowing they belonged to you, but you hadn't claimed your rightful inheritance. Yes, I built a life for myself. But I was hemmed in by the reminder that you weren't here, so it wasn't the life I wanted."

"Then my father passed, and circumstances meant I had no choice but to return to the one thing I actually had to my name. This land. And it got worse for you…when I came back."

"This last year hasn't been easy."

Alfred's breath shuddered. "I was certain you'd be bent on revenge. I should have known better, you being the person you are. I should have realized you would still be the same good woman I left behind. I'd apologize, but it's far too late for that."

"It's never too late for an apology," Harriet said, "whether it's accepted or not."

"Would you have taken it if I'd offered it, Arlene?" Alfred's eyes glistened in the illumination from the pendant lights over the island.

Arlene hesitated. "A year or two after you left, I don't think I would have. I had my own shame to overcome. I was the unlovable one, the woman who wasn't worth marrying but was profiting from the fact you were gone. Or so people thought."

Alfred shifted on his stool and lowered his head into his hands.

"We started out as friends in our school years," Arlene continued. "I know better than to expect anything like we had, but could we at least be good neighbors to each other?"

Alfred lowered his head to rest in the arms he'd crossed on the island. Finally, he looked up and lowered his hands to his lap. "I'm afraid that won't work for me."

Arlene raised her chin and closed her eyes, as if holding back tears.

"Being good neighbors is okay with me," Alfred went on. "We'll start there, if that's all you'll allow, and you have that right. But if you're willing to accept as many years of apologies as I can give you and forgive a foolish man's straying from the fold, and if you're daft enough to still love me, you're the woman I want to be with for the rest of my days."

The corners of Arlene's mouth twitched. "Well, that depends," she said.

Alfred stared at her. "On what?"

Arlene met his gaze squarely. "Do you truly and fully believe that I have never once wished ill on you or on your animals?"

He blinked in surprise. "Yes. Of course."

A smile broke over Arlene's face, like the sun emerging from behind the clouds. "Then yes. And as a reminder from thirty years ago, I do appreciate a hug from time to time."

While they celebrated the miracle of forgiveness with the sweetest embrace Harriet had ever seen, she wondered what her attitude would be if Will all of a sudden told her he couldn't marry her. If she had to let go of the joy he brought her and the promise of their life together, serving God side by side.

Her admiration for Arlene's tenacity and faith glowed inside her.

Harriet slouched on her stool at the island, overcome. And wondering whether they might make it to the altar before she did.

She hoped so. They had lost enough time.

"Now, tea?" Arlene asked, pulling out of Alfred's embrace.

"I'm parched," Alfred answered.

Harriet fingered the edge of the tarp while Arlene poured tea over ice and added a mint leaf she must have plucked from her garden.

The fuel can that captured Harriet's attention had been moved to the stoop outside the mudroom so its odor wouldn't be an issue. But there were other items on the island that interested her now. Bits of this and that, including a snippet of aged leather, and some pieces of what looked like cork. She observed the "debris field" as if it represented the scatter of hurt and longing that decisions from long ago had spread across those two lives.

Some of the items were unrecognizable. Some would take years, perhaps, to piece back together. But they'd started.

Harriet reached for something that caught her eye. A bauble of some kind? Something left in an ancient nest by a jewel-stealing bird like a magpie? She turned it over in her hands. A button.

She gathered a few other items that she thought would be helpful for identification. A few pieces of cork, a handkerchief, and that piece of leather looked like...

"Here's your tea, dear." Arlene set a mug on the island in front of her, careful to avoid any items of interest.

"Thank you, Arlene."

"You're most welcome." Arlene leaned over her shoulder. "What's that you've found?"

"I'm not sure."

Alfred nudged her with his elbow. "You and the pastor coming to Cliffside Chippy tonight with us to celebrate the pending nuptials?"

"I can check with him and let you know."

"Of course," he said. "He might have a prayer meeting or something."

"Maybe."

Arlene said, "She's a bit distracted, Alfred."

"By what? What you got there?"

"Whatever it is," Arlene said, "it's seen better days."

"Haven't we all?" Alfred quipped.

If Harriet hadn't been so engrossed in her discovery, she might have been startled to hear him joking so lightly. But humor would have to wait until she had answers.

CHAPTER TWENTY-FIVE

The excitement of being on the cusp of answers to more than one mystery propelled Harriet as she returned to the safety and familiarity of her beloved Cobble Hill Farm.

It was both a sadness and a gift, in a way, that she brought back one more goat that had exhibited symptoms before she left Alfred's.

She'd called Polly to ready the surgical suite before her arrival.

The room, sterile and well lit, somehow seemed more somber than usual this Thursday evening.

"Everyone ready?" Harriet asked.

"Ready," Brody said.

"You ever pumped a goat's stomach before, Doc?" Alfred asked anxiously.

"Alfred, please wait in the reception area. Arlene's out there. You can keep her company."

"I've a right to be worried, don't I?"

"Certainly. But your worry won't help me with this procedure that requires my full concentration. The reception area, please."

"Whatever you say." He headed toward the lobby, muttering under his breath.

"Can I get that in writing?" she called after him.

"Don't worry, Harriet," Arlene called back. "I'll keep him out of trouble."

"The anesthesia's doing its work, Doc. I think we're ready to begin."

"Good. Thank you, Brody. Now for the hard part." She mentally forgave herself for ever considering that Brody could have been poisoning Alfred's goats. If the doe's stomach contents showed what she suspected, all suspicions could be laid to rest.

Less than twenty minutes later, she had cleaned up and prepared her response as she headed to where Arlene and Alfred were waiting and working on a crossword puzzle together.

Alfred stabbed his pencil on the puzzle. "Twenty-two down. Ethereal," he said. "I'm right, aren't I?"

"You seem to be." Arlene looked up first and spotted Harriet. "I thought this would help us pass the time."

Alfred's gaze snapped to hers. "Give it to me straight, Doc." He grabbed Arlene's hand.

"She did very well. She's strong and healthy. I see no ill effects. She may have ingested some of the fuel, but we were successful in removing all of it. Now we—"

"Let me guess," Alfred said. "We wait for the lab."

Harriet smiled. "You do know the routine, Alfred. But the stomach contents have confirmed that, at the very least, the green leaves and acorns have been part of the problem. With this goat, at least."

"Can she come home with me?"

"She'll need to stay here tonight for observation. Ordinarily, I'd send her home with you after that procedure, but we're unsure what else we're dealing with. The lab will be instructed to look specifically for some kind of fuel in the toxicology screening."

"At least we finally know it couldn't have been Arlene," he said, a smile playing around his mouth. "She's too short to reach as high up as we found that petrol container."

Arlene nudged his arm. "You old fool." But she too was smiling.

Harriet rubbed her temples. "It's been a long day, friends. We have a lot more investigating to do. But at least we have a solid lead about these random and intermittent illnesses."

The doe would have to wait a while before Harriet introduced food or water, just to be safe. It might be a long night observing the goat's behavior, but she also itched to start the minimal lab tests.

As soon as the thought crossed her mind, she was struck by how interesting her occupation was and how crazy it might seem to others for her to get excited about examining a goat's stomach contents.

A text message pinged as she said goodbye to Arlene and Alfred and locked the front door behind them. It pinged a reminder a few minutes later when Brody and Polly left out the side door, Polly protesting all the way that Harriet should have let her settle the goat in the kennel.

"I can do it," Harriet assured her. "You've done enough staying this late for me."

She locked that door also and then went into the exam room, where the goat was just getting to its feet. Brody had lowered her to the floor earlier and tied her lead to the leg of the table. Harriet gave her a quick going-over before untying her and walking her into the office to shut down the computer before heading to the kennel. When her phone pinged another reminder, she sighed and took it from her pocket. The message was from Will.

"I'VE COME HERE WITH NO EXPECTATIONS, ONLY TO PROFESS, NOW THAT I AM AT LIBERTY TO DO SO, THAT MY HEART IS, AND ALWAYS WILL BE, YOURS." —EDWARD FERRARS, FROM SENSE AND SENSIBILITY, THE 1995 MOVIE—THE ONE WITH EMMA THOMPSON. MY MOTHER MIGHT NOT APPRECIATE THAT I'M USING A QUOTE THAT NEVER APPEARS IN JANE AUSTEN'S BOOK, BUT IN MY DEFENSE, THE QUOTE IS VERY GOOD, AND IN THIS CASE VERY TRUE.

She sank into her desk chair, savoring the sentiment as well as his thoughtfulness in sending it on such a day. No matter what else was unsure in her life, his love had proven rock solid.

It took Harriet a while to come up with her response, short as it was. She wanted to respond just as lovingly, but even if she weren't at the end of a long and trying day, she would have trouble matching that.

Finally, she texted, FULL DAY. FULL HEART. THANK YOU FOR SENDING ME EXACTLY WHAT I NEEDED. I LOVE YOU.

SWEET DREAMS, he answered in response.

Should she tell him it might be another sleepless night for her? Or that she was about to peer through a microscope at a drop of goat-stomach contents? Or that she was currently watching a goat recovering from gasoline poisoning or green oak leaf poisoning, if the tests proved as much? No, she shouldn't. Even she was more romantic than that.

He'd quoted a movie adaptation of a Jane Austen book. She had yet to find time to search for a Jane Austen book to give him in memory of his mother. The goat could wait another few minutes while she pulled up a search engine.

Success! A signed first edition, or so it claimed. A mere £239,317, plus tax. And shipping. Somehow, the £25 shipping charge seemed fitting. She clicked another page, less hopefully this time.

Pride and Prejudice. Written, apparently, in three volumes. Second edition. That was fine. It would still be meaningful to Will. *One of the most sought-after titles in English literature,* she read in the description. And only £38,000.

Wait. What was that one?

A recent publishing date, but could this be what she was searching for? *The Prayers of Jane Austen.* Yes. Perfect for Pastor Will. In a few clicks, the slim volume was on its way to Cobble Hill Farm.

If only Alfred's goat wasn't headbutting the back of her office chair. At least she was feeling better.

On Friday Harriet used one of her breaks to finish composing an email to thank her parents for sending the second payment for the caterer. At their ages, Harriet and Will had no problem assuming the bride and groom would pay for all the wedding expenses. She'd been living frugally and saving for years—for what, she hadn't known until she met Will. But her parents had insisted on being allowed to contribute some things for their only daughter's wedding.

She quickly clicked Send on her thank-you note and update to her parents. The catering was no small matter, and it turned out they could keep both the chicken and beef options for their guests. She and Will were genuinely grateful.

She was about to scrub in for surgery on a beloved service dog when Polly caught her in the hallway, eyes wide.

"Harriet, we have a problem."

"Can it wait? This procedure is important."

"I know, but unfortunately it can't. It's a big problem. Remember the letter you received from the RCVS a couple of weeks ago?"

"Yes." Harriet's heartbeat quickened.

"They're here."

"What?" Harriet glanced toward the reception area. "Why?"

"Your guess is as good as mine. They wouldn't tell me anything, although, believe me, I tried to get them to." If Polly, who could open up the most recalcitrant personality, hadn't been able to get them to talk, the situation must be serious indeed.

"I can't imagine that we're in any real trouble." Every business had disappointed customers who felt obligated to report their aggravation to someone higher up. The clinic had a stellar reputation. One her grandfather had spent decades building. Was she about to lose it in just a matter of months?

Harriet was itching to get through the scheduled surgery. The procedure itself was crucial to the dog's quality of life, and every surgery Brody assisted her with taught him things he'd be able to take into saving countless animals in his own career. Not to mention she was anxious to dive into the historical research about what she'd found lodged in the tree Alfred and Arlene shared.

But first, she must face the music, whatever the tune, with the Royal College of Veterinary Surgeons.

She walked out to the reception area and greeted the two men who had no animals with them and thus were likely not there for appointments. "Good morning, I'm Dr. Harriet Bailey. Would you like to talk privately?"

They followed her back to her office.

She gestured them into the two chairs across the desk from her own. "Now, what can I do for the RCVS?" The sooner she got this over with, the better she'd feel.

Alfred had lived with daily regret for decades. No matter what these men told her, Harriet knew she had done her best, even when the outcomes hadn't turned out as she'd hoped. She leaned on that now as she prepared herself for what could be an unsettling conversation.

"Dr. Bailey, I'm Dr. Nathan Lutz, and this is my colleague, Dr. Stan Irwin. You received a letter from us not long ago."

"Yes. I replied via email that I was grateful to have been made aware of some complaints you received. Should I have taken any additional action?"

"On the contrary. We're here to apologize in person for you having received it at all. It's our custom to verify complaints as legitimate before correspondence of that nature is sent. That step, we regret to say, was not implemented in this case."

Harriet's breath came more smoothly now, but it seemed odd that they would go to the trouble to deliver the apology in person.

Dr. Irwin spoke up. "The accusations, we now know, were not only completely unfounded, but originated from a single source. And that source has since admitted to having falsified all claims."

"Let me guess. Alfred Ramshaw?"

"Who?"

"Alfred Ramshaw." Harriet glanced from one representative to the other. "It wasn't him?"

"No. We're not at liberty to reveal the source, but rest assured we've put a stop to the complaints. Your clinic, and you, Dr. Bailey, are held in high esteem in RCVS circles."

"Thank you. I appreciate that."

Dr. Lutz leaned forward. "We know you've been in this role in White Church Bay for only a little over a year, but a flood of commendations have come to us, far outweighing this recent unfounded and unfortunately unvetted surge of complaints. We've been aware of your work as well as your grandfather's."

Dr. Irwin nodded. "We would like to extend an invitation for you and your family to be our guests at our annual awards ceremony. Normally it's in July, but it's been postponed until the fall this year, as you may be aware if you receive our newsletter."

"Yes, I am aware, and I'm grateful for the invitation. But really, you don't have to do that just because of a letter that was a mistake."

"Actually, that's not the only reason we're extending this invitation. Your grandfather will be posthumously honored at that banquet," Dr. Lutz said. "A scholarship is being formed in his name for promising young veterinary students interested in rural practice."

Harriet was speechless for a moment. Then she took another moment to get her emotions under control so she could speak without her voice trembling. "I can't think of anything that would honor him more. Thank you."

"You'll receive a follow-up letter with details about the banquet soon. Please rest assured, if the RCVS logo is in the return address, it will be good news this time."

Harriet thanked the men and walked them to the front door. It would be hard to focus on the surgery now. Or so she thought. But within minutes, she was back in the groove of animal medicine, her surgical and diagnostic skills overtaking her mystery-solving interests. She was once again able to concentrate on each case, each need, each pet, as if it were the only one in her line of vision.

After all, she wanted to honor her grandfather's memory too.

"What a day!" had become a routine reaction. This one was no different. But she was grateful that the animals she saw over the next few hours presented with relatively simple medical needs. She discharged each one in order.

Finally, the last wagging tail left the building. She no longer had to wait to dive into her questions about what had been retrieved from the cavity in the old oak tree.

With any luck, she would find the answers to more than one question.

CHAPTER TWENTY-SIX

He could not fail at this.

His head ached. His stomach rumbled. He'd been sure he could make the whole trip without food, which would weigh down the flying machine unnecessarily. He couldn't afford even a life jacket's bulk. Instead, he wore a cork jacket, not that it would help. He and his creation had to be nimble to conquer gravity.

But now, grounded in Calais, he needed water and food. The race prize was reserved for continuous, nonstop flight as deep as possible into Europe. Calais, France, barely on its fringe, was no victory. Others had accomplished that easily.

He had no choice. Despite naysayers discouraging him from doing so, he refueled in Calais so he could return to the starting point and make one more attempt before the day ended.

He could not listen to his wife's voice in his head warning of the risk. What could ever be accomplished without risk? She'd understand that one day, wouldn't she?

Elizabeth, this is for you. For us.

His small notebook bore a few more scratches from his stubby pencil. Date and time. Fuel load. He'd jettisoned everything he could think of to lighten the load even more. If he could have managed the trip without petrol, he would have. Alas, it was a necessary evil.

In Calais, a mere twenty-one miles from Dover, holiday trappings throughout the seaport reminded him that Christmas was on everyone's mind but his.

As he prepared to take off to return for one more attempt, he allowed himself the briefest thought that laying the prize before Elizabeth would make up for all he'd put her through.

CHAPTER TWENTY-SEVEN

Harriet could feel the late July evening deepening around her that Friday, even as her inquisitive nature kept her in her study way too late. Charlie and Maxwell had stayed in the kitchen after she'd replenished their bowls and given Maxwell a final tour of the garden for the night. Her own meal, now cold, was ignored in favor of continuing the list she'd started. What a way to end one of the most rewarding Fridays she'd had since moving to Yorkshire.

Not counting Friday evenings spent in Will's presence. Tonight he was attending to details for his absence from the pulpit for their wedding and honeymoon.

She turned her attention to the list.

Harriet wrote a note to remind herself to visit the gallery. She still wanted to see if she'd just been imagining that the word *codswallop* was on the back of Grandad's painting. But it was too late tonight.

Weariness all but consumed her. It would not, however, keep her from the last item on her curiosities list.

"You. What shall we do with you?" She turned the leather object over in her gloved hands. "Do you have a story to tell? Is it the one I'm considering? If so, I have some phone calls to make in the morning. And let's hope those I need to talk to are working on a Saturday."

She laid the item gently on an absorbent cloth on her desk. Its time in the cavity in the tree had not been kind to it, but then again, portions of it were in better shape than she would have assumed.

"And you." She picked up the metal button retrieved from that same cavity. "Are you a coincidence, or a connection?"

She slid the button under the microscope.

Brought it into focus.

And gasped.

She couldn't lose too many more hours of sleep and still hope to be able to function. Eventually, Saturday morning's dawn pulled her from bed to resume her search for answers.

Harriet started the day's search at her microscope. The lettering on the button was worn but obvious. Couldn't that be said of so much going on around her? Worn down over the years like a coin rubbed almost flat but still recognizable. Like the stones turning to pebbles turning to sand on the beach far below Cobble Hill Farm's lofty perch, wave-washed until they lost their original shape but always reflective of their origins.

Harriet mourned that it was still not quite seven thirty. Most of the people she was waiting to contact wouldn't be at work for another half an hour at the earliest. By that time, she'd be opening the clinic for her real, paying job, as she reminded herself.

But it all tied together, didn't it? Who she was as a vet was enhanced by who she was as a mystery-solver and amateur investigator. Will and her friends were quick to reassure her of that, even if it did concern her parents.

Any medical field—human or animal—required sharp investigative skills.

She had only one remaining mystery to solve.

Her phone didn't ring until midmorning. Harriet excused herself from Polly and her waiting clients and retreated to her study. She'd sent digital images of the items in question to several sources, along with a map of the area with Alfred's property highlighted.

The first to respond was a forensic pathologist from Kensington, a recommendation from Van.

"Is it possible there might be DNA that could be recovered?" Harriet asked him.

"It's possible," he said. "But not probable, I must caution you. With an item that old, our only hope would be to match any DNA we could collect with DNA of a close living relative, and I don't imagine that would be easy to acquire."

"We can certainly try," she said. They weren't talking about fossils, after all.

The second call came midafternoon, from a man who confirmed what she'd read on the internet and corrected a bit the internet had gotten wrong. As to the items themselves, he could only assure her what they were, not where they had come from or who they belonged to. And a visit to the location would not make his answers any more definite. But he did express extreme interest in anything she was able to discover about their history.

She called Alfred and asked if she could stop by after work. She cautioned him not to disturb any of the other items from the cavity in the tree. She hoped to retrieve them all for further investigation, if not by her, then by historical experts much more informed about such things than she was.

"It's just a bunch of junk," Alfred said, clearly perplexed. "Random pieces and scraps. You're welcome to it all. I'd like my kitchen island back."

She was halfway through solving "the mystery that was Alfred." More than halfway? She hoped, anyway. The rest of that story could unfold slowly as she watched him settle into the wonder that he was loved. All Arlene had borne while waiting for him, all the loneliness followed by his return—but not directly to her—was easing, Harriet could tell.

Alfred's farm was not only safe again, it was on its way to a new era of abundance. The wall around his heart had been torn down— not by anyone's chiding, but by his realization that love endures all things.

The past weeks of observing and analyzing had been challenging in so many ways. But it had been the most important wedding preparation she could have attended to.

She couldn't wait to fill Will in on all the details—how her heart had been prepared for him, for them.

And she couldn't wait to celebrate this new possibility of heritage and redemption in one story.

No certainties. But Harriet could hope.

Harriet kicked at Alfred's back door with her wellied foot. And again. And once more.

"Are your arms broken? I said come in," Alfred said as he opened the door to her. "Oh."

Harriet turned sideways to wedge herself and the large package through the opening and into his mudroom.

"What you got there?" Alfred asked. "If it's a cod, it's a mighty thin one."

"It's a gift. I know I should save it for your wedding, but I can't wait. Is Arlene here?"

"Right behind you," came the familiar voice in a singsong. Arlene hauled in her own offering, a crockery pot of something that smelled delicious. "Thought we'd share some leek-and-spring pea soup before Alfred and I take another swing of the hammer in the space behind the kitchen."

"*Spring* peas?" Alfred asked with a pointed glance toward the calendar on the kitchen wall.

"I froze them in the spring. That counts," Arlene replied archly.

He chuckled. "Here, Doc. Let me take that monstrous package from ya."

"Be careful with it, Alfred."

"Oh, thank you," he said. "I was planning on tossing it wherever like a sack of potatoes." But his gruff tone lacked its usual acid, at least to Harriet's ear.

"What do we have here?" Arlene asked, setting her pot on the walnut butcher block so she could get a better look.

"It's a wedding present from me to the two of you, although you'll think it leans a little more toward the man of the house." Harriet suddenly felt a nudge of remorse. After their first engagement had come to ruin, would they feel it was ill-advised for her to jump the gun that way, so to speak?

But Alfred and Arlene simply smiled at each other, and the tension in Harriet's chest eased.

She eyed the findings from the cavity in the tree, except for the fuel tank they'd moved to the machine shed, out of the way of goats and human noses.

At her direction, Alfred laid the package on the other half of the island.

"Do we need to wait until the wedding to open it, Harriet?" Arlene asked eagerly.

"You most certainly do not."

"Good. Oh, we've made a decision," Arlene added. "We don't want to interfere with your big doings. Ours will be a September wedding. We'll work it in around preserving vegetables and getting the homesteads ready for autumn."

Harriet blinked in surprise. "You don't have to do that."

"You think it's just for your sake?" Arlene said. "I plan to take notes at your wedding for my own lavish affair."

"She thinks I'm gonna wear a suit," Alfred said. "Can you imagine?"

"It's already ordered, Alfred," Arlene said, pressing a kiss to his cheek. "Take good care of it, and you can use it for your funeral too."

He scowled, but his eyes twinkled. "Grab me that cleaver, my love, and I'll tear into this package."

"No!" Harriet blurted. "I mean, you'll need to open it more gently than that, so it doesn't get damaged."

"Still the same gullible Doc Bailey." Alfred chortled.

"Please forgive my fiancé's rather mischievous sense of humor, Harriet, dear," Arlene said, nudging Alfred in the ribs with her elbow. "Behave, you."

His teasing stopped when he opened the box and lifted the kraft paper off the item inside. "Oh my." He felt behind him for a stool and lowered himself onto it. "Doc, how did you...?"

"Is that the one?" Harriet asked, beaming.

"It sure is," he whispered.

Arlene leaned closer. "That's beautiful. Is it one of your grandfather's paintings, Harriet? No one paints like he did."

"Yes," Alfred answered for her. He picked the frame up in his large hands and carefully flipped it over. "'Codswallop.' There it is. Just like you said, Harriet."

"The colors will go wonderfully with our themes for the living room, won't they, Alfred?" Arlene laid a hand on his arm.

He set the painting reverently on the island. "Harold..." He swallowed hard and began again. "Your grandfather knew I'd be back one day. He told me as much. I told him it was impossible for a person like you, Arlene, to forgive me, for my parents to ever see anything good in me, for my life to amount to anything."

"Hence, codswallop," Harriet guessed.

"That's it. That's his penmanship."

"It sure is." But Harriet knew there was deeper meaning in her instinct to make sure Alfred had the painting. "There's more. Grandad kept journals about his painting, and he'd jot down notes about each one—where he got his inspiration for it, who it reminded him of, things like that. So last night I looked through them and found this. I don't think he'd mind that I tore the page out of his journal to give to you." She took the note from her pocket and handed it to him. She already knew what it said.

To Alfred,

When you finally return to the pitch where you belong, remember: "Press on toward the goal to win the prize for which God has called me heavenward in Christ Jesus." Philippians 3:14.

Your good friend and biggest competitor,

Harold

Alfred swallowed hard. "We thank you and Old Doc Bailey, for this fine gift. Oh, don't go crying, Arlene."

"As if you're not on the verge of tears yourself," Arlene retorted, sniffling.

"Well, sure, but I've got a reason. What's yours?"

She beamed at him. "You said 'we.'"

CHAPTER TWENTY-EIGHT

Spoons clinked against ceramic bowls as they dug into the delicious leek-and-spring pea soup Arlene had brought. Alfred rounded out the meal with a loaf of hearty bread and more of his excellent goat cheese.

At his first bite of soup, his eyebrows rose. "You put tarragon in this."

Arlene smiled serenely. "I remember how much you love it."

He squeezed her hand before turning back to the meal. "Now, Doc, I believe you came out here for more than just bringing us far too lavish a wedding gift."

"I did," Harriet admitted. "How about I lay out the story for you?"

"I can't think of anything better to go with this meal than a good tale."

"First of all, Alfred, I'm so very sorry for the misery you've gone through with your goats and the stress it's caused you."

"I appreciate that."

"But I'm also very much *not* sorry for the part our quest to find the answers has played in restoring the relationship between you and Arlene."

Alfred's spoon stilled. "It was all worth it," he said.

"I believe it may also lay to rest another concern that has been a mystery far too long. And we wouldn't have been tipped off to it without the illness we couldn't explain."

"Go on," Arlene urged, selecting a slice of bread.

"More than a hundred years ago, a young man had an insatiable appetite for flight."

"Not many were flying more than a hundred years ago, Doc," Alfred said.

"That's right." Harriet drew a deep breath. "One of those few was a man named Conrad Stokes. Have you heard of him?"

"No," Alfred said, and Arlene shook her head.

"He was an early British aviator. One of the first and most inventive."

"How do you know about him?" Arlene asked.

"I'm getting to that. I think you'll be as interested as I am in his story. According to the historians I spoke to, Conrad Stokes entered an early aviation competition in 1910 right before Christmas, which challenged participants to fly across the English Channel and as deep as they could into Europe. The winner would be the one who flew the farthest without stopping."

Harriet paused to take a bite of soup. Then she said, "He took off from Dover and crossed the channel, but fog prevented him from making it any farther than Calais. His pride wouldn't take that. He wanted the honor, the recognition, and the cash prize. He was determined to try again, the same day."

Arlene gave Alfred a playful nudge. "Hmm. Stubborn, just like someone else I know."

"Conrad refueled in Calais to return to England so he could start over. I have to warn you there's a sad ending to this story, but the happy part is that he won the prize, which was about four thousand pounds, I think. So all his hard work paid off."

"I don't think I'm going to like the rest of this story," Arlene said.

"You're right, you're not," Harriet said. "Conrad had to wait a few days to collect the prize money—to make sure he maintained the record—and then he flew to Calais in preparation to return home. Despite warnings, he left Calais in a heavy fog for the forty-minute flight to Dover. He never made it. Conrad and his flying machine disappeared without a trace. Everybody assumed he was lost in the waters of the English Channel."

"Oh, dear," Arlene murmured.

Harriet sipped her tea then said, "They searched for him but couldn't find anything. Part of a pair of aviator's goggles and a cap washed up in southeast England a few days later, close to the Isle of Sheppey where he may have trained. But they were too common to have been linked specifically to Conrad."

"This is a sadder story than I expected it to be, Doc," Alfred said.

"The mystery of what happened to Conrad Stokes remains unsolved to this day," Harriet said. "But I believe it may be related to *your* mystery." She gestured to the artifacts on the other end of the island.

"You're not saying—"

"I'm saying it's possible these items are related to his crash."

"How could he have gotten so far off course?" Arlene asked.

"He was headed for Dover, according to reports," Harriet said. "He had plenty of fuel for that. I think it's likely he became disoriented in the fog and ended up way off course."

"What if he took ill?" Arlene asked. "What if he wasn't thinking properly, couldn't sort out his thoughts or his surroundings?"

Harriet nodded. "He was likely running low on fuel by the time he got as far as White Church Bay, and then somehow get turned around back to the channel."

Harriet tilted her head with the thought. "The only thing I can figure is that when he went over the farm, some things fell out of the plane and got caught in the tree. Then the tree grew over the years, around the items."

"Can that even happen?" Alfred asked.

Harriet shrugged. "As Hamlet said, 'There are more things in heaven and earth, Horatio, than are dreamt of in your philosophy.' I wouldn't want to say it was impossible."

"What about these things you found in the tree, Harriet? What do they tell you?" Arlene looked at her eagerly.

"As you can see, there are pieces of wood, some strips of leather, and bits of cork. We know from people who saw him in Calais that his life jacket was made of cork. I've seen images of the plane before his flight. It was downright skeletal. What we have to remember is that airplanes back then—biplanes—pretty much consisted of two wings and a chair. Things falling out seems not only possible, but very probable."

"Cork." Alfred stood and retrieved an irregularly shaped scrap of something from the collection. "Like this?"

Harriet took it. "Yes, like this. Cork would have no problem surviving for more than a hundred years inside a tree cavity. The tree growing around everything helped preserve the contents at least a bit, until the fuel tank finally began to leak, slowly enough that it wasn't visible at first, but then more, then enough for it to drip onto the leaves and acorns that then fell prematurely, and for the goats to grow ill from eating them."

Arlene sat back in her chair. "Imagine these scraps being all that was left to show how a person died."

Harriet reached for Arlene's hand. "Somewhere out there was a family who mourned Conrad's death but didn't know what happened to him. How long did they wonder? Do they think about his story even today, the younger generations of Stokeses?"

She was ready to lay her last card on the table. "We have some DNA."

"From the fuel can?" Alfred was as incredulous as she'd ever seen him.

"From the life jacket?" Arlene asked.

"No, the DNA comes from what I believe is a strap from his goggles. It would have gone around the back of his head and rubbed against—"

"His hair!" Arlene said excitedly.

"That's right, and it pulled some out, including the root. We need someone from his bloodline to see if there's a close enough match to assume it's Conrad's, but everything else points to it."

"Is that all we have?" Arlene asked. "It's a wonder to have that, I suppose, but it does seem to be a long shot."

"We also have a button," Harriet said. "Not a shirt button. A silver button given to the participants in the aviation competition. It's barely legible, but under the microscope, I could read it clearly."

Alfred slapped the surface of the island. "So this stuff has to be his!"

Arlene snapped her fingers. "The prize money," she said. "We haven't even asked what happened to it. If he had it with him when he took off, and he never made it home, did it fall out of the plane too?"

Alfred inhaled sharply, and Harriet looked at him, concerned. Was this all too much for him?

He stood and paced the room. "Remember, Harriet, I told you about the gold coins my great-grandfather supposedly found?"

Harriet nodded, feeling her heart beat a little bit faster.

"What if it's not just a tall tale?" he said. "What if he was telling the truth, and there really is more gold somewhere?"

"But, Alfred," Harriet said, "who would have found it? And if someone found it, why would they hide it and not tell anyone about it?"

Arlene held up her hand. "If, a hundred years ago, I found four thousand pounds in gold, I'd hide it. Here in White Church Bay, how could I have spent a gold coin without raising a lot of questions?"

"That's true," agreed Alfred. "Especially if people are talking about a missing pilot who had four thousand pounds worth of gold with him when he went down."

Harriet smiled at him. "Maybe you really do come from a family of considerable means," she said.

Arlene squinted at him. "What was the rest of that saying from your great-grandfather?"

"'Look to the sky and it will light your way,'" Alfred said.

Suddenly a picture formed in Harriet's mind.

"Alfred," she said. "I think I need to climb that ladder again."

Albert pushed aside enough tools, equipment, and cardboard boxes in various states of decay to create a path deeper into the crowded machine shed. Although plenty dusty, the shed wasn't as dark inside once Alfred flicked on a couple of bare bulb lights overhead.

The skylight was a good twelve feet above the floor. Harriet changed her mind about the ladder when she saw an old tractor sitting directly underneath the skylight. She thought she could reach the rafters by climbing on it. After all, she didn't need to reach the skylight itself. It was obvious that nothing was attached to it.

"Alfred, do you mind if I climb up on this tractor instead of using the ladder?" she asked.

"I'm not sure you should be getting up there, Doc," Alfred said. "I don't think I can catch you if you fall."

"And you could have caught me when we were at the tree?" Harriet grinned at him. "It's a little late to tell me that, don't you think?"

Alfred shrugged. "There were more people to cushion your fall then."

"Don't listen to him, Harriet," Arlene said. "You're more than capable of seeing if there's something up there. Just be careful, and you'll be fine."

Harriet stepped over a curious assortment of objects and slid others out of the way until she reached the antique tractor with enormous iron-ribbed wheels. She found her grip, testing each handhold and foothold as she gingerly climbed onto the machine, finally reaching a box-like apparatus that must have served as the cover for the engine. It was dented but solid. And just large enough to hold her in a stabilizing stance.

From that position and height, Harriet could look over the rafters. "I don't see anything up here," she said, disappointed.

"Can you feel along the tops of them?" Alfred asked. "There could be a hidden compartment or something, right? If I were hiding the money, I wouldn't just set it on top of a rafter where anyone could see it who looked."

Harriet reached up and gingerly ran her hands over the nearest rafter. They were made of rough lumber, and she sure didn't want to get a splinter in this not-so-clean shed. "Nothing here," she said. Two more swipes of two more boards yielded the same result.

"See if you can reach the one behind you," Arlene suggested.

Carefully, Harriet pivoted on the engine cover, testing each step before putting her full weight down. Once she felt secure, she reached up and ran her hand along the rafter above. And there was…something different… Her fingers dipped into a recessed part of the wood and felt cold metal. "There's something here," she said, trying to work her fingers under the metal object.

"What is it? Is it money? Is it gold?" Arlene was almost dancing in her excitement.

"Just wait a minute, it's heavy. I need to get it out." Finally, she was able to get her fingers far enough into the hold and along the side of the object to pry it out. "It's a metal tin. And like I said, it's really heavy. I won't be able to carry it while I climb down, and I can't just toss it to you."

"Give me a minute," Alfred said. "I'll move that mattress over here and then you can drop it."

It took more than a minute in that clutter. And Harriet had to hang on to the rafter to keep herself from losing her balance. But getting a ladder set up safely in that spot would have been even more difficult.

With the mattress draped awkwardly over the items beneath it, Harriet leaned over as far as she could and dropped the tin. It landed with a thud.

"You're right, it's an old tin," Alfred said. "Looks like one my grandmother used to keep odd buttons and such in."

But Harriet wasn't through. She ran her hand farther down the same rafter...and felt another opening in the board. "There's a second one," she called.

She went through the same procedure with another tin.

Once she was satisfied there were no more discoveries, Harriet climbed down from her perch and joined a stunned Arlene and Alfred on the ground below.

Alfred was holding both tins. "Should we open them inside the house where we can see better?" Harriet suggested.

"Great idea," Alfred said. "Might want to brush some of those cobwebs out of your hair first."

Harriet laughed as she complied. A few cobwebs in her hair were nothing when they might have finally found the last piece of the puzzle.

CHAPTER TWENTY-NINE

W hat's it say?" Arlene asked, rotating one of the gold pieces in her hand. "I should get my reading glasses."

"It's in French," Harriet said, making out the words *Republique Française* on one side and *Liberte-Egalite-Fraternite* as well as *20 Fcs* and *1910* on the back.

"And it says 1910." Alfred held another like it in his hands.

"Unless I miss my guess, this is how Conrad Stokes was paid, in gold coins." Harriet tried to estimate how many coins lay in the battered velvet pouches inside the tins. And made of pure or nearly pure gold? They were worth a fortune at today's prices. "I don't think these are all the coins though. I don't know what the conversion rate was back in 1910, but I'm sure four thousand British pounds in gold would have been more than this. Certainly, it would have weighed more. Conrad didn't even have a compass on board to minimize air resistance and weight. But he tried to bring his prize money home in his plane—no wonder he couldn't keep it in the air."

Alfred's countenance was unusually pensive. "So our best guess at what happened is that as he flew over our farm, at least some of his prize money and a few other things flew out of his plane and landed here. He might have been struggling to keep the plane up, but whatever happened after that, he was lost to history."

Arlene took his hand. "So are you thinking that your great-grandfather must have found these coins scattered on the ground, gathered them, and then hid them?"

Alfred nodded. "We'll never know if he spent any of it or just squirreled it away."

Harriet had a mental picture of Betsy with her metal detector. "I bet he missed a few, and those were the ones that were found and that started the rumor," she said.

Alfred smiled. "At least we can set Betsy's mind at ease, and she can stop looking for the buried treasure." He chuckled. "At least I hope she will."

And then he sobered. "I suppose it will take a while to find out who these coins really belong to."

"We've got time," Harriet said, "The important thing, Alfred, is that the mystery of what's been making your goats ill has been solved. And the bonus is now we know more about the mystery of Conrad Stokes. I'm sure his descendants will be thrilled to know what we've found."

"So much history behind us," Alfred said.

"So much future ahead of us," Harriet added, with an unveiled reference to now two weddings on the very near horizon.

Suddenly, she wasn't afraid of being a pastor's wife anymore. Just as He had in every circumstance of her life, God would give her what she needed—when she needed it—to fulfill whatever future He called her to.

Will, I can't wait until we begin our adventure as husband and wife, serving this unusual but undeniably rich community.

Solving the mystery of what had affected Alfred's animals had led Harriet to solving at least some elements of a confounding aviation mystery. It would soon be completely in the hands of the aviation museum and historians.

The artifacts belonged to history. The story was one she would treasure forever.

FROM THE AUTHOR

Dear Reader,

Long before I was asked to write this novel, I fell in love with all things British. I'm no expert, but I often turn—in my very Midwestern USA family room—to British archaeological videos, British royal history videos, British house/home/castle renovations, and *The Yorkshire Vet*. Since you're reading this, I think it's safe to assume you're the same way.

My passport is still waiting to reflect a trip to the fells and moors and narrow cobbled streets and charming houses that lean a bit because they're hundreds of years old. But it wasn't hard for me to imagine Harriet's enchantment with the sea, the gardens, or the people of White Church Bay and Cobble Hill Farm. It was a joy to explore the legends, lore, quirks, and in this case, quacks and squawks and bleats of a rural seaside community.

As authors often do, I found myself drawn into the emotional and spiritual growth moments of the characters—what makes them who they are, what complicates their relationships, the wonder of love ignited or rekindled, the mystery of forgiveness and second chances…

I drew from some of my own knowledge about knitting, wool, and sheep from my years working for an internationally renowned knitting expert and wool supplier. It was so fun to dive back into the feel of lanolin from natural wool and those glorious shades of undyed fleece.

I was personally encouraged, as I hope you have been too, that even ancient walls can virtually come down, even if their presence has been a part of the landscape for eons.

Signed,

Cynthia Ruchti

ABOUT THE AUTHOR

Cynthia Ruchti has been telling stories hemmed in hope most of her life, starting with a scripted radio broadcast heard on forty-eight stations across the country. Shortly before that broadcast retired, her first novel was published in 2010. She's been publishing fiction and nonfiction ever since, delighting in the joy of rearranging words on a page to engage readers' hearts and minds and offer hope in every circumstance. In addition to the more than forty-five books she's authored, coauthored, or contributed to, her bookshelves now also hold books of the authors for whom she serves as a literary agent. Her tagline is "I can't unravel. I'm hemmed in Hope."

TRUTH BEHIND THE FICTION

I don't remember now what first intrigued me about British aviation history and led me to the story of the real "Conrad Stokes," a man named Cecil Stanley Grace, whose adventures and misadventures in Britain's primitive aviation days eventually brought resolution to our fictional Alfred Ramshaw's mystery. Cecil's story tugged at my heart, as it might yours.

Cecil emigrated to England from the US and became an English citizen in his youth. He was fascinated with experimental aviation and threw himself into it, spending some of his training time near Dover on the Isle of Sheppey, where a handful of early aviators (Cecil was issued the fourth-ever pilot license) experimented with flight and aeroplane design.

The first crossing of the English Channel by Louis Blériot had taken place just a year and a half earlier than the 1910 Baron de Forest race, an endurance and distance competition that Cecil was determined to win. For a hefty monetary prize and the notoriety it would gain him as a serious aviator, Cecil was willing to risk the dangers of the challenge.

The prize was irresistible to him. He was so confident that he flew over the Royal Navy's battleships in fog to prove his expertise—and perhaps entice the navy to notice the value and possibilities of aircraft in military use.

On the day he attempted to win the Baron de Forest prize, thick fog enveloped him soon into the flight. But he pressed on, reaching as far as the Belgian frontier, but then was forced to return to Calais, France, due to high winds.

Most would have given up. But Cecil Stanley Grace refueled for a return trip to Dover and a second attempt. The fog was even thicker by that time. He never reached his destination, nor was he able to recross the English Channel and fly deeper into Europe for the prize. As a matter of fact, he disappeared altogether. Of course, for my story, I needed him to win the prize, and so I took some artistic license with history.

After an extensive search, authorities concluded that no hint of what happened to Cecil would ever be found. To this day, it remains an unsolved mystery in early British aviation. Cecil was the second aviator to give his life, it's assumed, in pursuit of flight.

At an aviation memorial museum on the Isle of Sheppey in Kent, stained glass windows honor both Cecil Stanley Grace and another aviator lost at sea, Charles Stewart Rolls. The stained-glass panels are labeled *Fortitude* and *Hope*. Below one is the inscription, *Having done all, to stand*, a reference to a passage from Ephesians 6. Below the others are the words, *Turn you to the Stronghold, ye prisoners of hope*, from Zechariah 9:12.

In reality, the strong clues authorities needed to confidently report what happened to Cecil are likely in the depth of the English Channel, farther off course than anticipated in the vast North Sea, or perhaps tucked in another spot no one has yet checked. Perhaps even the hollow of an old oak tree.

But without Cecil's efforts and innovations, aviation's progress would not have been the same.

If you want to read more about Cecil's determination and courage, you can find several accounts of his story online.

YORKSHIRE YUMMIES

Sticky Toffee Pudding

Ingredients:

For the Pudding Sponge/Cake:

6 chopped Medjool dates

1 cup milk plus two tablespoons

2 large eggs

¾ cup dark brown sugar

½ cup room temperature butter

1½ cups all-purpose flour*

1 teaspoon ground ginger

1½ teaspoons baking soda

1½ teaspoons baking powder

3 tablespoons molasses

*For gluten-free pudding, substitute cassava flour for the all-purpose flour

For the Sticky Toffee Sauce:

½ cup (4 tablespoons) butter

¾ cup dark brown sugar

1 tablespoon molasses

1¼ cups heavy cream

Directions:

To make sauce:

Warm butter, brown sugar, and molasses in saucepan over low to medium heat until sugar is thoroughly dissolved. Don't let it cook too long or it will turn stiff. Remove from heat. Stir in heavy cream. Reheat for serving.

To make the cake (or sponge *in British terms):*
Preheat oven to 350 degrees Fahrenheit.

Soak chopped dates in 2 tablespoons milk to soften.

Mix remaining ingredients except milk in large bowl and stir until well combined.

Add 1 cup milk and softened dates (plus any milk in which the dates soaked) into the bowl in stages, stirring well after each addition.

Pour mixture into greased 9x13 casserole dish.

Bake 30 to 40 minutes. Remove from oven and cool slightly before serving with the warmed sauce. It's great with vanilla ice cream.

*Read on for a sneak peek of another exciting book
in the* Mysteries of Cobble Hill Farm *series!*

Borrowed Trouble

BY SHAEN LAYLE

"Harriet, we have a problem."

It was midafternoon on Saturday, and August light poured through the church's back window where Harriet Bailey and her wedding party had adapted into a dressing space. Harriet turned from the mirror, where her mother had been carefully pinning her veil into place, and faced her matron of honor, Polly Worthington, and bridesmaid, Ashley Fiske.

Polly lived in White Church Bay and was Harriet's right-hand woman at the veterinary clinic that Harriet ran, while Ashley had flown to England from the States with her preteen son, Trevor. The last time Ashley was in town, she had helped Harriet solve a decades-old mystery. Today was all about celebration though. So why did both of her friends wear matching expressions of concern?

"Uh oh. What's wrong?"

Harriet's stomach tightened as her thoughts ran ahead. Had something gone wrong with the flowers? Or the music? What if Will had taken sick at the last minute? She had waited so long to find the love of her life. She certainly didn't relish the thought of a delay in their wedding ceremony.

"It may not be a big deal at all," Ashley rushed to explain. "The hotel staff assured us they're taking care of things."

Harriet and Will had planned to have their reception at Ravenscroft, a lovely historic castle-turned-B&B on the outskirts of White Church Bay. It was romantic, historic, and large enough to comfortably seat all those invited. But if Ashley's vagueness about the reception hall was meant to ease Harriet's worry, it wasn't working.

Harriet braced herself before continuing. "Details, please?"

"They're having some issues with birds in the main hall." Polly picked up where Ashley had left off. "They think they got in during renovations."

Harriet had been thrilled when the hotel manager informed her of the venue's upcoming renovations. Things would be in tip-top shape for the reception. But then when the renovations dragged out, stretching closer and closer to their booking date, she'd gotten jittery. Maybe she'd been right to feel so.

Harriet's mother chimed in as the voice of reason. "If the staff said they would take care of it, I'm sure we have no reason to worry. I'll call them after the ceremony, Harriet, while you're getting pictures with Will. We'll have it straightened out in no time. The worst thing that could happen is the reception starts a few minutes late."

Aunt Jinny smiled reassuringly. "Every wedding must have a hiccup or two. It makes for a fun story later."

Polly and Ashley echoed their reassurances and hurried from the room to get in line for the processional. Harriet's mother returned to smoothing the filmy, translucent folds of Harriet's veil over her shoulders. "Sweetheart, you look lovely."

Harriet reached back to place her hand over her mother's, which was resting on her shoulder. It was so good to have her here. Since Harriet had moved to England a year and a half ago, in-person visits with her parents had been few and far between, and video calls just weren't the same. Having her mother and father close at hand for her special day meant so much. Of course, she enjoyed having her White Church Bay family close at hand too. Today represented not only Will and her joining together in marriage but also the melding of Harriet's American and English lives. Had she really been in Yorkshire running Granddad's veterinary practice for only the past year and a half? The place and people now felt so familiar to her, it seemed she had been in White Church Bay forever.

"You're prettier than a picture, lass." Aunt Jinny echoed her sister-in-law's sentiment.

Harriet squared to face the mirror again. She normally shrugged off compliments, but today she believed her mother's and aunt's words. She couldn't help but feel beautiful on her wedding day. Radiant happiness had a way of painting the world in sunshine, and that was how it felt to finally be marrying Pastor Fitzwilliam Knight.

She smoothed the front of her dress, and its pearl-encrusted fabric glimmered in the glass. Within the hour, she would be walking down the aisle of White Church and reciting her vows before God and all her nearest and dearest friends and family. She couldn't wait. Some brides got cold feet, but she wouldn't. How could she doubt that God had brought Will and her together?

"All right, final touches." Her mother handed her the bouquet of English roses mixed with aromatic lavender. "It's almost time to go. Are you ready?"

Harriet nodded but paused when Aunt Jinny held up a finger.

"Wait, I have one more thing for you." Aunt Jinny riffled through the handbag that she'd plopped down on a nearby chair. She removed a small jewelry box tied with a ribbon and handed it to Harriet. "Consider this as your something old *and* your something borrowed."

Harriet untied the ribbon and opened the box. Nestled inside on a bed of wispy cotton was a gemstone brooch. It had a gold underplate, and its top was set with vibrant emerald stones and fashioned in the shape of a heart.

"It's beautiful," Harriet breathed. She turned the brooch over in her hands. It was heavy and showcased the craftsmanship of a bygone era. "Did it belong to a family member?"

Aunt Jinny nodded. "Yes, though I don't know who first owned it. It's called an endearment brooch, and it's quite old. Mum is the one who passed it down to me, but she didn't know the details of its history. I suspect, however, that this—" She reached over to unhinge a tiny clasp that had escaped Harriet's attention, and the front of the brooch swung open. "—is the original owner."

"How clever. It's like a locket." Harriet peered at the picture that occupied the brooch's hollow space. It was of a young man and woman dressed in opulent clothing. Whoever the couple were, they appeared completely in love. They sat next to each other on a velvet settee with clasped hands and tender expressions. Were these some of her relatives from generations back?

"I recognize the look on their faces." Harriet's mother smiled. "I've caught you and Will glancing at each other like that a time or two."

Aunt Jinny pressed Harriet into a hug. "Your grandmother would have wanted you to have this brooch for your special day. I think it's a paste piece, but it's still quite pretty and sentimental."

"I love it," Harriet assured her. "Help me pin it on?"

Harriet held still as Aunt Jinny and her mother worked together to pin the brooch into place at the neck of her dress. She reached up to make sure it felt secure before turning this way and that in the mirror to admire the effect.

Harriet's mother and aunt helped her finish getting ready, and she set aside her earlier worries about the reception venue. Nothing could dampen the brightness of her outlook right now.

She was marrying Will.

If Harriet had any doubt of Will's affection for her, it was immediately cast aside when she stood at the entry to the majestic stone church's sanctuary. As Harriet's seven-year-old cousin, Sebastian, carried the couple's rings on a satin pillow and his twin, Sophie, scattered rose petals in the aisle, Harriet caught Will's eye.

The look of love written on his face made her feel as if she floated, rather than walked, on her father's arm to the melodic strains of Clarke's Trumpet Voluntary. Familiar faces in the crowd passed by in a happy blur. Countless parishioners of Will's from White Church. Harriet's kind neighbor, Doreen Danby and her family. Harriet's mother and Will's father. Aunt Jinny, sitting beside her son, Anthony, and his wife, Olivia—parents to Sebastian and Sophie.

Low laughter rippled through the crowd as Sophie blew kisses from the front of the sanctuary. Little matter that her flower girl role was finished. She was obviously eating up the attention.

Harriet's focus, however, rested on Will. It was as though the two of them were suspended in time. The only people in the world.

Harriet's father lifted her veil and pressed a kiss to her cheek. Then he left her at the altar before Will and Jared, Will's seminary roommate, who was performing the ceremony.

"You look beautiful," Will whispered, so low that only Harriet could hear.

"You don't look so bad yourself," she whispered back.

Her eyes misted with emotion as she joined hands with him. How special this day was. Her family and friends in attendance and Will's as well. All those they loved best, in one room.

What a winding road had led her here. Just a short while ago, Harriet had wondered if marriage was part of God's plan for her. A broken engagement had nudged her to relocate from her hometown in Connecticut to England and take over her late grandfather's business and estate. It was a radical move, and one that made her wonder even more at what her future held. Then she met Will, and his tender attention healed her broken heart. Looking back over the pattern of past months, God's plan was clear. In His perfect timing, He brought Will and her together, and today was the fulfillment of that promise.

After Jared's opening remarks and Will's cousin Emily had sung the song she'd written for the occasion, Harriet and Will took turns reading from the Alfred, Lord Tennyson poem, "Marriage Morning."

Light, so low in the vale,
You flash and lighten afar,
For this is the golden morning of love,
And you are his morning star...

Next, they said their vows, joining a long line of couples throughout history who have made the same sacred promises to each other. Harriet smiled as she thought of the brooch pinned to her dress. The commitment of those who had gone before her filled her with gratitude.

The ceremony complete, Jared invited Harriet and Will to face the congregation. "I present to you Fitzwilliam Ringo Knight and Harriet Grace Bailey-Knight."

As the crowd applauded, Will squeezed her hand. "Ready to face the world, Mrs. Bailey-Knight?"

"With you? Always."

After the ceremony, the photographer pulled the members of the wedding party aside to take more pictures. She kept raving about the "golden hour" and how perfect the light was for photography. Hopefully, that meant the pictures would turn out well. Harriet cheesed with Will through what felt like hundreds of photos, and by the time they finished, her cheeks ached from smiling. Finally, it was time to wrap things up at the church and head to the reception.

"Your carriage awaits, my lady."

Past the happy gauntlet of well-wishers throwing confetti, Will led Harriet to the stylish black car waiting to transport them to the reception venue. Their driver opened the rear passenger door and waited while Will helped tuck Harriet and her dress's voluminous tulle inside. Then Will circled around the back of the vehicle to take his place opposite his bride.

"What do you think of her?" he asked Harriet as she fastened her seatbelt.

Harriet frowned at him. "*Her?*"

"Yes, her. The car." Will grinned. "She's something, isn't she?"

All Harriet could offer was a bemused smile. What was with the "she"? Was it like with boats, where men personified them into people?

She shrugged. "I don't know. It's a nice car, I guess." She could tell from the leather interior and sharp details that it was a step above a common vehicle, but her answer must've surprised Will. His eyebrows shot up.

"A *nice* car? You *guess?*"

"I don't know much about vehicles."

"First order of business then." Will winked. "I'm happy to teach you, if you're interested in learning. I've been fascinated by vintage cars since I was a lad."

Will set aside light conversation as the driver eased the vehicle into motion, and both Harriet and he waved through the windows at the group of wedding guests still milling in front of the church.

Harriet flinched as a sudden cascade of confetti showered down the windshield. Wait a minute. Weren't they done with that?

When the view cleared, however, she could see what had happened.

Apparently, Sophie and Sebastian hadn't gotten the message that the time for throwing confetti was over. Harriet and Will shared a chuckle as Olivia and Anthony lunged to stop the twins from chucking any more at the car. A smile pulled at Harriet's cheeks. The twins were as thick as thieves, and as mischievous too. But what else could you expect from seven-year-olds?

With the twins constrained, the driver honked the horn at the crowd. Then he eased out of the parking lot, leaving Will free to turn back to the matter at hand: sharing his passion for vehicles with Harriet. "For your information, this is more than a 'nice car.' It's a Jaguar E-Type."

He said the last part emphatically, as though it was supposed to mean something. She decided to humor him. "Is that different from a regular Jaguar?"

"Different?" Will nearly came out of his seat. It was really quite amusing. She'd had no idea of his rabid interest in cars before. "I'll say. It's an absolute classic. One of the first cars with disc brakes on all four wheels, as well as monocoque construction."

Amazing. It was like he was spouting Greek. "I'm sorry. What?"

"Monocoque construction. It means that the body and chassis of the car are integrated into a single unit. Plus, it's the same kind of vehicle Joe Root drives. When he's not chauffeured around, that is."

"Now that's a job I'd jump at." The driver angled an amused look at them in the rearview mirror.

"You and me both," Will replied.

Now, Joe Root, Harriet knew. Will enjoyed watching cricket in his spare time, and Joe Root was his favorite player. "Ah, well. If it has a cricketer's ringing endorsement, it must be quite impressive."

Now Will seemed satisfied. "That it is. And I rented the car for the entire week. We'll be touring in style for our honeymoon."

She reached across the back seat to lace her fingers with his. Who would have thought? Her new husband had a penchant for vintage cars. Just an hour into marriage, and here she was, learning something about him that she hadn't known before. One of the many things she would certainly learn about Will over the years.

How she hoped there would be many of them.

A NOTE FROM THE EDITORS

We hope you enjoyed another exciting volume in the Mysteries of Cobble Hill Farm series, published by Guideposts. For over seventy-five years, Guideposts, a nonprofit organization, has been driven by a vision of a world filled with hope. We aspire to be the voice of a trusted friend, a friend who makes you feel more hopeful and connected.

By making a purchase from Guideposts, you join our community in touching millions of lives, inspiring them to believe that all things are possible through faith, hope, and prayer. Your continued support allows us to provide uplifting resources to those in need. Whether through our communities, websites, apps, or publications, we inspire our audiences, bring them together, and comfort, uplift, entertain, and guide them. Visit us at guideposts.org to learn more.

We would love to hear from you. Write us at Guideposts, P.O. Box 5815, Harlan, Iowa 51593 or call us at (800) 932-2145. Did you love *Stray from the Fold*? Leave a review for this product on guideposts.org/shop. Your feedback helps others in our community find relevant products.

Find inspiration, find faith, find Guideposts.
Shop our best sellers and favorites at
guideposts.org/shop
Or scan the QR code to go directly to our Shop.

Loved Mysteries of Cobble Hill Farm? Check out some other Guideposts mystery series! Visit https://www.shopguideposts.org/fiction-books/ mystery-fiction.html for more information.

SECRETS FROM GRANDMA'S ATTIC

Life is recorded not only in decades or years, but in events and memories that form the fabric of our being. Follow Tracy Doyle, Amy Allen, and Robin Davisson, the granddaughters of the recently deceased centenarian, Pearl Allen, as they explore the treasures found in the attic of Grandma Pearl's Victorian home, nestled near the banks of the Mississippi in Canton, Missouri. Not only do Pearl's descendants uncover a long-buried mystery at every attic exploration, they also discover their grandmother's legacy of deep, abiding faith, which has shaped and guided their family through the years. These uncovered Secrets from Grandma's Attic reveal stories of faith, redemption, and second chances that capture your heart long after you turn the last page.

History Lost and Found
The Art of Deception
Testament to a Patriot
Buttoned Up

Pearl of Great Price
Hidden Riches
Movers and Shakers
The Eye of the Cat
Refined by Fire
The Prince and the Popper
Something Shady
Duel Threat
A Royal Tea
The Heart of a Hero
Fractured Beauty
A Shadowy Past
In Its Time
Nothing Gold Can Stay
The Cameo Clue
Veiled Intentions
Turn Back the Dial
A Marathon of Kindness
A Thief in the Night
Coming Home

SAVANNAH SECRETS

Welcome to Savannah, Georgia, a picture-perfect Southern city known for its manicured parks, moss-covered oaks, and antebellum architecture. Walk down one of the cobblestone streets, and you'll come upon Magnolia Investigations. It is here where two friends have joined forces to unravel some of Savannah's deepest secrets. Tag along as clues are exposed, red herrings discarded, and thrilling surprises revealed. Find inspiration in the special bond between Meredith Bellefontaine and Julia Foley. Cheer the friends on as they listen to their hearts and rely on their faith to solve each new case that comes their way.

The Hidden Gate
A Fallen Petal
Double Trouble
Whispering Bells
Where Time Stood Still
The Weight of Years
Willful Transgressions
Season's Meetings
Southern Fried Secrets
The Greatest of These
Patterns of Deception

The Waving Girl
Beneath a Dragon Moon
Garden Variety Crimes
Meant for Good
A Bone to Pick
Honeybees & Legacies
True Grits
Sapphire Secret
Jingle Bell Heist
Buried Secrets
A Puzzle of Pearls
Facing the Facts
Resurrecting Trouble
Forever and a Day

MYSTERIES OF MARTHA'S VINEYARD

Priscilla Latham Grant has inherited a lighthouse! So with not much more than a strong will and a sore heart, the recent widow says goodbye to her lifelong Kansas home and heads to the quaint and historic island of Martha's Vineyard, Massachusetts. There, she comes face-to-face with adventures, which include her trusty canine friend, Jake, three delightful cousins she didn't know she had, and Gerald O'Bannon, a handsome Coast Guard captain—plus head-scratching mysteries that crop up with surprising regularity.

A Light in the Darkness
Like a Fish Out of Water
Adrift
Maiden of the Mist
Making Waves
Don't Rock the Boat
A Port in the Storm
Thicker Than Water
Swept Away
Bridge Over Troubled Waters
Smoke on the Water
Shifting Sands
Shark Bait

Seascape in Shadows
Storm Tide
Water Flows Uphill
Catch of the Day
Beyond the Sea
Wider Than an Ocean
Sheeps Passing in the Night
Sail Away Home
Waves of Doubt
Lifeline
Flotsam & Jetsam
Just Over the Horizon

More Great Mysteries Are Waiting for Readers Like *You*!

Whistle Stop Café

"Memories of a lifetime...I loved reading this story. Could not put the book down...." —ROSE H.

Mystery and WWII historical fiction fans will love these intriguing novels where two close friends piece together clues to solve mysteries past and present. Set in the real town of Dennison, Ohio, at a historic train depot where many soldiers set off for war, these stories are filled with faithful, relatable characters you'll love spending time with.

Extraordinary Women of the Bible

"This entire series is a wonderful read.... Gives you a better understanding of the Bible." —SHARON A.

Now, in these riveting stories, you can get to know the most extraordinary women of the Bible, from Rahab and Esther to Bathsheba, Ruth, and more. Each book perfectly combines biblical facts with imaginative storylines to bring these women to vivid life and lets you witness their roles in God's great plan. These stories reveal how we can find the courage and faith needed today to face life's trials and put our trust in God just as they did.

Secrets of Grandma's Attic

"I'm hooked from beginning to end. I love how faith, hope, and prayer are included...[and] the scripture references... in the book at the appropriate time each character needs help. —JACQUELINE

Take a refreshing step back in time to the real-life town of Canton, Missouri, to the late Pearl Allen's home. Hours of page-turning intrigue unfold as her granddaughters uncover family secrets and treasures in their grandma's attic. You'll love seeing how faith has helped shape Pearl's family for generations.

Learn More & Shop These Exciting Mysteries, Biblical Stories & Other Uplifting Fiction at **guideposts.org/fiction**

Printed in the United States
by Baker & Taylor Publisher Services